SHRUNK: THE EXILE OF MAURICE

Neighborlee Book 8

Michelle L. Levigne

www.YeOldeDragonBooks.com

Previously released as ***Divine's Emporium,*** 2010
Revised

Ye Olde Dragon Books
P.O. Box 30802
Middleburg Hts., OH 44130

www.YeOldeDragonBooks.com

2OldeDragons@gmail.com

ISBN 13: 978-1-952345-21-0

Published in the United States of America
Publication Date: July 1, 2021

Welcome to Neighborlee, Ohio.

Where? Somewhere on the North Coast of Ohio, south of Cleveland, right off I-71, north of Medina, in the heart of Cuyahoga County.

What is it? That's a little harder to explain.

Neighborlee is a place you need to experience.

The most important thing you need to understand: Neighborlee is ***magic***. Some people say the town is alive. It exists to protect the weird and wonderful (and sometimes a little bit scary) from the cold, practical, material world.

More important, Neighborlee protects the outside world from the weird and wonderful that come to visit … and sometimes come to stay.

First stop: Divine's Emporium, a four-story Victorian house sitting on a hill overlooking the Metroparks. Whatever you really need, you can find at Divine's. Even if you don't know what you're looking for when you walk in the door. The shop is often bigger inside than it is outside. Angela is the proprietor. Please stay on the first floor. You don't want to find out what is hidden and locked safely away upstairs. Like Aslan, Angela is good, but that doesn't mean she's safe. And neither are the secrets and wonders and doorways to other worlds that she protects … and keeps securely locked.

Come in and explore. Meet the people who help Angela guard Neighborlee. Share their adventures of magic and wonder, danger and sacrifice. You never know who or what you'll run into as you walk the streets and listen to the stories of their lives.

Chapter One

Two months and three days after establishing the curiosity shop, Heart's Desire, Maurice struck gold. All the work and planning, all the discomfort of living inside a disguise, seething every time he saw poor Forsythe get kicked around the town that by all rights, he should own. It all paid off the moment Jordan Price laid his gold credit card down on the counter.

The cheating schemer, Jordan Price, who made bad old Dad look like an amateur. His father had cheated Forsythe senior out of his property when they were college boys, but Price went further and made sure Forsythe junior never got a decent break. When his wife stumbled on evidence Forsythe owned the property the town was built on, the Price estate, and the gold mine that financed Price Industries, he drove her into a nervous breakdown to silence her.

In the tiny mountain town of Sunrise, Price could have anything he wanted without paying a fair price. But Maurice and his store weren't for sale, although he intended to exact a heavy payment from Jorgan Price.

Maurice was Fae, born with magic in his blood, a long life ahead of him, and a driving need for entertainment. Tormenting bullies was his latest, most satisfying hobby. Everything in Heart's Desire was illusion, just like the illusion the people of Sunrise were decent, hard-working, charitable folk. A few people in town still had hearts and listened to their consciences. Maurice watched how they treated poor, downtrodden Forsythe. He cheated the cowards and rewarded the ones who dared to help Forsythe while Price and his cronies watched.

Today, after all his hard work, planning and plotting, watching and waiting: end game.

Price slapped his credit card down on the counter. All he saw was the illusion of a crooked, white-haired woman perched on her stool, wrapped around Maurice like a mask. Despite his alleged superiority, Price sweated. Three drops on his left check. Four on his right. A veritable rainforest springing to life at his hairline.

Which, if Maurice was correct, he had just noticed was

receding at an alarming rate.

"I want--" Price stopped, his voice cracking. He licked his lips, coughed to clear his throat. "That photo." He gestured at the photo in an antique silver frame hanging on the wall behind the counter.

Underneath the magic wrapper lay a plastic dime store frame, painted to look silver, with a photo filler of one of those generic, happy families playing at the seashore.

Maurice was exceedingly proud of the spell on that frame. The image was always different, depending on who looked at it. His spell dove into the mind of the observer and dug out the most life-destroying memory and superimposed it on the photo.

He could have looked into Price's mind to see what mortified and frightened the town bully, but Maurice had standards. He had done enough stupid, selfish things in his long life, he didn't want to see what others had done. That didn't mean he wouldn't or couldn't take advantage of the hundreds of guilty consciences in this self-satisfied little town. So far he had sold that frame to sixteen men and forty-three women. Either women had more money or they listened to their guilty consciences a lot sooner.

Everyone who touched the frame got a subliminal kick in the pants to urge them to be nicer to their fellow man, starting with Forsythe. Then the frame returned to Maurice. They had a couple hours of terror when they couldn't find the incriminating photo they had just purchased. When they returned to the store, they didn't see it hanging behind the counter again, waiting for the next bully or cheat to come in and pay to ensure no one would learn their horrific secrets.

"It's not for sale," Maurice said, his disguised voice frail.

"Everything is for sale." Red flushed Price's face. The rain on his forehead became a deluge. "Everybody has his price."

"Especially you?" His disguise shook and shivered, to taunt Price, who despised the frail, and despised little old women the most. His grandmother had been the only person in his life who'd ever told him no. Maurice chose his disguise to remind the bully of his grandmother, who had survived several suspicious accidents that would have killed a less stubborn, cantankerous old biddy.

"What do you want for the photo?" Price tried to growl. His voice caught and broke.

"I want to tar and feather you, for starters." The words came out in Maurice's normal voice.

He stumbled back from the counter, hit the wall, knocking the photo to the floor, and slapped both hands over his mouth. He hadn't meant to say those words. He had been thinking them, but he hadn't planned to say them.

Price stared at him, eyes wide, the red seeping from his face, and sweat dripping down his cheeks, soaking his silk collar and...

No, wait a minute. Nothing was dripping. No color seeped.

"Oh, heck," Maurice snarled, as his old woman disguise shredded. "Come on, let me finish!"

Blackness took over. It could have lasted for a heartbeat or a year, or a decade.

That was the irritating thing about the Fae realms, and life in the Fae enclaves. Time didn't run in synch with the Human world. Other Fae didn't have the respect for clocks and calendars, and the baseball and television seasons, that Maurice did.

He blinked and found himself sitting on a backless wooden stool, pinned under a spotlight inside an ocean of blackness. He was in his own body. At least his captor let him wear comfortable clothes, his favorite slate gray cashmere sweater and matching slacks and his new Italian loafers. He had iron manacles around one wrist and both ankles, attached to iron chains. The leg chains extended into the darkness beyond the pool of silvery-blue light. The arm chain led up into the air, vanishing in the darkness beyond the stream of the spotlight.

Common sense said not to get off the stool. It was more than possible there was no floor, ceiling, or walls.

"Come on, guys! Do you know how much work I put into that scheme? Let me finish the game, at least. The guy was a bully. He deserved what I was going to give him."

Maurice winced as his words seemed to hit a wall a hundred miles away and were absorbed. Chances were good that whoever had yanked him away from Sunrise wasn't even listening. Or if they were listening, they weren't going to respond.

That was standard practice for the Fae Disciplinary Council. Lock up the miscreant, leave him alone for a while to squirm and sweat, and then bring him out for judgment. Eventually.

It was the *eventually* part of the formula that worried Maurice.

Fortunately, he wasn't so deathly allergic to iron that he got poisoned by the touch of it or sickened by the smell, but he was allergic enough for a bad rash. And iron squelched his powers to minimal levels. He could use his trickle of magic to conjure up a book to read or his new iPod for some music, but that would use up all the automatic magic that fought the hives and sneezing that always came with the touch of iron. If he tried to hoard his magic until he had enough to burst one manacle, he would be miserable, sneezing and scratching and wheezing and seeping (and bored), and what good would it do to break just one manacle? He would be wiped out, magic-wise, and his captors could come back at their leisure and restore the manacle while he waited for enough magic to break the other two manacles. His allergic reactions would get worse, and he would still be bored.

So Maurice sat there, as still as he could so his sweater and socks stayed between his skin and the iron manacles. He thought very hard about his possible judges, the possible charges, and his possible punishments. His imagination was even more acutely developed than his sense of irate justice.

"Yeah, Willy Shakespeare, you didn't know squat when you talked about 'now my soul's palace is become a prison.' I really think you were three sheets to the wind when you wrote that line. And good old Lovelace was off his rocker when he said 'Nor iron bars a cage.' I'm allergic to iron! He didn't know squat about iron chains."

For punctuation, Maurice sneezed five times in a row, until his head felt like it would snap off his neck. He nearly hit himself in the face with the manacle when he tried to hold onto his head. In the waiting room before judgment fell, anything could and often did happen, so he wasn't taking any chances.

The crusty old fogies on the Fae Disciplinary Council weren't taking any chances on him getting away, were they? He was stuck, no two ways about it.

"Hey, I know you can hear me!" He tipped his head back to look up at the source of the light. "Isn't there something in the Fae Disciplinary Rules about cruel and unusual punishment?" His words didn't seem to be absorbed so entirely this time. Was that a good sign, or bad? "Come on, guys. I was just having a little fun."

Yes, but your idea of a good time coincides unpleasantly with others' ideas of a bad time, an unfamiliar, creaky voice whispered in the middle of his head.

All right, so he was wrong. The Council was keeping an eye on him every second until they brought him up for judgment.

But to be fair -- would anyone be fair? -- he got caught when he stopped to help someone who wasn't having a good time.

All right, he hadn't exactly stopped. More like put on brakes and sank roots and stayed to torment that bully, Jordan Price. It had seemed like the right thing to do, at the time. Price's insistence on not only tormenting Forsythe, but taking away every chance he had for a little fun, a little comfort, and a decent life -- that riled Maurice. And it took a lot to rile his righteous indignation. So he had set up shop in the guise of a slightly dizzy old woman, and had opened a store that promised to fulfill everyone's dearest wish.

Amazing the number of greedy souls in one tiny town. He could have become a millionaire in a matter of months, but he'd drawn the line at taking the money of people who couldn't afford to have the rug ripped out from underneath them. Too bad the dusty old fuddy-duddies on the Council wouldn't take that into consideration. Maurice suspected the amount of fun he had had would cancel out all the good he had done.

The darkness congealed around Maurice, revealing a long, dark room with a vaulted ceiling of churning black clouds. A door appeared at the far end and swung open. The iron manacles and chains on his ankles vanished. An iron ring appeared in the air, attached to the other end of the chain on Maurice's wrist. It slid through the air, toward the open door.

Maurice had to follow, sneezing and itching abominably as the manacle slid off the insulation of his sweater and settled on his wrist. His eyes watered and his nose dripped and he couldn't even snap his fingers and conjure a handkerchief. No way was he wiping his nose on his cashmere sweater.

The door leaped forward and swallowed him.

Twenty tiers of seats rose up through the rainbow-streaked shadows as the room solidified around him. His Italian loafers tapped on a jeweled tile floor. That dratted iron ring hovered in the air over his head, making him hold his arm at right angles to his body.

Thirty members of the Fae Disciplinary Council were hard at work in the stands. They wore various robes and wigs and other costumes denoting judges in various cultures and centuries, with casual disregard for proper colors and styles. Stacks of papers appeared in front of them and drifted down to the tables, to sparkle and vanish as soon as they were read and signed.

Most of the Council members kept working, ignoring Maurice. All except for two: Chief Council Speaker Asmondius Pickle, wore lavender, with lavender owls perched on his shoulders. Strictus Hooper, sitting two seats to the right of Pickle, wore sour cabbage green with a neon green Georgian wig sitting crooked on his bald head.

"Maurice..." Asmondius sighed as he rested his elbows on the table in front of him. "Lad, you are a problem. Always have been. There's something to be admired in a Fae who doesn't like injustice or bullying. But when you turn into a bully yourself, and have too much fun in the pursuit of justice, well..." He shrugged, his robes shifting into saffron in places.

"Your sentence is exile," Strictus snapped. He sniffed. "Since you seem to like Humans so much, you are sentenced to two years of exile in the Human realms. No communication with the Fae enclaves, no visits home."

That didn't seem so bad, but Maurice knew there had to be a real stinger hidden under the supposed mercy of the Council. He braced himself.

"Two years in reduced circumstances." Strictus smiled, and that worried Maurice. The last time Strictus had smiled... Come to think of it, he couldn't remember the last time Strictus had smiled. Not that he spent time voluntarily in the old sourpuss's company, but such an unusual event would have been reported in the *Magical Mumbler*.

Reduced? His brain snagged on that word, images of what it could mean flitting through his thoughts.

"Humans think we're only five inches tall and have wings like butterflies." Strictus steepled his fingers and leaned back in the tall chair so his wig flattened and lifted off his bald scalp for a moment. "You shall spend your time of exile as Humans think the Fae are. And the scope of your magic shall match your size." He snapped his fingers, and an enormous cabbage-green gavel appeared out of thin air and slammed down on the table in front of him.

Maurice's mouth dropped open. He couldn't think of a single

word to say. The reverberating thud-clang of the judgment gavel would have drowned out any sound he made, anyway.

The reverberations continued, growing louder, making the room shake. The iron manacle fell off his wrist, but before he could gather up his magic and try to slip into a sideways dimension, something squeezed down on him. His back itched abominably. He opened his mouth to shout, to deny what was happening... A squeak emerged instead of the shout he'd intended. He dropped to his knees.

The lights flickered, and he landed on a marble floor.

Around him were a ball-and-jacks set, all the pieces larger than his head, a glass jar of rainbow-colored rocky candy sticks taller than he was, and an iridescent globe that looked like a transportation and communication globe, set in a brass stand shaped like a coiled dragon, with rubies for eyes. An old-fashioned brass cash register towered over him like a three-story building.

"You must be Maurice," a woman said, and her voice came from high overhead.

Okay, he liked tall women, but this was ridiculous.

Before his neck could get a cramp from looking up and up and up, Maurice's perceptions changed. This heart-shaped face and waterfall of hair in ten shades of gold and cinnamon weren't particularly tall. He was very, very short.

Unable to resist, he looked over his shoulder. Wings. Butterfly-shaped, glistening, iridescent, lacy, rainbow-streaked wings, fluttering like the lashes of a flirting maiden. Maybe if he turned around and pretended they weren't there, they would fade away? Fae hadn't had wings for centuries.

How could they do this to him?

"Cute, but not you," she said. Laughter sparkled in her big blue eyes, and put a rich tone in her voice, but she didn't smile. Somehow, her sympathy and attempt not to hurt his feelings just made the whole situation worse. "Especially not with those Italian shoes. I hope you won't end up with permanent holes in that sweater. Cashmere?"

He barely restrained his tongue and changed his words to something less offensive. "Who the heck cares?" Maurice had always been a quick study. He put all the pieces together within a few seconds, despite his head reeling from the utter indignity: five inches tall, and wings no self-respecting Fae would wear to a costume ball! "I suppose you're my probation officer?"

"Angela." She nodded, and didn't do him the indignity of offering a finger for him to shake. She wore a slightly faded, long blue dress in a shapeless style Maurice thought had been referred to as a granny dress. "This is Divine's Emporium. I can't understand why Asmondius wants you to spend two years here, but I've known him long enough to know he has his reasons. Why he would consider Divine's a punishment..." She shrugged.

A communications globe shimmered into being just above the globe in the dragon stand. Angela's lips quirked up a little more and held out her hand. A scroll popped out of the globe to land in her hand, then the globe popped like a soap bubble and vanished. She sat down on a wooden stool behind the counter in what looked like an old-fashioned general store.

Maurice took a good look around while she read the scroll.

No general store he had ever known looked like this place. For one thing, if he moved his vision sideways a little, he could see the slits in reality where extra rooms and slides into other dimensions hid, waiting to be opened up and used. The actual physical rooms themselves contained a mish-mash of different styles of shelving; wrought iron, glass, chrome, plastic, and wood. Antiques and toys, penny candy and dozens of styles of dishes, handcrafted wooden furniture, kites, wind chimes, candles, were piled willy-nilly on them. The list went on and on. And scattered through everything, he caught the glimmer of magic waiting, resting, poised to spring into action. The place reminded him a lot of his shop.

Maurice had the dreadful feeling Angela was one of those do-gooders who existed to grant the wishes of others and made a regular nuisance out of themselves, insisting that people who were perfectly happy were actually miserable and didn't know what they wanted or needed. Usually by the time these do-gooders threw up their hands in defeat and fled town, they had ruined a dozen lives.

Too bad. Angela looked like she had an actual sense of humor, which most do-gooders, in Maurice's experience, lacked.

Oh, Maurice, old boy, you are in one heck of a lot of trouble.

"So Asmondius wants to teach you a lesson." Angela rolled up the scroll and tucked it into a pocket of her dress. "Because the shop you set up to teach those villagers a lesson was a parody of my shop--"

"Can't parody what you don't know exists," he offered.

"Granted." Another twitch of her lips, another smile stifled. "Asmondius thinks you need to squash bullies and help the underdog, but you also need to learn discretion. To study and think before you leap into a situation." She gestured for him to follow as she stepped away from the counter. "Let me show you around."

Maurice almost snarled for her to wait for him. It was a doggone long drop to the floor, and he wasn't sure how to get down. Then he remembered he had wings. Did they actually work? He fought down the urge to lean back against a sharp corner and scratch hard, and flexed his shoulder blades. With a gust of cotton candy-scented air -- *oh, please, did they have to be that cruel?* -- he was airborne.

He followed Angela into the back of the store and through a storage room. She led him outside, for a good look at a snowy slope going down into a winter wonderland of forest and meadows and a wandering, ice-coated river. Turning around, he saw the shop was in a big Victorian house, gold, with cupolas and lacy olive-green gingerbread trim and dozens of windows. Sideways vision showed him more slits where magic could come in and out and doorways inside the shop led to other places and times.

"Divine's Emporium exists to heal and assist those who come here looking for help. We guard other worlds and times, secrets and dangers. We don't force help on anyone, we don't take over anyone's life. A lot of people you would probably label misfits come here because they know they'll be loved and accepted here." Angela's voice went stern. "I don't want you mocking any of my friends, understand?"

"Understood." Maurice had the strangest urge to salute, but he knew Angela would not be amused.

"You're here for two full years, Human time. You have to find opportunities to help Humans. I'm not allowed to give you specific orders, but I can make suggestions. And give lots of guidance." She gestured for him to follow her back inside.

The evening was spent in fitting out his quarters and giving him a tour of all the rooms that belonged to Divine's Emporium. Angela didn't suggest he move into the antique dollhouse, and he was grateful. Instead, his apartment fitted out with dollhouse furniture was set up in a hutch, with plenty of room for him to float from one floor to the other with the doors closed, providing him with a sense of privacy.

In the toy room, he found a dozen sets of clothes for male dolls that fit him. The magic that made his wings appear created slits in the clothes when he tried to put them on, and mended them when he took them off. Even his cashmere sweater, to his relief.

Except for his size and the wings, nothing else about him had changed. He had feared the Council would change his hair, but it was still a short, curly mane of jet black, and he still had his fencing/rock climbing/track-and-field physique. He had worked hard for that, rather than using magic to keep himself looking good, and he felt his first flicker of gratitude that the Council hadn't taken that away. For instance, making him a reedy wimp with lavender hair and weak ankles.

That night after dinner, Angela gave him a verbal tour of the town. She brought the globe in its dragon stand upstairs to her apartment, as a visual aid. The globe was known as the Wishing Ball. Quite a few of the town's children believed in magic and regularly wished on it, so some of the more alert children might be able to see him. Meaning he had to proceed with caution when there were children in the shop.

While she talked about the town, images appeared in the Wishing Ball. Divine's Emporium sat on the edge of the town of Neighborlee, Ohio, overlooking the Metroparks. Willis-Brooks College was over 150 years old and took up a good portion of the town. The center of town had a square with the requisite Civil War monument, playground, and gazebo, and was surrounded by a lot of old-fashioned-looking buildings, giving the moonlit downtown area a sense of belonging in the previous century. Maurice decided he liked Neighborlee, just before it occurred to him that a quiet town would make it hard to find people to help.

Chapter Two

"Mistletoe?" Maurice perched on the top shelf behind the store counter, where the coffee shop shimmered on the edge of becoming solid. It was Saturday morning, one day into his exile.

He wrinkled up his nose at the mistletoe Angela was hanging from the pull cord of the ceiling fan. "You're wasting mistletoe on Humans, Angie-baby. They can't see into the parallel dimensions, and even if they could, they have to be pretty quick to reach through the slits and pull their dreams-come-true back into reality with them. Not one Human in a million can do it."

"We Humans have a magic of our own," she responded serenely, and climbed down the ladder. Angela looked up at the gold balls and red ribbon, bits of green leaves and white berries, and smiled. She had hung mistletoe in every room of the shop.

"Yeah, and how long has it been since you were an ordinary Human?"

"I don't exactly recall." Her smile faded a little. "But even at the beginning, I doubt I was ever ordinary."

"You're one weird chick."

"Coming from someone five inches tall and wearing wings Tinkerbell wouldn't be caught dead in, I think I'll take that as a compliment." She stepped up behind the counter, to give the Wishing Ball one last polish with Windex and a paper towel.

Maurice couldn't be angry. He burst out laughing instead. He watched her polish the rainbow-smeared metallic ball for a few seconds. Angela confused him, and strangely, he almost liked it. This period of exile, shrunken body, shrunken magic, and being invisible to almost everyone wouldn't be easy. He sensed having Angela for his probation officer would make all the difference. For the first time in his life, he had limits he couldn't charm or scheme his way around, but maybe that wasn't so bad?

"How come you make magic so easy to come by here?" he had to ask, after she opened the first of three boxes of ornaments that looked, and sparkled with real magic, like the Wishing Ball.

"Magic *is* easy to come by for Humans who know to look for it and know to want it. Most are so caught up in their physical world, they think it's the only one, and they miss the magic. I just make things a little more obvious. Divine's has a reputation for amazing things happening. People who don't believe in wishes elsewhere believe here. I take them back to simpler, happier times, when the world was filled with possibilities." She smiled and brushed a loose strand of hair back over the shoulder of her gold-trimmed, crimson velvet gown. "Perfect. Almost time for the party."

"Doesn't look like a party." He glanced around, half-expecting food, chairs, and decorations to appear from a sideways dimension.

"It's my annual decorating party." She flicked her fingers at the winkies slipping back and forth through the ceiling. It raised another two feet. "Keep a sharp eye out, Maurice. You could get your first assignment this afternoon."

"Assignment." He huffed. "Am I supposed to be Santa's helper, or just a vending machine for all your hopeless Human friends?"

Angela's eyes darkened, sending a shiver of apprehension down his back. His wings fluttered faster, despite his best efforts to keep them still. It occurred to him that if she wanted to stomp on him, he didn't have the magic or wing speed to get out from under her foot in time.

"Attitude will get you nowhere. If you don't straighten out, I'll make you spend the entire Christmas season as the angel on top of the tree." She gestured in the corner, as if the tree was already there.

"Yeah? You and whose army?" Belatedly, he hoped she would take it as a joke.

Angela just smiled at his words, but he had the feeling the joke was on him. He gulped hard and offered his most charming smile. Of course, how charming could that smile be, when it was probably about half an inch wide?

"Okay, I take that back. Lesson learned."

"You hope." She looked around the room, gave a nod of approval, and sauntered out of the room.

The first person who showed up certainly didn't look like she was ready for a party. She was pale under gallons of rusty freckles and cold-reddened cheeks, short, with bowed shoulders and hips that looked a mile wide under a down jacket that hung past her knees and made her look like the Michelin Man.

Maurice winced, too fascinated by the pitiful creature to turn away when Angela called her name and greeted her with a hug.

"I rescued some more books," Holly said as she handed over three bulging plastic grocery bags to Angela. "They didn't even put them in the Friends of the Library sale, just tossed them. Sacrilege."

Angela put them on the counter, pulling out a few from each bag. "Just because the binding and cover are a wreck doesn't mean the words inside are any less precious. Let's see if we can work our usual magic and find a new home for these treasures."

Maurice hovered overhead while Angela and Holly looked through the battered, ragged old books. He dropped down to study a faded illustration, and Holly nearly closed the book on him. She didn't react when he yelped.

"So... if nobody can see me, they can't hear me, either?" He sighed and settled down on the shelf, where he could watch what they were doing without overtaxing his new wings.

People who come in here are a lot closer to believing in magic and other worlds and the Fae. They're my friends, so no straining their sense of reality, you hear me? No nasty tricks, no hiding things, no illusions and sound effects. Got me? Angela said into his mind.

Full of surprises, Angela definitely was.

He gave her a stiff, military-precise salute. "Got it. It's the angel on the tree until New Year's, if I don't fly straight and true."

Angela glanced over her shoulder at him, eyes sparkling with laughter, and nodded once. Then she went back to work on the books with Holly. They decided all the books could be salvaged with a little work and tender loving care. Holly took them upstairs to deposit in one of Angela's workrooms.

From some of the things Holly said as she and Angela examined the rescued books, Maurice guessed she was a librarian. He kind of liked her for rescuing books that were about to be discarded, for Angela to mend and put on her shelves. He did love to fall into a book and travel through his imagination.

Come to think of it, Holly looked like a librarian. She needed wire-rimmed spectacles and a skirt down below her calves, instead of patched jeans, faux-fur boots, and an oversized white Mickey Mouse sweatshirt. Her hair, when she pulled off her Cleveland Browns stocking cap, disappointed him. He expected frizzy red to go with all those freckles. It was dishwater brown, straight, with a few specks of ginger.

"So... I love a good book," he said, when Holly stepped out of the room. "But please, please don't tell me she's my first assignment. I don't do makeovers."

"You might be surprised, if you got to know Holly. Maybe she doesn't need a makeover at all."

"Yeah? Without one, how am I ever going to dupe some dweeb into falling in love with her?"

"You have a lot to learn," Angela responded quietly. "How about you get an eagle's eye view of things?"

Her smile turned sweet. Maurice had the awful feeling a sticky sweet Angela was more dangerous than the entire Fae Disciplinary Council with malfunctioning magic, jazzed on diet cherry cola.

~~~~~

Christmas at Divine's Emporium was a study in merry chaos. Ken Jenkins retreated to the sidelines and watched a dozen people help Angela decorate the tree and string pine garland from room to room. He had done his part, bringing the granddaddy pine tree to the shop and manhandling the monster in through the side door. A side door that only seemed to appear at Christmastime.

The ceiling seemed higher than usual, too. Things always seemed to work out just the way Angela needed them to, inside her shop. Sometimes it seemed like the walls adjusted to comfortably fit everything she put inside the store. Too bad the rest of the world didn't reshape itself to accommodate Angela's friends.

Ken snorted softly at his flight of fancy. He had given up on magic long ago. Not that he wouldn't appreciate a bit now. This first Christmas without Brittney was one of those *grit your teeth and face it like a man* situations, since this should have been his first Christmas *with* Brittney.

It would be a lot easier if he wouldn't see her traipsing around the company Christmas party in two weeks, on the arm of Allistair Somerville.

Ever since nursery school, Allistair believed whatever Ken had was his to take. If he couldn't steal it from Ken, he lied or whined until someone gave it to him to shut him up. All through school, no matter how big or small, whatever Ken prized or needed, Allistair went after. Then used up, destroyed or discarded it a day or a month or a year later. Ken's rubber ball. His tricycle. His basketball. His BMX bike. His homework. His prom date. His expected
~~~~~

promotion to junior vice president at Myerhausen.

Allistair had mostly ignored Brittney, who had come close to drooling after him, Ken realized in retrospect. When she finally gave up and started dating Ken, Allistair saw the light and went after her in a big way. Big gifts. Derailing Ken's plans for dates. Trying to get him transferred out of state.

Ken wished now Allistair had worked faster, or Brittney had given in sooner. Like between the engagement ring and the wedding. They had barely been married four months when she met Allistair for lunch. Two of Ken's buddies from college had seen them and told him. Brittney lied when he asked, and Ken chose to believe her. He thought she had better taste. Until she dumped him at their ten-month anniversary.

Merry Christmas? Ken didn't think so.

All he wanted for Christmas was a date to the company party. A girl to make Brittney jealous enough to dive headfirst into a vat of ice cream and not come out until she had lost her uber-slim super-model look. He especially wanted a girl with the brains and good taste to laugh in Allistair's face when he made a play for her. Because he *would* make a play for her, just because Ken had her.

He had considered asking Lanie Zephyr to pretend to be his girlfriend. He thought she was great. If he didn't have a raw wound where his heart used to be, he might pursue her as a girlfriend someday. However, that wheelchair got in the way. Even if Lanie were pretty enough to elicit jealousy from Brittney, his soon-to-be-ex-wife was too shallow to see the woman inside the wheelchair. She would only see the handicap and wouldn't be jealous. The whole point of finding someone new and wonderful was to make her jealous. On a positive note, Allistair thought anybody in a wheelchair had a communicable disease, so he would never try to take Lanie from Ken. Although it would certainly be fun to see her shred Allistair with her sharp, lunatic sense of humor.

"Perfect," Angela sighed as she stepped back from the tree. "Thank you, everyone. I don't know how I would have done it without your help." She turned, her long, gleaming golden hair swirling out from around her like a satin cape.

"You don't need anyone's help, Angela." The speaker was a kid in baggy jeans, ball cap, and oversized gray sweatshirt, sitting on the front counter. "If we hadn't stopped in to help, you would have just called the elves, and they would have decorated."

His remark earned laughter from the others around the tree. Ken laughed along with them. The boy was right. Angela always managed to work miracles, and Divine's Emporium seemed to be a source of never-ending strange and wonderful things and occurrences. Angela always had advice and something to suit everyone's need, so when she needed help, there was always someone ready and willing.

Metallic, rainbow-streaked balls, miniatures of the Wishing Ball hung on the tree. Ken admired the ornaments and longed for the ability to believe in magic and make a wish. But if magic was real, then belief was the key ingredient in making it work. If he couldn't believe, no matter how strong and real the magic was, it wouldn't work for him.

"Just for that, Jo," Angela said, "you get the first wish."

Ken caught his breath. *Wishes?* He laughed silently at himself. Even if there was no more magic left in the world for him, that didn't mean other people couldn't believe and enjoy.

"Make a wish?" Jo's voice cracked with a cold. The kid hopped down off the counter and stepped over to the Wishing Ball. The rainbow metallic ball in its stylized dragon stand seemed to glow with a light of its own.

"Not there." Angela gestured at the tree. "Here. Hold an ornament in both your hands and make a wish."

"That's easy." Jo wiped his hands on the seat of his jeans and reached for an ornament. "I wish I had a job. Better than my paper route." He grinned over his shoulder at Angela. "Better hours, and indoors, please."

Ken could have sworn he saw the Christmas tree angel lean down and shake glitter on the boy's baseball cap.

Shaking his head, he wondered if he had been working too hard. Now he was hallucinating, from fatigue and the shifting lights in the shop. Maybe instead of worrying about his date for the company Christmas party, he should just ask for the entire month off and go to some place quiet and restful.

"Oh, no you don't," Angela said, when Jo made a move to put the ornament back on the tree. "How can your wish come true if you don't take it home with you?"

"I don't have a tree."

"It's still three weeks until Christmas." She closed the boy's hands around the ornament again. "Something might happen between now and then." She met Jo's eyes until the boy gave in and tucked the ornament into the front pocket of his sweatshirt. Angela nodded, and looked around the room. "Ken?" She winked at him when he startled. "Your turn next."

"But --"

"You don't have to say your wish out loud. It won't negate what you wish for." She glanced at Jo.

The boy stuck his tongue out. Under the smears of dust and strands of cobweb hanging from the brim of his ball cap, his face looked delicate. Ken couldn't remember seeing him in the shop before. Maybe he was new to town? Sickly?

Make a wish. Ken fought a snort of skepticism. That attitude didn't belong at Divine's. He walked up to the tree. When he picked his ornament, he glanced up at the angel.

It winked at him.

He flinched. *I wish... I need a date for the company Christmas party. Someone classy. A real lady. Someone wonderful, who'll stick around forever.* After all, if he was going to take a chance on wishes, why not go for broke? *And if Allistair shows his true colors in front of the boss, that'd be great, too.*

He watched Jo while the rest of the decorating party made their wishes. Some aloud, others silent. Ken remembered when he had been part of the laughing and teasing, the complaints about the crowds at the malls, comparing plans for holiday celebrations. It felt like a lifetime ago.

Jo didn't join in the teasing, which reinforced Ken's suspicion the kid was new in town and didn't know many people. Poor kid, looking for work while he was still in school. He wondered if Jo was from the orphanage. Angela mentored the kids who lived there, finding jobs for them in her shop or other shops in town.

If you want good things to happen in your life, his mother used to say, *you should make good things happen for other people.*

"I swear," Diane, one of Angela's clerks said, laughing, "you get a bigger tree every year, but it's never a problem."

"We don't believe in problems at Divine's Emporium." Angela looked positively prim in her smugness. "You've worked for me long enough to know that."

"Just solutions and miracles," Jo said. "Christmas is the right time of year for miracles, that's for sure." He smiled, but there was something wistful in his expression, and that decided Ken.

"Hey, Jo." Ken dug in his wallet for a business card. He held it out to the boy, whose eyes were bright blue among the dust from lugging boxes of decorations up from Angela's cellar. "Go see the Human Resources director at Myerhausen. She'll find you a job."

Jo's eyes widened and his long, delicate fingers twitched as he took the card. "Thanks -- uh," he glanced at the card, "Ken. That's really nice of you."

"That's one wish already come true," Angela said.

"I haven't even applied yet." The boy laughed.

"Oh ye of little faith. Where's your Christmas spirit?" She wrapped an arm around Ken's shoulder for a brief hug. "I think I can guarantee your wish will come true."

"I didn't do it to make my wish work," Ken muttered. He hated it when his face got so hot. Brittney had always teased him about being able to use his face for a warning beacon.

"That's exactly why it'll work." Angela winked and walked on past to talk to Jane Wilson.

"Good luck." Ken held out his hand. He caught his breath when a spark shot up his arm at the touch of Jo's warm, smooth hand.

His last task before he left the decorating party was to haul two garbage bags to the back storage room and put them in the wheeled garbage bins. Angela was waiting for him when he picked up his coat from the pile in the book room.

"I hope you don't think making that wish was a waste of time." She rested a hand on his arm.

"I'm not exactly in a mood for believing in wishes and magic." He felt almost ashamed to say that to her. What was Divine's Emporium, if not a magical place?

Angela sighed, and the sympathy in her eyes was warming, and didn't tie him up in knots inside like the sympathy he saw in other people. That was part of the magic of this place, too. A magic he could still believe in, maybe even needed, desperately.

"Just because Brittney used you to get Allistair's attention doesn't mean you, Ken Jenkins, are worthless or a fool. There is still magic in this world. There is still true love. And those who are willing to look for magic and love will find them. Take a chance."

~~~~~

Jo sighed as the last few people left the decorating party. Only she, Angela and Holly were left in the main room, though she thought she heard Lanie and her brothers talking in the book room. She watched Ken stride out the front door, into the swirling snow. His shoulders were bowed like Santa Claus carrying an impossibly heavy pack.

He seemed like Santa Claus right now. In the three years since she had moved to Neighborlee to take care of Aunt Myrtle, Jo had made many wishes at Divine's, but none had ever come true this fast and this clearly before.

She laughed silently at herself when she felt the business card crumple in her fist and watched Ken tugging his Willis-Brooks College varsity jacket closer around his shoulders. Her smile faded, remembering the stress lines around his mouth and eyes. Somebody needed to do something nice for him. How many people nowadays lifted their heads out of their own problems to help someone else?

"Hey, Angela?" She yanked her baseball cap off, letting her sweaty, toffee-colored curls fall down around her shoulders.

"What do I know about Ken Jenkins and Myerhausen?" She leaned forward on her partially cleared counter, blue eyes sparkling. "Myerhausen is about eight miles north of Neighborlee. It handles a lot of the shipping, logistics and warehousing for companies around Cleveland. As for Ken..." She sighed and shook her head. "Ken is a nice guy who always lends a helping hand, but never seems to get a break."

"That's what I thought," Jo murmured. She thought of Ken's big, chocolate brown eyes, his snub nose and his short-cropped hair. Something warmed deep inside.

"The two of you would make a nice couple." Angela almost sang the words, under her breath.

"Don't even go there. Until Auntie's hospital bills are all paid up, I'm too busy working three different jobs to have a social life, much less..." Jo sighed.

"Get distracted by a truly nice guy?"

"Hormones. Especially if I end up working with, or even for, my Santa Claus. So Myerhausen does warehousing and shipping, huh? Well, that suits me. All my clothes look like this." She slapped
~~~~~

at her grime-streaked clothes. "Working all the time has been great for my diet, but not my wardrobe."

Jo had worn her oldest clothes today to help haul boxes out of storage. Her good clothes weren't much better. She had lost a lot of weight since coming to Neighborlee, so her baggy clothes made her look like a ragamuffin. That hadn't mattered before, because her paper route and other odd jobs didn't leave her time for socializing. With Aunt Myrtle's bills to pay off, she didn't have the money to shop for a new wardrobe now, either.

"You are not aiming at a dirty warehouse job," Angela scolded. "I have some nice dresses in the back, just perfect for an office job." She hooked her thumb over her shoulder, in the direction of the secondhand clothing room. "Holly, you helped me hang them up, you know where they are. Don't let her leave until she has something nice."

Holly saluted. She wiped her hands on the seat of her jeans as she crossed the room. When Jo didn't follow her immediately, she growled teasingly and grabbed hold of her hand. They went laughing through the doorway, Holly pretending to drag her.

The moment they vanished down the hall, the light in the main room lost some of its warmth. The Christmas tree shuddered. Angela's smile flattened. The angel shot off apple green sparks, fluttered his wings, and slid down a succession of branches until he was eye-level with Angela. He used the last branch as a springboard and did a quadruple twist through the air to land on the counter in front of her.

"Maurice."

"Angela." He gestured at his angel outfit. "Mercy? Haven't I been a good boy most of the day?"

"Most of it." Her lips twitched as she fought a smile.

His gold and white robes changed to the camouflage clothes he had stolen from G.I. Joe. Maurice sighed in relief, then glanced sideways at her.

"You know what I'm like. You read that report Asmondius sent you. You asked for it when you sentenced me to the top of the tree in that ridiculous get-up." He crossed his arms and returned her glare for five seconds. Then they both grinned. "Come on, Angie-baby. If I have to help Humans, I can have a little fun, can't I?"

"A 'little fun' is what got you sent here." She stepped back and looked him over. "People see more at Divine's."

"Uh, duh," Lanie Zephyr said, wheeling into the room. "First winkies, now … mini-Legolas?"

"Hey, babe." Maurice saluted, bending over far enough to make himself turn a somersault in mid-air. "Thought I saw you seeing me."

"Nice to know everything we went through this summer hasn't driven me bonkers just yet."

"Lanie, could you let Maurice and me deal with some business?" Angela said, never taking her gaze off Maurice.

"Hey, sure. Just wanted to make sure I wasn't …" She twirled her forefinger by her right temple. "I gotta run, committee meeting. You're not into Star Trek, are you, Maurice?"

"Please." Angela rolled her eyes, but her lips twitched, fighting a smile. "That is the last thing we need. Most of the people who might be able to hear or even see Maurice belong to your club. It might not be wise. Not yet, at the start of his exile."

"Exile?" Lanie looked like she was going to ask more questions. She took a deep breath, shook her head, and turned to head out of the room. "They'd be less likely to notice at our Christmas party. Someone's always trying to spike the fake Romulan ale …"

"Lanie, go!"

She flashed the Vulcan salute and her wheelchair sped down the hallway and out of sight. Without touching the wheels.

"Okay …" Maurice nodded. "I see what you mean. Didn't see that coming. I do like Star Trek …" He clasped his hands under his chin and fluttered his eyelashes.

Angela sputtered, fighting laughter. "We'll see. If you behave yourself for the next couple weeks. Now, to business. The guardians can handle the reality of you, in theory. With others who are sensitive enough to see you, we must tread lightly. To avoid tipping them in the wrong direction."

"Like Ken?"

"Perhaps. Ken noticed something, even if he isn't sure what. You don't want to get off to a bad start."

"I think I'm off to a great start. Helping two lonely hearts has to make big points with the Fae Council, don't you think?"

"Did you make Ken--"

"Nah, he thought of that all by himself. Guys like that need full-time keepers, helping others and ignoring themselves." His frustrated look faded into sympathy. "They'd look good together, you think?"

"I think those two would be very good together, yes." Angela tugged Maurice's outfit straight. "And I think they could do with a little help. *A little*. Not interference. A few nudges. Clearing a few obstacles out of their path. That sort of thing. Nothing drastic to catch the attention of Humans, and no strong use of magic."

"What strong magic?" he snarled. "When the Council pasted these stupid wings on me and shrank me, they shrank *everything*."

"If you don't fix that attitude, you can spend the entire Christmas season on that tree." She fought not to burst out laughing when terror blanched his ruddy complexion.

"It's kind of hard not to have an attitude when you're used to being over six feet tall and you're condemned to five inches for two Human years," he moaned He glanced toward the doorway and leaped into the air, before vanishing in a shower of purple sparks.

Jo came back into the room, accompanied by Holly. She wore a royal blue calf-length knit shirt-dress that hugged her slim frame. "What do you think?" She turned around, making the skirt flare out.

"You are going to knock them dead. They'll have to make you secretary to the president when you interview," Angela said.

"I'll just be glad to have a job with regular hours, indoors, and no newsprint or diesel fumes or engine pieces all over the floor."

"Go on back into that room," she made a twirling motion with her hand, "and don't come out until you have at least one outfit for each day of the week. That's an order."

Jo and Holly picked out three more dresses, two skirts, two pairs of dress pants, and several sweaters and blouses. They chattered excitedly as they left together, hauling Jo's new clothes out to her car.

Angela curved her hands around the Wishing Ball. The dragon's ruby eyes glowed softly in the dim afternoon light. "I wish for you a happily ever after," she whispered. Sparks spun up out of the Wishing Ball and shot out across the shop, through the front door. They split into two streams outside, following the paths Jo and Ken had taken.

Chapter Three

Monday morning, Jo arrived at the Myerhausen front office half an hour after she calculated the office staff would show up. If she wanted the HR manager to be in a good mood when she applied for work, she would let that manager get his or her coffee and sit down and gear up for the day. Then she could attack, beg, grovel, whatever it took to get that job.

Connie, head of HR, was a comfortable-looking woman who wore sensible shoes and little jewelry. She smiled when she saw Jo sitting in the reception area, filling out the requisite application form. Jo said a prayer of thanks yet again for Angela bullying her into buying new clothes. The blue dress made her feel elegant and sensible at the same time as she followed Connie into the office for her interview.

~~~~~

While Jo filled out the Meyers-Briggs test, Connie stepped across the hall to refill her coffee cup.

Mrs. Myerhausen toddled down the hall, shaking a few loose snowflakes from her crimson coat and matching scarf. She let out a little yelp when she nearly ran into Connie, who was busy watching Jo and sipping her coffee as she crossed the hall.

"Oh, Mrs. M. Sorry!"

"Not a problem, dear." She chuckled. "No harm." With her dark green skirts and her red boots and hat, rosy cheeks and white curls, she looked like a modern Mrs. Claus. "You looked pre-occupied." She glanced into the office and smiled, seeing Jo bent over the third page of the test. "Please tell me that lovely young lady is applying for the secretary position," she said just above a whisper.

"Well... She's just applying in general, but from all her experience, I'm tempted to offer her the job."

"Good. She looks like someone with a sense of balance. All those girls who coat their faces in makeup and starve themselves to be fashionable are just poisoning their brains. I like the look of her."

"Ken must have, too."

"Ken?" Mrs. Myerhausen's gaze sharpened. "Mr. Jenkins?"
~~~~~

"He sent her over to apply."

"That's a boy with a good head on his shoulders." She nodded. "If he recommended her, that's good enough for me."

"I'm going to Arthur's office and have a little talk with him, just to make sure he doesn't mess this up." She tugged her scarf off her neck and folded it as she resumed her trip down the hall.

"Mrs. M..." Connie didn't look worried, just thoughtful.

"That old bear might know how to run the company, but when it comes to the backbone of the company, the young women who run the office... He's hopeless. He hired Felicia, didn't he? And look what a mess she made of things."

~~~~~

Eight more days until the company Christmas party.

Friday afternoon, Ken marked another day off his desk calendar, closed his eyes and leaned back in his chair with a long sigh of exhaustion. During the holidays, a majority of Myerhausen's customers slowed down or even shut down. That meant less work for his division, less stress, fewer crises. The entire month of December, he could usually be out of the office by 5, instead of working until 6.

When he and Brittney were first married, he had looked forward to going home at a decent hour and taking her Christmas shopping, decorating their apartment together, maybe hitting the toboggan chutes in the Metroparks. Spots on his calendar that he had filled out months ago, marked "pick up Brittney's present" and "first Christmas portrait sitting" had Xs through them.

Next to the calendar, the invitation for the company Christmas party waited for Ken to fill out the RSVP. Today was the deadline for responding. If he didn't answer, Connie in HR would hunt him down and ask for an answer. Most likely in front of several co-workers. Admitting he wasn't coming to the Christmas party would be bad enough, but everyone would know he wasn't attending because Brittney would be there as Allistair's date.

They would pity him. A few would call him smart. Allistair's friends and supporters would call him a coward and wimp.

Sighing, he picked up the invitation and paused, with his pen poised over the "not attending" box. He couldn't do it. A tiny scrap of something inside him still believed in wishes coming true. He was holding out for that miracle girl who would make Brittney
~~~~~

green and Allistair's eyes pop out of his teeny tiny skull. He tossed the pen down. He still had another hour before Connie would come looking for it.

"Oh, straighten up, you whiny sap," he muttered.

The new girl paused in his open office doorway and looked in with a smile. Other than Arthur Myerhausen had snatched her up as his new secretary on Monday and she had started work on Tuesday, he didn't know anything about her. Felicia, the previous secretary, had left under a black cloud. According to the secretarial pool, she had sabotaged the files in retribution. The same sources said the new girl had been scrambling since she got the job, trying to straighten out the mess Felicia left behind.

Felicia had been Allistair's office paramour. Everyone suspected she delayed the requests and reports of other executives to make them look bad and help Allistair look good. Rumors said she had suffered a nervous breakdown when Allistair had snagged Brittney and dumped her.

When Ken had fought temptation and refused to help her sabotage Allistair's career, Felicia lost her slippery grasp on reality and decorum. Mr. Myerhausen had terminated her employment immediately, and security had escorted her from the building.

The mess she left behind had driven away the last two replacements, and the tangle had only grown worse. Ken hadn't learned the new girl's name, since she might only last two weeks before she gave up.

However, today was Friday and she was leaning against the doorframe, smiling, and didn't look frazzled or exhausted. In fact, she looked great. Her toffee-colored hair was pulled back in a simple ponytail and her blue eyes sparkled without the help of layers of makeup. Unlike Felicia. Or Brittney.

"Sorry," he said, offering a smile that he hoped would assure her he wasn't a lunatic. "I wasn't talking to you. Honest."

"That's okay. It's the end of a really long week."

"You're Mr. M's new secretary, aren't you? Yeah, I can imagine it's been a trial by fire, with the big mess left after -- Sorry, shouldn't talk badly about the departed." He was pretty sure that rule applied more to the dead than a vindictive-witch-dragged-out-screaming, but like his mother always said, *Never say behind someone's back what you wouldn't say to his face.*

"You're the only one who won't." Her tired smile brightened. "I've heard about Felicia from everybody. Starting with *Mrs.* M. I really wondered what I was getting myself into."

"Will I scare you away if I tell you that it's slow right now, because of the holidays?" At the back of his mind, a little voice told him to shut up, he was only making things worse. The thing was, he wanted to keep her talking to him for as long as possible. Even if he sounded like an idiot. "Most of our clients are shutting down until after New Year's. Usually I'm here until after 6, but all of December, I usually get out before 5, sometimes 4."

"Then this is late for you," she said, gesturing at the clock that read just after 5. "Why are you working so late?"

"No reason to go home, I guess." He tried to smile. There was no way he was going to confess to her that he hated going to his un-decorated, wifeless apartment. Then she would know for certain he was a loser, not just suspect it.

"Come on, I refuse to let my Santa Claus be depressed. Especially on a Friday, with a whole weekend ahead of you."

"Santa Claus?" He shook his head, not sure he had heard right.

"Oops. Sorry. Getting ahead of myself. Honestly, I've been so busy settling in, but I've been trying all week to catch up with you."

"Excuse me? Am I in trouble? Whatever nasty notes Felicia left behind, they're a pack of lies. I swear." He fought down that shiver of panic that regularly hit since Allistair had snagged a job here, just two months after Ken had graduated from warehouse supervisor to the executive ranks.

"From what I've heard about Felicia, if she left notes calling you Jack the Ripper, then I'd know you were a saint. Which I already thought before I even got the job."

"Sorry," he shook his head, "must be more tired than I thought. I'm totally lost."

"I wanted to thank you." She stepped into the office and held out her hand.

"For what?" Ken stood and shook hands without thinking.

"I wouldn't be here, if it wasn't for you."

"Oh, please, don't blame me for that!" Ken wanted to keep her standing close enough to smell her vanilla perfume and retain his grip on her elegant, long-fingered, warm hand.

"Blame?" Two tiny frown lines appeared between her eyes.

"You have the toughest job in the whole company, untangling that mess, and standing guard at the boss's door."

Then she laughed and blushed a little as she looked down at her hand, still caught in his grip. She didn't pull her hand free, and Ken took that as a major victory.

"You don't remember me, do you?"

"Wish I did." He wished he knew something suave to say.

"You gave me your business card at Divine's last weekend, and told me to apply for a job here. I'm sure it was because *you* sent me that they hired me so quickly."

"I gave -- no, that was a kid -- Jo? You're Jo?" Ken gaped and nearly forgot to let go of her hand as he sat down again. The shape of her face, the sound of her voice, her eyes, her smile. She was definitely the kid he had met and tried to help, but vastly improved. "I thought you were a boy in junior high, and you'd get an after-school job in the mailroom."

"I was aiming for a job in the warehouse," Jo said, with a delightful little chuckle.

It took his breath away, how relieved he was that she laughed instead of getting offended.

"Angela made me aim higher and invest in a new wardrobe. And I've been trying to get in here all week to thank you."

"I'm glad I could help." Ken really wished he knew the suave lines now.

"Well, no matter who you thought you were helping, I want to thank you. If there's anything I can do to repay you..." A sighing laugh escaped her. "Within reason, of course."

"Without getting tangled in office politics? Actually --" He swallowed hard and scolded himself not to be such a coward. "How about going to the company Christmas party with me?"

"Really?" She blushed.

"You act like nobody ever asks you out."

"Well, no, they don't." Jo laughed again before he could even think to feel sorry for her. "Probably because most of the time they think I'm a skinny school kid." She gestured down at her dress. "I've been working night shift jobs and delivering papers and such for years, and my wardrobe hasn't gone beyond jeans and sweats."

"Then they were blind." Ken stood again and held out his hand. To his delight, Jo put hers into his grasp again. "I was blind last week. And I'd be grateful if you'd go to the party with me, Jo. It'd be nice to go with a friend."

"A friend." She blushed. "I'd like that very much."

~~~~~

Hovering outside Ken's window, Maurice goggled at the scene that had just played out. How had that happened? He had come to Ken's office with a great plan: knock Jo's next load of papers out of her arms right in front of Ken, and when he stopped to help, sprinkle them with some glamour dust to jump-start an infatuation.

If they jumped ahead of him in the program, how was he going to get any points for helping them? Both Jo and Ken had their wishes now, and he hadn't been involved at all.

Sometimes a guy just couldn't get a break.

~~~~~

"Well, if it ain't good old Ken." Allistair sauntered up to Ken in the hourly employees' lunchroom on Monday. He carried a takeout box and wrinkled up his nose at Ken's brown bag lunch. "I thought for sure you'd give up schmoozing with the grunts, now that you have the inside track." He sneered as his gaze slid over the four dock crew workers at the round table in the corner.

"No idea what you're talking about." Ken continued across the lunchroom to join his friends.

He could usually count on their presence to keep Allistair in the executive lunchroom. Allistair had a phobia for the 'great unwashed,' as he referred to the blue-collar employees. The smell of sweat earned through honest labor clearly repulsed him.

"Yes you do. Kissing up to the old man's new secretary. She's not your type. Must be pretty desperate, lowering your standards."

Ken saw red. Harsh self-control let him put down his bag and three cartons of chocolate milk before he squeezed and destroyed his lunch. He didn't look at his waiting friends. He didn't need to see their faces, neutral but for the disgust in their eyes for Allistair.

Knowing they would let him handle his own fights helped Ken reduce his interior temperature by ten degrees. He nudged the chair out, preparing to sit, and took a deep breath.

"If you're referring to Jo, I think I've improved my standards."

Allistair had it coming. Brittney was a bag of bones compared to Jo. Ken had never understood her obsession with starving herself to attain *the look*. Jo had curves like a real woman, yet was sleek enough to pass for a boy. Knowing Brittney would shriek at what he had said made him grin. It helped his blood pressure.

"See, that was your problem with Brittney. You have no grasp of reality," Allistair sneered. His new Italian loafers left another black streak on the lunchroom floor as he turned to leave. "It won't do you any good, kissing up to the new girl. If anything, you're just kissing your career good-bye. From what I've heard, the old man's taken quite a liking to her himself. If you know what I mean." He stomped into the executive lunchroom.

Maurice landed on the edge of the ice cream vending machine and pointed his finger at Allistair, making him trip on the metal strip where tiled floor met carpeting. He stumbled, losing his grip on his takeout carton. It flipped over three times and landed upside down on Mr. Myerhausen's feet. Creamy noodles and seafood spattered the black, shiny tips of his shoes.

Mr. Myerhausen was white-haired, heavy-set, usually jolly and relaxed, but his mouth went into a hard, flat line under his bushy moustache, and his eyes came close to shooting sparks.

Jo and her new office friends, Debbie and Karen, had stopped in the opposite doorway. They muffled giggles as Allistair dropped to his knees and used his gray silk handkerchief to hurriedly wipe clean his boss's shoes.

Slapping his hands together with satisfaction, Maurice took a running leap off the ice cream machine and glided, his wings spread flat. He landed on an artificial tree in the corner. It gave him a good view of Jo and Ken in both rooms.

"Wish the big man had been here to hear him say that," Jake muttered.

"You can bet Mr. M. isn't anywhere around," Doug added, nodding toward the door between the two lunchrooms. "Otherwise he'd have kept his filthy mouth shut."

"What's his problem?" Mike said through a mouthful of meatloaf sandwich. "That Jo's one foxy lady. And really sweet, too." He swallowed and leaned closer to Ken. "So, is it true, buddy? You and the lady are getting it on?"

Maurice leaned forward, eager to hear the answer to that one. He caught a glimpse of Jo and her two friends peering in from the doorway, their eyes wide, just as interested.

"I asked Jo to the company Christmas party. And no, we're not getting it on. Because she's a *lady,* understand?" Ken fought to keep his tone light, and not throttle Mike.

Maurice clearly saw that little smile Jo aimed at Ken. *She likes him. He likes her. He stood up for her. She heard him. This is going great!*

Chortling in satisfaction, Maurice vanished, to reappear in Allistair's office. Jo and Ken didn't need any help, but there were no rules against frustrating the enemy whenever possible.

Allistair faced an afternoon of chaos. Drawers refused to open. His computer turned off before he could save documents. His phone squealed every time he picked up the receiver. Ink cartridges sprung leaks whenever he tried to print something. And his coffee mug cracked, leaking all over the reports for tomorrow's meeting.

Maurice checked in on Allistair half an hour before closing time and found him fighting to get a clean report reprinted. He had his phone tucked between shoulder and ear, trying not to get ink onto the phone or his clothes. Maurice got a great idea. He snapped his fingers and connected the speaker to half a dozen other phones scattered throughout the company, letting others listen in.

"You're not listening to me," a female voice whined.

"Of course I am, babycakes," Allistair protested. "I heard every word you said."

This had to be Brittney. Maurice had heard enough about Ken's soon-to-be-ex to loathe her just as much as Allistair.

"I don't want to wait until Christmas. I need the new necklace for the opening night party at the Playhouse."

"You got it. Don't I always come through for you, sugar?" Allistair scowled at the printer while drops of sweat beaded on his forehead and darkened his shirt collar.

"But this is important."

"Everything you say is important." He flung the ink cartridges into the garbage, snagged the last handful of tissues from the box on his desk, and cleaned his hands, somehow managing not to lose his grip on the phone caught between shoulder and ear. Allistair sat down at the desk and reached for a notepad. Maurice made the ink go dry in the pen. "Now, which store did you say it was at?"

"Allistair!" The phone speaker squealed, and Maurice swore it gave off sparks. Allistair dropped the phone.

"I'm just double-checking, honey-doll," he said after he picked it up. "I don't want to go to the wrong store."

"You better not. I have to have that necklace tonight!"

"You'll have it." Allistair wiped sweat off his forehead. There was still ink on his hands. He reached for the now-empty tissue box.

"Over my dead body," Maurice muttered, and vanished in a shower of poison green sparks. Next stop: the parking lot.

He popped back into the office five minutes later, reasoning that Allistair would stay longer at work if his computer and printer actually cooperated. It was worth the extra magic taken out of his daily budget to see Allistair jerk and nearly fall out of his seat when the printer started working.

An hour later, Allistair sat in his car in the empty parking lot, cursing under his breath and rocking in the driver's seat, having a miniature temper tantrum. The car ground and growled and the engine almost clicked over, but never quite caught.

Maurice conjured up ice skates and drew pictures of Ken and Jo's smiling faces in the paint on the roof of the car, never losing his place in the delicate operation, despite the furious rocking of the car. When Allistair tried yet again to use his cell phone to call for help, it sparked and squealed.

In fury, he slammed the steering wheel with both fists. The horn sounded -- and kept on sounding, echoing off the warehouse buildings and the ice coating sections of the parking lot.

More than an hour later, Maurice was doing the backstroke through the air, keeping three yards precisely in front of Allistair as he struggled to get into the mall against the current of departing shoppers. His pants were wet from the knees down, there were oil smears all over his expensive overcoat, one glove was torn, and the other glove was missing altogether, along with his hat.

"You know, Allistair, a guy could almost feel sorry for you." Maurice turned over, switching to the Australian crawl, leaving little ripples of red and green and gold light in his wake. "Almost."

A few children in strollers saw the light and let out cries of delight. Maurice waved at them and they waved back, giggling.

Allistair escaped the crowds and stepped into a wing of the mall with only one-third of the traffic. Maurice spotted the upscale jewelry store, with its security gates lowered almost two feet. The manager was in a hurry to get out of there, obviously.

The contents of the display cases hadn't been moved into the safe. If Allistair saw the jewelry still on display, he probably wouldn't notice the gates ready come down like a guillotine. A clerk stepped into the back room of the store, carrying a big cardboard display. The manager remained out front. Joy of joys, he had hearing aids in both ears.

Instantly, Maurice had his plan in place. Allistair was still six stores away from the jewelry store. He'd slowed down with a relieved smile at the sight of his goal, still lit and open for business.

"Not yet," Maurice muttered, as the manager stepped over to the controls for the security gates and pressed a conspicuous red button. There was a loud *click* as the gates unlocked. "Give the poor guy some hope. "

Sparks surrounded the gate mechanism. It resisted when the manager tried to pull it down. Maurice slowed to let Allistair catch up with him, then hitched a ride on his shoulder, watching carefully for just the right timing.

When Allistair was two stores away from his goal, Maurice snapped his fingers. The security gate slammed down, hitting the floor and snapping into the locking mechanism with a loud, final snap. Gold sparks shorted out the manager's hearing aid. Maurice zipped up to the ceiling as Allistair gripped the security gate. He called to the manager, who had opened the first display case and picked up the velvet-lined tray of rings to carry into the back room. He never paused, never heard Allistair's pleas for mercy.

"And then take that hope far away." Maurice turned a backward somersault. "The good guys can sleep a little better tonight, knowing another soldier of the evil empire has been frustrated." He vanished in a burst of green and red sparks.

~~~~~

Tuesday morning, Jo was surprised to see Ken come into the reception area outside Mr. Myerhausen's office. She forced a smile, despite a choking sensation of impending doom.

Was he coming to say he had changed his mind and didn't want to take her to the company Christmas party? Jo had heard how respectful he was to the other secretaries, and he treated the blue-collar dock and warehouse workers as equals. She knew he would be kind when he delivered the dread news. He would probably claim a conflict had come up and he wasn't able to go to the party, and then he would probably stay home to avoid embarrassing her if she went by herself. Which she wouldn't do,
~~~~~

but she couldn't tell him that, could she?

"Hi, Jo." Ken stopped three feet away from her enormous desk. Mr. Myerhausen had joked on her first day that it could serve as a barricade in case the workers rioted. "Is Mr. M. in?"

"Oh -- uh -- yes." She glanced over her shoulder at the closed door. "On the phone, I think." She checked the switchboard and saw the green light was still lit. "Is something wrong?" Relief hit her like a shot of laughing gas: he hadn't come to dump her.

"I have no idea. I had an e-mail that he wants to see me when I finished the meeting with the dock supervisors." Ken stepped to the right to settle into a chair.

Jo dared to hope he chose that chair just because it was closest to her desk.

Oh, get a grip, you nit! This isn't high school.

The scolding helped her calm down. Ken really was comfortable to be around. Despite being so nice-looking, she could relax around him. She liked knowing he went around the office in his shirt sleeves, with his tie loosened, instead of buttoned up all day long like the executives Mr. Myerhausen referred to as stuffed shirts. She especially liked the way he rolled up his sleeves, raked his fingers through his hair and leaned against a wall when he talked with the guys from the warehouse and the dock.

"What was that?" She blushed when she realized Ken had spoken to her and she hadn't heard a word.

You idiot -- you dream about hearing him say your name, but when he does talk, you're out in la-la-land!

"I just wanted to know if you picked out your dress for the party." He offered a lopsided smile. "Everybody else has been planning their wardrobe since the date and place were announced."

"I've been a little busy. Maybe I'll go to Divine's after work and..." She swallowed down a groan. Admitting she only bought her clothes secondhand was no way to impress a man.

"Angela always has the perfect thing." He nodded. "I bet you'll be gorgeous, whatever you find."

"Ken, are you flirting with my new secretary?" Mr. Myerhausen called from his office.

"Ah... No, sir. Just talking about the Christmas party." Ken leaped up from the chair as if something had bitten his behind.

Jo muffled a tiny giggle as he hurried into the office. After only a week, she could read her boss quite well. He was a dear, pretending to be gruff to keep the snobs in their places. But he chatted easily with the truck drivers, mechanics and warehouse workers about their families and the company basketball league.

His wife had visited the office on her first day of work and they had hit it off immediately. Jo had felt like she had found a long-lost aunt. It helped when Mrs. Myerhausen told her firmly not to let "that old bear" pick on her. Mr. Myerhausen had pretended to be indignant, but Jo had caught him pinching his wife's ample bottom a little while later, getting a squeak and a giggle from her, and a quick kiss. She'd been delighted with their teasing and the signs that the romance was still alive.

~~~~~

"Sir, you should know I asked Jo -- Miss August -- to the company Christmas party. If that's a problem, sir, I'll back down." Ken cringed. Was he babbling? Sweat beaded on his back, sticking his shirt to his skin.

"Hmm, and leave me to explain how the previous ugliness in the outer office is affecting her? I think not." Mr. Myerhausen leaned back in his burgundy leather chair. "Don't worry about what those idiots down the hall might say. Miss August told me you asked her, as soon as she realized that others in the company might try to cause you trouble because of your very kind invitation."

"Sir?" Ken felt like the air had just been put back into the room. He finally obeyed Myerhausen's gesture to take a seat.

"I think this company will soon owe you a great deal for your simple act of kindness to a stranger." He chuckled when Ken just shook his head and frowned, still confused. "I'm quite impressed with your track record over the years, Ken. And I'm quite aware that others have used your initiative as a springboard for their own careers, without giving you any credit."

Something dropped in his gut. Should he be pleased or worried? He supposed he came across as weak, for not protesting when sneaks like Allistair stole the march on him. He didn't like to be a whiner. He had always felt that griping whenever something didn't go his way meant people would be less prone to listen when something really crucial happened.
~~~~~

Chapter Four

"I assume that's good?" Ken ventured. "You don't think I'm a wimp?"

"I think you care a little too much about coming across as a whiner and schemer, like others in this company I could mention. There's nothing wrong with bringing it to the attention of the proper authorities -- me -- when others steal your hard work and pass it off as their own. Even when those unnamed others have the skills to erase all the evidence."

"I always figured I should save my complaints for important things. Kind of like not crying wolf."

"An executive who thinks about something besides his own advancement is a rare thing. Now, back to what I was saying. Miss August tells me that you sent her over here to apply for work."

"Sir, at the time, I thought Miss August was a *boy*, and I was thinking of the mailroom," Ken hurried to say.

Myerhausen laughed. "And that, son, is exactly why I'm not worried you'll try to gain undue influence over the inner sanctum. Unlike Felicia and that whole ugly scene. I may be eighty-plus, but that doesn't mean my eyesight and my ears aren't as sharp as they always were." His eyes twinkled with humor.

Ken settled back in his chair and let go of the armrests. "If you'll excuse me, sir, why did you call me in here? I was sure I was going to be called onto the carpet for something I didn't realize I did."

"Hmm, and I suppose Allistair dropped hints all morning?" His smile cooled. "Some people rise to the level of their incompetence or their immaturity. Have you ever heard of the principle of giving someone enough rope to hang himself?"

"Uh... Yes, sir."

"Let me say, then, that I have complete confidence you will never hang yourself, son." That smile reappeared. "We'll soon partner with Flagstaff Promotions Manufacturing, and you have the difficult but key responsibility of being our liaison."

"Sir?" Ken grinned, despite something cringing deep inside. An image filled his head, of Allistair stepping in and taking the liaison role in a year, after Ken had done all the sweating and suffered all the headaches and ulcers. "Sir? Um... I thought-- That is, everybody already assumed Allistair --"

"Mr. Somerville's opinion about his skills and intelligence is just that. His opinion. Neither accurate nor true. And don't worry about having this project taken away from you, once you've done all the hard work, laying the foundations. This project needs someone who can commit and stick, not flit from one golden opportunity to another. You've proven you're someone to be relied on for the long term, Ken. I can guarantee you'll have the position until you decide you don't want it anymore." He chuckled. "Or until we take on another tricky, valuable partnership that can only be trusted to someone like you."

~~~~~

Maurice nodded in satisfaction. He liked Ken, even if the guy had a little too much Dudley Do-Right in his blood. He vanished from the top bookshelf in Myerhausen's office, to reappear in the fern in the corner of the reception area, where he could watch over Jo's shoulder. That girl sure could type fast. Footsteps approached. Maurice flew over to the doorway to look down the hall and cursed. What did the Slime King want now?

Maurice hovered in the doorway, watching Allistair saunter closer, and considered making the fire extinguisher malfunction all over him. He trusted Jo not to fall for the creep's lines, but she was just a little too nice and patient and didn't know how to tell him to get lost. The girl needed some rescuing.

He snickered as he got a brilliant idea. He flew across the office to land on the sleek, multi-buttoned intercom on Jo's desk. Open every channel and let the whole building witness the bilge from Allistair's collagen-enhanced lips?

No. Save that for later. Right now, only one person needed to hear.

~~~~~

"Is Mr. M. busy?"

Jo smiled as she turned from her monitor. What was it about smooth, deep voices that made her feel so good? Yet the sight of Allistair's chiseled, airbrushed-tan features made her stomach take a nosedive. She remembered the nasty sneer, the threat in his cold voice, echoing out of the lunchroom into the hallway.

She had caught her breath when she heard Ken respond so calmly. She'd cringed when she heard his friend ask if they were 'getting it on,' and had been relieved, disappointed, and flattered, by his response. Ken had talked about her as if she were a real lady, worth respect, not a grubby kid scrambling to make ends meet.

"Yes, very busy." Jo reached for the pink message pad and a pen. "Did you want to leave a message for when he's free?"

"Who's he with?" Allistair flashed a smile that might have made her melt if she hadn't already seen his true personality.

"I'm sorry, but Mr. Myerhausen has impressed on me the importance of confidentiality."

"You know that doesn't include me." He winked and leaned forward, resting one manicured hand on the edge of her desk.

"Actually, I don't know any such thing. I've found that it's always best to take my directions from the highest authority."

"Tell you what. Why don't you let me take you out to lunch, and I'll help you get the hierarchy at Myerhausen all straightened out in your cute little head?"

"No, thanks. I have work to finish." Jo barely stopped herself from nodding at her computer screen, which held the final revisions on the Flagstaff dossier.

"All work and no play makes Josey a dull girl." He hitched his hip up on the edge of the desk and leaned a little closer. "Let me rescue you from the cafeteria."

"I brought my lunch." She barely kept herself from clutching the collar of her green wool dress, so he couldn't look down her neckline. What was with this guy? How could someone so slimy have climbed so high in the company?

"I'm sure you're a great little cook, but it just can't compare with this cute French bistro in Medina." Allistair winked.

"No. Thank you."

The door opened and Allistair slithered back onto his feet. Now Jo knew how he got away with so much dirt. He moved fast and knew how to present an appearance of innocence.

Her heart skipped a beat as Mr. Myerhausen and Ken emerged. Ken looked daggers at Allistair. Almost as if he knew what Allistair had been saying.

"Miss August." Mr. Myerhausen gestured at the computer. "How soon can you have that dossier printed up for Mr. Jenkins?"

"I'm about one page away from sending it to the printer. How many copies do you need?" Jo refused to whine and blame Allistair for the delay in finishing her project. Even if Allistair was to blame.

"Just the one, for now. I'm sure you would have had it done ten minutes ago, if you hadn't been distracted." He rocked back on his heels and flashed a stern glance at Allistair.

Jo nearly choked. How had he known? Warmth and appreciation flooded Jo. Nothing could get past Mr. Myerhausen.

"Sir." Allistair pasted on a smile just two degrees short of being a smirk. "I'd like to talk to you about the Flagstaff project. I have a few ideas, that might help --"

"Save your suggestions for the organizational meeting. What date did we agree on, Ken?"

"January 15, sir." Ken nodded to Jo. "I'd like to get together with you to discuss putting a few meetings on the calendar, whenever you have a chance."

"Ken?" Allistair nearly choked. "Sir, I must have mis-heard, but it sounds like --"

"Mr. Jenkins is our liaison with Flagstaff." Mr. Myerhausen's chest thrust out like a proud father. "I'm sure the new project is in more than competent hands."

From the fury in Allistair's eyes for two heartbeats, Jo knew he had put mental dibs on that project. She would have to warn Ken.

"Miss August, whatever Mr. Jenkins here needs to carry out his new duties, I'd like you to personally handle. If you don't mind?"

"Oh, no sir. No problem at all." Her face got hot as she met Ken's gaze, and he smiled at her.

"I think once that dossier prints, it would be a good idea for the two of you to have lunch and discuss it. Away from the office, and any distractions." He nodded, and Jo could have sworn he winked. "Go to Clarice's, and put it on the company account."

"Thank you, sir," Ken nearly stammered.

"I'll get that dossier printed up right now." Jo turned to her computer and glanced through the last page. She didn't miss the momentary slip in Allistair's smooth, yes-man mask.

"Ken, when you have time," Allistair began, his voice strained.

"Mr. Myerhausen doesn't want me discussing the Flagstaff project until January." Ken sounded calm, no triumph or irritation. "There's a lot to get up to speed on, and we want to move forward with the new year."

"How are you going to handle your old duties?" Allistair nearly growled.

"That's what tomorrow's executive meeting is about," Mr. Myerhausen said. "Dividing up Ken's responsibilities among the rest of you. Some people seem to have an amazing amount of free time. A little more work might keep them out of trouble."

"Sorry, sir. I do have some things that need to be done before lunch." Allistair departed.

Jo hit the print button for emphasis and bit her lip to keep from laughing. Bad experience had taught her never to gloat over her enemies' misfortunes.

Mr. Myerhausen laughed. Soft, yes, but a hearty sound all the same. Jo turned and saw him and Ken grinning at each other.

"Miss August, before you go to lunch, I suggest you call maintenance." He headed for his office. "There's something wrong with your intercom." He nodded to them and closed his door.

"My intercom?" Jo flinched when the printer banged and started spitting out the dossier.

"We heard everything Allistair said." Ken sat on the edge of her desk. Funny, how his warm, crooked smile took away the feeling of threat that she had when Allistair sat in that same spot.

"I didn't turn it on."

"We know. There was a lot of static and he couldn't get through to you. And then we heard what was going on and we decided to... Well, in Mr. M.'s words, give Allistair enough rope to hang himself." He gestured at the printer. "How much longer?"

"It's a pretty big document. One hundred pages." She gestured at the printer. "It's fast, so we won't lose too much of our lunch hour."

"Take an extra half hour," Mr. Myerhausen said, his voice clear and static-free through the intercom.

Jo and Ken grinned at each other for a few seconds, then they both laughed. She liked his laughter, warm and low and rumbling.

~~~~~

Two hours later, Allistair followed Ken into his office, so close on his heels he ran into his back when Ken stopped to hang up his coat. "Have a nice lunch?"

"It went pretty fast. There was a lot Jo needed to explain to me.
~~~~~

I can see now why Mr. Myerhausen told her to work with me. She knows everything that's going on, because she put the dossier together." Ken ordinarily wouldn't have given that much information to Allistair, but better to distract him than give him time to think of something nasty to say.

"Why didn't the old man put her in charge of Flagstaff, then?" He settled on the edge of Ken's desk, just as he was about to sit.

Ken refused to concede dominance to Allistair in his own office. He stayed standing and crossed his arms. Let Allistair lecture him again on body language, and he might just learn what sort of communication a fist and nose could make.

Stop that, Ken scolded himself. *You're not a kid in high school.*

Yeah, another part of him retorted, *but does Allistair know that?*

Nothing could take away the glow that remained after his pleasant lunch with Jo. There was nothing like talking with a smart young woman who had a sense of humor and couldn't wait for Cleveland Indians spring training to start. She had laughed when she got in Ken's car to ride to the restaurant and saw the vintage Carlos Baerga bobblehead doll sitting on the dashboard. They almost forgot to talk about the Flagstaff project at lunch, in favor of discussing last year's Tribe.

"Got to admire you, Ken, old buddy," Allistair said, with a slightly sour twist to his mouth.

Uh oh. He never admires anybody unless he's about to zing them.

Allistair paused, but Ken refused to rise to the bait and ask. "Bringing in that ringer to butter up the old man," he finally said. "Got to admire that long-term planning. I know you hated Felicia. When she got herself run out of the company, you had your chance to get the inside track."

"I guess fair is fair. You had Felicia in your pocket for so long, it's only right that someone else has a turn," Ken said in as light a tone as he could manage, when his chicken club and vinegar fries were trying to do a mambo in his gut.

He felt only a slight flicker of triumph when Allistair paled, then went dark red.

"For your information, I didn't bring Jo in to take Felicia's job. She got her job through her own skills and not through any string-pulling or threats on my part." Ken thought longingly of his intercom. What were the chances he could hit the connect switch without Allistair seeing and realizing?

No, that would be a coward's trick. A wimp and a whiner tries to embarrass his enemy. A real man lets his enemy shoot himself in the foot.

Ken just wished Allistair wouldn't take so long destroying his career.

"Threats?" Allistair's voice strained, making his tone of innocence even less believable. "Are you saying I use threats?"

"Did I say anything about you?" Ken could play innocent much better than Allistair, because most of the time, he actually was innocent. It amazed him how some people could spend so much energy and time covering up their schemes and lies, when it was far easier to be honest all the time. No worry about contradicting cover stories or filling in the holes.

"Just you wait, Ken old buddy. We'll see how long you last in your cushy new job. There's a reason why I was named junior vice president instead of you, when all the dupes in this company thought you would get the job."

Yeah, it's called having a computer nerd in your back pocket to hack into other people's computers to steal their work and put your name on it. Ken made a mental note to warn Jo not to leave any Flagstaff work in her computer where unfriendly eyes could spy and unfriendly hands could sabotage.

He kept quiet and tried not to cheer as Allistair slid off his desk and stomped out of his office. He waited until his nemesis slammed the door, then let out a deep sigh, and sank into his chair.

He yelped when he heard a tap on his door. It opened and Jo stuck her head in. She offered a tentative grin. Something inside him that had felt bruised and half-asleep for months stirred to life when he realized that light in her eyes was concern. For him.

"It's okay. No blood, no broken bones."

"How does a snake like him get away with so much?" she seethed, quietly, as she stepped into his office.

Ken opened his mouth to warn her not to close the door because of the company policy on avoiding sexual harassment lawsuits. If no one closed their doors when alone in a room with someone of the opposite sex, then nothing improper could occur. In theory. He stopped short, the words on the tip of his tongue, when Jo caught the door and left it open a good six inches. Then his attention caught on her smooth stride and the sway of her hemline around her calves.

Why had he ever thought that Brittney's bony features and her swagger were beautiful? Jo reminded him of deer gliding through the shadowy forest. He grinned, remembering their talk of baseball all through lunch, and knew she was the kind of girl who would gladly slide into jeans and sneakers and spend a rainy April evening sitting in the bleachers at Progressive Field, cheering herself hoarse -- and not worry about her hair.

"Excuse me?" Ken blinked, torn out of his daydream when he realized Jo waited for him to answer her. He offered a crooked grin when she repeated herself. "He knows all the tricks. The only way to beat him at his game is to refuse to play, and even then, it's fifty-fifty that you'll come out with your skin intact."

"I heard what he said. Too bad there wasn't another malfunction with the intercom." She shuddered, then slid a three-inch thick accordion file across the desk to him. "Here's the master file, everything that's come in and gone out to Flagstaff."

Ken restrained a whistle. "It's a good thing everything else is off my plate. I can see some late nights with this baby until I'm up to speed." Then he remembered what he had just been thinking, about Allistair, sabotage and spying, and warned Jo.

"That occurred to me." She nodded. "It's too bad you're too nice a guy to grab every chance you can to zap him."

"Thanks. At least, I think that was a compliment."

The music of Jo's laughter remained in the office for the rest of the afternoon. Ken didn't care if it was sappy, he was glad she thought he was a nice guy.

~~~~~

Mrs. Myerhausen came into the office half an hour before her husband expected her, at the end of the day. She was struggling with a dozen shopping bags. Her cheeks were rosy from the cold, and the mischievous sparkle of her eyes matched the snowflakes gleaming on her scarlet beret. Jo leaped up from her desk and hurried to take most of the bags from her.

"Oh, thank you, dear. Is the old bear in his den?" She settled down into the closest reception chair.

"Out doing his afternoon walkthrough, right on schedule. Where does all this go?" Jo hefted the bags.

"Any place you can hide them." She fanned herself, overheated
~~~~~

from her shopping expedition. "He's like a little boy, when it comes to Christmas. I buy twice as many presents as he deserves, just so he'll have something to open on Christmas day that he hasn't already gotten into. He'll drive himself mad, trying to find where I hid his presents at home." Mrs. Myerhausen giggled like a teen. "And all the while, they'll be here, right under his nose. You're a positive genius, dear, suggesting I hide them here."

"My aunt was the same way." Jo blinked away the threat of tears. After eight months, it still hurt to think about her dead aunt. "I worked midnight shift dispatch for a towing service, and my boss let me hide her presents at work. She was so thrilled that I finally outwitted her, she didn't care that they smelled like a garage."

She crossed the office to a wide wall of filing cabinets, all dark wood to match the office décor. Jo had explored the room top to bottom her first two days there, just to figure out where everything was. Nearly two-thirds of the filing cabinets were empty. Her new friends speculated that Felicia had destroyed records to protect herself. Jo had lots of space to offer Mrs. Myerhausen.

Her employer's wife chattered about the shopping and the weather, and how different shopping was when she was a child. Back before the super malls and shopping strips, it was a grand event to go Downtown Cleveland and spend the day at the major department stores. Mrs. Myerhausen's mother and aunts and cousins all dressed up with fancy hats and sturdy shoes. They took the Rapid into the Terminal Tower, enjoyed the window displays at the May Company and got lunch at the soda fountain at Woolworth's. If there was time, they took a trolley car down Euclid Avenue to see the grand, beautiful houses of Millionaire's Row.

Jo listened and asked questions and packed away the store-wrapped presents as quickly as she could. Mr. Myerhausen was no fool, and if he couldn't find his presents at home, only two weeks before Christmas, he would know his wife was up to something. If he realized how much extra time she spent in the office, he might suspect Jo of helping to hide his presents.

She paused a moment to knuckle the tears from her eyes. After feeling alone and helpless for so long, buried under Aunt Myrtle's bills, it was still a bit overwhelming to have double the salary, and to be treated like a niece by her boss's wife. All because Angela had teased her into coming out to help decorate the tree, and because

Ken had heard her wish for a new job.

Angela, Diane and Holly at Divine's had been her only real friends, and that was mostly her fault because she spent so little time with other people, when she wasn't working. Now, though, Ken was becoming…what was he becoming? Jo wasn't quite sure, but she hoped the company rules weren't against it.

"Something on your mind, dear?" Mrs. Myerhausen asked, when Jo shoved the last drawer closed and turned around, dusting her hands off against each other.

"Me?"

"You looked a little distracted when I first came in. Is the old bear giving you too much work to do?"

"Oh, no, not that." Jo laughed. It was too easy to spill the whole story, from Ken coming in for the meeting to Allistair blowing a gasket after the two of them came back from lunch.

"That one isn't going to get away with his dirt for much longer, let me tell you." She nodded for emphasis. "Take a piece of advice, dear. Business or sports or playing soldier, it all boils down to the same thing with most men. A chance to pound their chests and make a lot of noise in the hopes of impressing each other. Arthur knows exactly what that Somerville brat is up to. That's why he didn't give the vice presidency to Ken this summer. Flagstaff was in the works, but very hush-hush. Arthur hated hurting Ken, because that boy deserves a promotion ten times over. But if he had promoted Ken back then, that Somerville brat would have been next in line when it came time to start work on Flagstaff."

"It's like keeping your best player on the bench until the big push during the last three innings," Jo muttered. She wondered if she could or even should tell Ken what Mrs. Myerhausen had said. After all, he hadn't whined about Allistair stealing his promotion, or gloated that he finally got rewarded.

"You like him, don't you?" Mrs. Myerhausen laughed when Jo's face warmed, startled by the question. "Arthur said Ken asked you to the Christmas party. I'm so glad. You do have a good pair of dancing shoes, don't you?"

"I don't know how to dance." Jo blushed, hating to admit that. There had never been time to learn to dance, or the pretty clothes to let her go out dancing.

"Well, let's hope Ken does. As long as he knows what he's

doing, you have nothing to worry about. Except for finding the mistletoe, of course." Mrs. Myerhausen's mischievous little giggle put all sorts of ideas into Jo's head.

~~~~~

Ken braced himself for some nasty, last-minute interception from Allistair at the end of the day. He kept all the Flagstaff project files on disks instead of saving it on his computer. He put everything Jo had given him into his briefcase, to take home for safekeeping. It was too bad he had to resort to such tactics to protect his job and the company. He was glad Mr. Myerhausen seemed aware of the nasty little tricks and political games being played, but why didn't the company's owner do something about it?

"Not your problem," he told himself as he reached to turn off his computer.

His gaze landed on a few crumpled pieces of paper in his wastebasket. He had roughed out some ideas for Flagstaff while he read through the dossier, then organized everything and saved the file on a disk. In case Allistair had a spy in Maintenance, who could sift through his wastebasket tonight, he retrieved the papers. Then he pulled the small portable shredder out of the bottom drawer of his desk.

He left the drawer open as he settled the shredder on top of the wastebasket and made sure all the Flagstaff notes were destroyed. His gaze landed on the photo frame lying face down in the drawer. It was a picture of Brittney. Why had he held onto it? How had he ever deluded himself into thinking that bundle of sticks in designer clothes was beautiful?

Maurice popped in amid a shower of silver sparks and settled on his shoulder while he puzzled over that period of stupidity. A moment of thought, then he put the frame face down on his desk and pried the back off. Brittney's photo went in the shredder.

"He shoots and scores!" Maurice turned somersaults through the air while Ken unplugged the shredder and put it back in the drawer.

The photo frame went into his briefcase. He considered getting a photo of Jo with him at the company Christmas party, to put in the frame. The more he turned the idea over in his mind while he put on his coat and locked the office door behind him, the more he liked it.
~~~~~

However, friendship with Jo would be seen as a conspiracy to deny Allistair more power. Ken would have to protect her as well as cover his own back. He didn't doubt Allistair would keep trying to rope Jo into helping him as Felicia had done. The question was if Allistair would try charm her or scare her into cooperating.

"Hey, maybe you should make sure Jo gets out of the building okay?" Maurice asked as he landed on Ken's shoulder.

Had Jo left for the day? Ken glanced at his watch. He knew she didn't drive. Over lunch, she had told him about a funny incident on the bus ride home yesterday. The walk to the bus stop left her vulnerable. Ken didn't think Allistair would physically attack her, but there were dozens of subtle ways to scare her.

Or seduce her.

He felt sick at the thought of Allistair or one of his suave, well-dressed friends making friends with Jo for the sake of getting that inside track in the company. Jo seemed like a common-sense type of girl, but she hadn't been in the company long enough to know how to protect herself.

"Not her job," Ken muttered, and strode down the hall, heading toward Myerhausen's office. With every step he took, he prayed Jo had left for her bus already. He should have checked the bus schedule. He should have offered to drive her home.

"If you call lunch all business, then you can get away with asking Jo out tonight." Maurice grinned and patted Ken's shoulder before leaping up into the air. "Have fun, buddy." Then he vanished in another shower of sparks.

Chapter Five

When Ken turned the corner, he spotted Allistair in the hallway, filling the doorway of Myerhausen's office so anyone who tried to get past him would have to squeeze up against him.

"This is really something that can wait until tomorrow," Jo said, as Ken got close enough to look past Allistair.

She stood in the office, coat on, a large canvas bag over her shoulder, snow boots on her feet, arms crossed, five feet away from Allistair. Ken silently applauded her for being smart enough to stay out of his reach.

"Now is that any way to treat a fellow worker? If I don't turn in that report to the old man first thing in the morning, it could affect three different departments. Domino effect, you know?"

Allistair was using his *I'm just one of the gang, let's be reasonable* voice. It had stopped fooling Ken when they were in junior high.

"Could get the old man really upset. Don't want to do that to him this close to Christmas. Especially when you haven't been here long enough to earn that Christmas bonus the rest of us are looking forward to. I hear you really need it, too."

Jo's impassive face twitched, just long enough for Ken to see dismay and a little fear. Anger predominated. Allistair had three underlings to foist work onto and blame if something wasn't done on time. The only reason Ken could see for Allistair trying to give the work to Jo was to inconvenience her. Maybe make her feel guilty for not accommodating him, so she would feel obliged to help him out some other time.

"My day is over. You should have thought of your report an hour ago," Jo said. "Which makes me think you're deliberately keeping me from leaving on time."

"Can't blame a guy for wanting to spend a little time with the new girl, can you?" Allistair took a step into the office.

"After your little performance, what makes you think I'd want to spend any time in your company?"

"Hey, we're all one big happy family at Myerhausen. I just wanted to make up for coming down so hard on you. You aren't to blame at all, sweetheart."

Jo's chin went up and her mouth flattened into a hard line.

Ken silently cheered.

"No, see, the guy to blame is Ken. He comes across as a good old boy, but he's a player. I don't want to see him playing you for a fool. I like you."

"Only because you know Mr. Myerhausen likes me." Jo gestured at the door. "Now, are you going to get out of my way, or do I have to call security?"

"Come on, sweetheart. How are you going to explain the big fuss, when all I want to do is talk?"

"I'm going to miss my bus."

"I'll drive you home."

That gave Ken an idea. He backed up about ten steps and came down the hall again, making his steps loud. He pretended surprise when he came to the doorway and found Allistair there, looking over his shoulder.

"Jo, sorry I'm late. I bet you thought I forgot I was giving you a ride home tonight." Ken gestured over his shoulder with his thumb. "There's a big storm in the forecast. Wouldn't want you to get caught outside when it hits. You ready?"

"Ready. Yes. Thanks." Jo took two steps toward the door and looked pointedly at Allistair, who scowled and stepped backward, out of the way.

For good measure, Ken reached in and pulled the office door closed, making sure it clicked and locked, then held out his arm, like an usher at a wedding. Jo hooked her arm through his. Neither said anything until they were out in the parking lot and they were sure Allistair hadn't followed them.

"My hero," she breathed. "You have no idea --"

"Yeah, I do, actually." Ken reluctantly let go of her arm so he could unlock the passenger door. "I heard a little bit of what went on in there."

"Umm... Why didn't you interrupt sooner?" She stayed perfectly still, not moving when Ken pulled the door open for her.

"I wanted to see if you were as smart as I think you are." He was more relieved than he liked to admit when Jo grinned. He managed to get his own grin down to a reasonable level by the time he walked around to the other side of the car and climbed in. "Big question. Where exactly do you live?"

On the way home, they didn't talk about Allistair or the situation at the office. Ken preferred to leave all those problems and concerns behind. Jo seemed to feel the same way. They talked about the decorating party at Divine's Emporium and discovered a few mutual friends in Neighborlee.

"You know," Ken said, when he pulled up in front of Jo's little house, "you're only five blocks away from my apartment."

He glanced at the white clapboard with the peeling paint and the flowerbeds buried under snow. The sidewalks were neatly shoveled, and he imagined Jo was just as careful with her flowerbeds and the rest of the house, inside and out. There were just some jobs too big for her, all alone. He hadn't snooped to the degree he knew Allistair and others would, but he had found out Jo had no one except her elderly aunt, who had died earlier in the year. Something ached inside when he realized there was no one to help her hang the lights outside. Then he wondered if she even had any outdoor lights to hang.

"That's nice." She offered him a little smile and put her hand on the door latch, but she didn't hurry to get out. That encouraged him.

"I mean... I hate to think of you racing to catch the bus in this weather. How about if I pick you up in the morning?" What felt like a sharp-edged rock lodged in his chest when her eyes widened. "You don't have to if you don't want to --"

"No. I mean -- yes. I'd love to -- I'd really appreciate a ride. Riding with a friend. That's great. Thanks." She blushed so bright a red, he thought he could feel the heat from her skin as she slowly climbed out of the car.

"I see you don't have any decorations up yet."

"I know. Aunt Myrtle was so into Christmas. We would have the lights out on the day after Thanksgiving and the tree up by Saturday and we wouldn't take anything down until February. I just can't seem to get up the energy to do it this year."

Ken swallowed hard. "I could come over and help."

"You're serious?" Her smile lit up the inside of his car.

"How about Sunday?"

"You don't have to -- but I'd really like that. A lot."

"Great. Then it's a date. After our date on Friday."

"It's a date."

"It's a date." He took a few deep breaths, fighting the urge to break out in adolescent giggles.

"Um... I'd better close the door and let you go home. I know you have a ton of work to do." She didn't make any move to step back and shut the passenger door.

"Yeah. A ton." Ken wondered if this was what people meant when they talked about drowning in someone's eyes.

"Tomorrow then? What time?"

"Time? Oh. Right. What time am I going to pick you up? Um ... eight?"

"Sounds great." She stepped back and shut the door and waited while he pulled out of the driveway and headed down the street again.

Ken looked back and waved. She waved, and then he was at the corner and had to turn.

He discovered two things when he got home. First, Jo had left her canvas bag with her shoes in his car. That was all right, since he was picking her up in the morning. Second, he realized he hadn't learned enough about her to get her a nice Christmas present. He definitely *wanted* to get her one. He hadn't thought he would want anything to do with Christmas this year. Thanks to Jo, and the wishes they made at Divine's, this Christmas was going to be nicer than he could have hoped.

~~~~~

Ken walked Jo to her office the next morning. He nearly stopped short when they walked past his office and he saw the door was ajar, just enough to be noticeable. He kept talking -- what about, he couldn't remember later -- and made sure she got safely to her office. Then he walked back to his office, with a lead weight of apprehension sinking deeper in his stomach.

He nudged his door and tested the doorknob. Nothing seemed wrong. Somehow, that wasn't a good sign. He stepped into his office and closed the door before turning the light on. No sense in letting the enemy see him react to whatever damage might have been done. But nothing seemed out of order. Ken kept looking around while he hung up his coat, folded his scarf and put it on the shelf next to his coat hook. Then he sat down at his desk.

The monitor power light was on. The tiny amber light meant the monitor had been turned on, but not the CPU. Or was it the
~~~~~

other way around? Someone had turned it off, but not the monitor? He leaned over and reached under his desk to put his hand on the dark gray plastic casing. He felt the residual warmth even before his fingers touched it. So, someone had been in his office this morning, searching his computer files.

He always locked his office at night. The only people who had the key besides Jo and security was maintenance, and they hadn't been in last night. That left him only a few guesses about what was up and who had been sneaking around his office.

There was a time to be a bigger man than his petty enemies, and there was a time to be sensible and ask for help. This was a problem for the whole company. If one person could circumvent standard office procedures and security, then so could others. And then Myerhausen had a real problem.

Ken called the head of security first, and then one of his weekend basketball buddies who worked in maintenance. The computer was still warm when Ted in security came in. He gave the go-ahead for maintenance to change the lock on Ken's office door. Then they both went to report to Mr. Myerhausen.

~~~~~

Jo laughed when she heard the doorbell ring only ten minutes after Ken dropped her off at home that night. She had left her shoe bag in his car for the second time, and had resigned herself to getting teased about her forgetfulness when he picked her up in the morning. Leave it to Ken to turn around and come back to give it to her tonight.

"Okay," she said as she yanked the front door open. "I take back all the things I ever said about guys being--"

"Being what?" Allistair grinned wide enough to show his back teeth. "Nice place. I'm glad you could keep it, after all the hospital bills you have to pay."

Jo bit back a retort that no, she doubted he was glad about anything on her behalf. It chilled her to know Allistair had researched her.

"Are you going to invite me in?" he continued, when a glare was all she could manage in her own defense. Then he held out a paper-wrapped bouquet of three pink roses.

"No, I'm not. I don't make it a practice to invite troublemakers into my house."
~~~~~

Jo held her breath, waiting for Allistair's next onslaught of charm. Several new friends at work had warned her about his two-faced attack method. She could handle nasty Allistair more easily than a charmer who didn't give her any ground to resist him.

"That's fair." His smile drooped and he backed away from her door. The bouquet hung at his side. "We got off to a bad start, and I do apologize. There's no reason for you to get caught up in a stupid contest between Ken and me. I really do want to be friends."

She opened her mouth to tell him she made it a practice never to be friends with co-workers, but that would be a lie. She wanted to be friends with Ken. Much closer than they were already.

But that wasn't helping her deal with Allistair, who would start gloating if she stayed silent much longer.

"I think this should be handled at the office. Coming to my home, uninvited, sends all the wrong signals."

"Ah. Good point." He nodded and backed up another step. "Honestly, I'm sorry for how badly things got started. I hope you'll let me be friends at work, at least."

"You could start by being friendly to *everyone* in the office, not just the people who can do you some good."

"Ouch." He offered a lopsided grin and started down the stairs. "I swear, the reformation starts now. See you in the morning."

"Not if I see you first," she muttered, as soon as she had the door closed. She shivered, listened to his footsteps on the driveway, then the thud of his car door slamming shut.

Ten minutes later, the doorbell rang again. Jo put down the can of soup she had just decided to make for dinner, and stomped to the door. If Allistair had returned, she was going to yank those roses from his hand and slap his smug face with them. She hoped the florist had left the thorns on.

"I cannot believe this." The woman standing there sneered when Jo pulled the door open.

Jo did not know this woman in a fur-trimmed black wool car coat and a red dress skinny-tight enough to make Twiggy gasp for breath. Who in the world took the time to match her boots with her hat, gloves and purse?

Answer: someone who had money and time to burn.

Jo allowed herself two seconds of jealousy, then pushed it away. Even if she had the money and time to spend on her wardrobe, there were better things to do with both. Her unidentified and unwanted guest was giving her a thorough inspection in return. From the ugly curve of her upper lip, this woman with her I-just-spent-six-hours-at-a-salon look didn't like what she saw.

"Let's get something straight. You don't have the style or the class to get your claws into Allistair, so just quit while you still have your eyes. *Comprende*?" The stranger flexed her red-lacquered nails for illustration.

"What makes you think I want Allistair?" Jo laughed, mostly from surprise.

"He followed you home." Glamour-Puss looked around the porch with its peeling paint and shredding doormat. Her expression said she expected to need a tetanus shot.

"He's trying to get in good with me so he can hijack Ken's new project. Why any woman would want that sleaze when she could have Ken -- well, she needs to get her head examined."

Idiot! That was the wrong thing to say.

The visitor's sneer went cold, she took a step backwards and looked Jo up and down again. "You're after Ken? Big mistake. Until those divorce papers are signed, Ken Jenkins is still my husband. He always was a softy, taking in strays and helping sad sacks, but with you he's scraping the bottom of the barrel. It's a good thing I shook free of that loser when--" She squealed when Jo's open palm connected fast and hard with her over-rouged cheek.

Jo gaped. She had never slapped anyone before. She didn't think she had it in her.

Then again, she hadn't known Ken was married, either. When the girls at the office talked about that skinny witch, Brittney, she thought the woman was just a girlfriend. What kind of woman would marry a wonderful guy like Ken and then dump him for Allistair Somerville?

With a yowl like a wet cat, the twitch leaped at her with both sets of claws spread and ready to rip. Jo screamed and ducked and turned, putting her elbow into the woman's almost nonexistent gut. But not before one set of claws raked her cheek.

"Get this straight, you filthy --"

"No, *you* get this straight," Jo snarled. "I wouldn't touch that idiot Allistair with a twenty-foot pole and I'm this close to pressing assault charges."

"Assault!"

"I could go to a hospital right now and get documentation and they'll call the police. You're on my property, threatening me, trespassing, and probably a dozen other charges I can come up with. Who do you think they're going to believe?"

Part of Jo stood back in amazement at the words spilling out of her mouth. She had wanted to think this fast, be this vicious when neighbors were nasty to Aunt Myrtle or the doctors lied and overcharged for treatments that didn't help, or a dozen other injustices. She had always been afraid to make waves, to stand up for her rights, fearing that if she didn't cooperate, she would lose what little help she and her aunt had.

Jo thought maybe she would like this new part of herself. Once she got over the shock.

"Maybe I should just call the police right now. I have your license plate," she lied. Jo pulled her hand away from her face and was shocked and satisfied to see blood streaking her palm. She showed her bloody hand to the twitch, who had gone so pale all her makeup showed up in stark relief like clown paint. "I'll give you until the count of five to get into your car. Then I'm letting the dogs out. Self-defense. No judge in the land will convict me." She took a deep breath.

The twitch didn't move.

"One." She prayed the woman moved soon, because she didn't have any dogs to let loose on her.

Jo kept counting, even as the woman slipped and stumbled down the steps and the paving stones to the driveway. She made a snowball and lobbed it at the red sports car, just as the engine roared to life.

It was true, what Aunt Myrtle had always said. The ones who shrieked the loudest and made the most threats had the most crimes to hide and the most to fear.

Jo stayed on the porch, memorizing the license plate before the car pulled into the street and screeched away. Then her hands started shaking. She made it through the door before her knees wobbled, but she managed to lock up and stumble to the couch.

She didn't cry. There was this odd, empty feeling inside, like she had been kicked in the gut, but numbness instead of pain.

That twitch said she was getting *divorced* from Ken. That meant she was Ken's *wife*. Legally, if no other way.

Ken had married her? Ken liked that kind of woman, with her clothes painted on, wearing an inch of makeup, driving a fancy sports car that probably cost more to service than the monthly mortgage on Aunt Myrtle's house?

They were getting divorced, weren't they? That meant Ken had seen the light. She had come here to drive Jo away from Allistair, so that anorexic idiot had left Ken for Allistair? What was wrong with her? Besides a hooker's taste in clothes and makeup?

But Ken had married her? What was wrong with *him*?

~~~~~

Jo wasn't at home when Ken came to pick her up the next morning. He rang the doorbell and walked around the house to look in the kitchen windows and see if she was all right. The wrinkled little man next door leaned out his upstairs window and told him Jo had left early for the bus. He warned Ken he'd better take care of Jo, because she was a good girl and took good care of her aunt before she died, God rest her soul.

Ken assured him he planned to take very good care of her, before he got back in his car, in a hurry to get to the office.

Had he done or said something yesterday to irritate Jo?

He heard her tapping away on the keyboard before he walked into her office with the bag of shoes. That reassured him. Would she be working so hard if something was wrong?

"Hey, Jo, are you okay? I stopped by your house --" He saw the scratches on her cheek. She had tried to hide them under makeup, but obviously she didn't have a thousand-dollar investment in makeup like Brittney did.

She had left similar marks on his cheek when she was leaving to move in with Allistair, and Ken had been too stunned to get out of the doorway fast enough to suit her. She had clawed Felicia in a catfight that had brought half the office staff running to intervene.

"Sorry." Jo flashed him a thin smile without meeting his eyes. "I should have called you and said I needed to get in early. Did you bring my shoes?"

Numbly, he held out the bag. She took it, thanked him, and put it under her desk.

"Please tell me you didn't run into Brittney," he said. All
~~~~~

Brittney's screaming and whining and ranting couldn't compare to that one hurting look Jo gave him.

"When I run into that-- Well, it'll be with a car and she won't get off so easily," she muttered. Then she blushed.

"What happened? I'm sorry. Whatever she wanted, it's -- well, why did she come after you? The sooner Brittney is free of me, the happier she'll be." The final divorce papers had been sitting on his desk at home for weeks. Ken didn't know why he delayed signing. He didn't want Brittney back, and she wouldn't care if he signed right away or never. "I should have signed the divorce papers weeks ago."

"Why didn't you? Are you --" Jo looked away.

"No, I'm not still in love with her." *Wow, that was easier to say than I thought.* "No, I'm just delaying to irritate her and Allistair. Not that they care whether it's right for her to live with him while she's still legally married to me. But why did she come after you?"

"Believe it or not, she came to warn me away from Allistair."

"Why'd she rake you?"

"That's what it felt like." She brushed her fingertips over her scratched cheek. "So that's Brittney, huh? I kind of guessed her name, but she didn't stick around to ask mine. For all I know, she still doesn't know who I am."

"Are you going to tell me before I have to shake it out of you?" That momentary surge of anger instantly turned into a feeling like laughter wanted to burst out.

Jo must have felt the same way, because they exchanged grins. He reached out to touch her cheek. "I've felt her claws myself. What made her think you were interested in Allistair? I mean, I know you have a lot better taste than to encourage him."

"I hope so!" She didn't pull back from his touch, and that encouraged Ken. "Allistair followed me home from work, and she must have followed him. Those two deserve each other."

"So Allistair made a play for you. He must be tired of Brittney already." *He always wants what I have. Does he think Jo is mine already? Please, God, I've been good. She'd be the best Christmas present I ever got.*

Ken mentally slapped himself for those thoughts, even as warmth spread through him.

"Thanks," Jo said, "but he's only interested in getting an inside track to either Mr. Myerhausen or the Flagstaff project. Or both."

"Don't be too sure." He regretted it, but Ken knew how it would look if someone saw him sitting on the desk, touching Jo's face, so he withdrew his hand. Did she look a little disappointed? "You're worth the trouble," he added, his voice a rasp he didn't recognize.

"Why didn't you tell me you were married?" She got up quickly to pull open a filing cabinet drawer three steps away.

Ken noted her blush. A hungry part of him woke up and howled victory. He hushed it immediately. This was just the first step in what would be a long, careful campaign. No more rushing in, no more getting swept up in dreams and facades. After Brittney, he refused to make that mistake again. Jo was real, honest, and genuine. Worth waiting for.

"Almost divorced. And that's a part of my life I prefer to forget, thanks very much." He got up off the desk and jammed his hands in his pockets.

"How could she leave you for that slimy Allistair?"

"Thanks." He laughed when she blushed at the throaty emotion in his voice. "He only wants what I have. Brittney couldn't get him interested until it looked like she wanted me. Then he went on the warpath. She's a real player."

"Yeah, I could tell. Kind of scary, when you think about the time she spends on looking just so..." Jo sighed, and a wistful look flashed into her eyes.

"Hey," he said, softening his voice, wanting to help her. "You don't need to spend time on looking great. That's what I like about you. You don't waste time on makeup and clothes and -- Uh, that didn't come out right. But..."

It helped that Jo went red and bit her lip, visibly trying not to laugh. It didn't help that Mr. Myerhausen chose that moment to stick his head out of his office.

"Ken, don't you have something to do besides fluster my secretary?" the old man asked, shaking a reproving finger at him.

"Yes, sir. Sorry." He backed toward the door. "Uh, Jo..."

"I'll see you at lunch," she said, her voice rich with laughter.

Ken hurried for the door. Out in the hall, it took all his self-control not to dance all the way to his office.

By the time he got to his chair, his chain of thought had switched, back to that wistfulness in Jo's eyes. She wanted luxuries, to be pampered and wear stylish clothes. Didn't she see how pretty she was right now? How much more appealing she was, simple, clean and neat, instead of coated in makeup and too-tight clothes? He knew when he finally took Jo into his arms, she would be soft in all the right places, sleek and firm. She'd smell like rain and wide-open spaces -- not a perfume factory.

But before he could start his campaign to win Jo, he had to free himself of Brittney. He kicked himself for not signing those papers immediately. Thinking he could irritate her by delaying, he'd been childish and blind. It wasn't like he wanted her back. Not if she begged him. The sooner he cut the last flimsy ties with Brittney, the sooner he could get to work on winning Jo.

How? Who could he go to for advice? Someone who knew Jo, obviously.

~~~~~

"I hope you aren't going to make a wish for Jo to love you forever," Angela said that evening, once Ken finished explaining the situation. He had come to Divine's immediately after work. She nodded at the Wishing Ball on the counter beside her.

He felt as if his stomach had dropped below his knees. His face got warm. "That'd be cheating, wouldn't it? I mean, how could I ever be sure it was her and not my wish?" He snorted. "Listen to me. Up until two weeks ago, I didn't believe in wishes anymore."

"That's because you gave up on love." Angela's small, warm smile returned. "You're already ahead of the game, just realizing that little detail. Love has to be earned and nurtured, not stolen or conjured up with wishes. Other people can wish for you two to love each other, to have happily ever after, but that's the kind of wish you can never make for yourself."

He needed to think that over. "You weren't surprised by anything I said, were you?"
~~~~~

Chapter Six

"Let's just say that I saw a connection between you and Jo when you reached out to help her." Angela stepped back from the counter and looked around the shop. "You want a nice Christmas present for her? Think about the type of person Jo is, her life. Simple. Hard-working. Dedicated to someone else. Never thinking about herself."

"Get her something she wouldn't get herself. Easier said than done."

"Hmm, maybe. Jo won a day of pampering at Jane's spa two months ago and she just raved about it. Facial, foot massage, manicure, haircut."

"Get her a gift certificate?" Ken felt torn. A gift certificate would be too easy. It felt impersonal. "Thanks for the idea, but that just seems too ... cold."

"It might be more than she would be willing to accept. Jo wouldn't feel comfortable receiving a large gift from you. But I bet if you went to Jane, she'd put together a nice little sample box, all the creams and candles and such that Jo would just love, without feeling guilty that you spent much money on her."

"And when I get over to Jane's, she'll probably have it half-assembled," Ken said with a nod and a wry grin. He laughed when Angela just gave him an innocent look. The mischievous sparkle in her eyes totally destroyed that façade.

~~~~~

"If only there were more guys like you around here," Jane said as Ken walked into her spa shop. She laughed when he stopped short on her doorstep.

The wind slammed the door against his backside, so he stumbled the rest of the way into the shop.

"Angela called me." She held up a wire mesh basket lined with crimson and gold shredded cellophane and crammed with sample tubes, tubs and bags. She dropped in two rose-shaped soaps to punctuate her words.

"I feel like the gift is more from you two than from me," he said, and didn't feel ashamed of the slight whine in his voice.
~~~~~

"You asked advice from her friends. That's more than most guys ever think of. They depend on the flash and glitz and lots of money to say what a little bit of thought and effort would express much more clearly." She turned to the worktable behind the counter, her long, sand-colored braid swaying like a pendulum down her back. In moments, she had wrapped the basket in pale green cellophane and tied it all together with gold cords.

"So, Jo will like this?" He tried to see through the layers of cellophane. It looked like there were at least twenty different packages, and little balls that were probably bath oils like his mother used to use.

"She'll love it. People who don't take any time for themselves just love it when someone pampers them. Especially if it's something she wouldn't get for herself." Jane studied him. "You really like Jo?" Her smile widened when he nodded. "Good. The two of you are--" The smile fell off her face as her shop door opened.

"Baby," Brittney cooed. Her stiletto-heeled boots squeaked on the floor tiles. "You really shouldn't have. I mean, we're still separated. It's a lovely gesture." She reached for the gift basket, eyes bright with avarice, and then pouted when it slid out of her reach without anyone touching it.

"We're not separated, we're divorced." Ken wished he could think of something cutting to say, but his mind blanked. He just wasn't a guy who enjoyed kicking others' feet out from under them.

"Oh, honey, that's not true. I know I was talking about it, but ... well, it's the holidays. Maybe we should try to fix things."

She's worried about Allistair. He nearly laughed when his next thought was, *I don't care.*

Brittney was only being nice to make Allistair jealous. Ken was glad he had signed those divorce papers and dropped them off with his lawyer at lunch. It was liberating to know Brittney and Allistair couldn't affect his life anymore.

"Those aren't my favorite scents." Brittney leaned over the counter to see into the basket. "Honey, you forgot what I like."

"This isn't for you."

"But --" Tears instantly welled in her eyes.

Just a few months ago, Ken would have been terrified by the waterworks she could turn on and off at a moment's notice. "How do you do that, without messing up your makeup?"

That earned a snort and a grin from Jane. Brittney shrieked, stamped her foot, and nearly fell off her stiletto heels. When Ken didn't leap to catch her, she stomped out the door. Just before the door closed, she let out a wail and went down, her feet sliding out from under her in two different directions.

Ken knew that sidewalk was clear of snow and ice, and even had a nice coating of salt. How could she have slipped?

"From her cursing, I think she broke a heel. That and breaking a nail are the only things that could make her talk like that."

"She sounds like a sailor after a bender. Not that I've ever been around such creatures." Jane fluttered her eyelashes at him. They shared grins, and she held out her hand to shake his. "Congratulations, Ken. I think you're finally over her."

"We all make stupid mistakes. The lucky ones live to walk away."

Jane winked at him and turned to ring up the gift basket. She chatted about the upcoming Christmas festivities in town. Ken thanked Jane and took his purchase, carefully cradling it in its white paper bag, and left.

~~~~~

Jane watched Ken go. She waited for a ten-count, then crossed her arms, and settled down on the high stool behind the counter.

"I know you're here, Maurice. You knocked Brittney off her pins and broke her heels, didn't you?"

She waited, but the Fae didn't respond. Sighing, she closed her eyes and took a deep breath. She went semi-transparent, looked around the shop, and leaped. Moving like a streak of light, she darted up to the corner of wall and ceiling farthest from the door and snatched at empty air. When her fist closed, Maurice materialized inside. He let out a yelp and a curse and pounded on Jane's fingers. She ignored him as she floated slowly back down to the floor and became opaque again. All but for the fist holding him.

"Angela warned me you were meddling with Ken and Jo."

"I didn't do anything to either of them. Just zapped the cow giving them grief," he grumbled. Then he tipped his head to one side and grinned. "Neat trick, babe. Please tell me you're single and looking." He scowled when she laughed and settled down on her stool again. "Hey, I'm not always going to be this size."

"I know. And you're kind of hunky. But I'm with Kurt, and his
~~~~~

gifts include being able to borrow my gifts. Meaning he can find you anywhere. Do you want to end your exile as a pancake, or last long enough to go back to normal size?"

"Can't blame a guy for trying, can you?"

"Concentrate on helping Ken and Jo. But don't interfere, understand?" She released him and let her hand go back to normal.

"I'm on the job." Maurice rose up in the air. He saluted and vanished in a shower of sparks.

~~~~~

Only an hour into the office Christmas party Friday night, Jo suspected someone had spiked the spicy lime punch. Everywhere she looked, a clump of mistletoe hung directly over her head. Either it hung from every light and in every doorway in this party center, or the silly bit of useless decoration was following her.

"Something wrong?" Ken came up behind her and held out a tall glass of amber liquid.

She opened her mouth to refuse, then saw the drink had bubbles in it. He was definitely her knight in shining armor. Tonight proved it. His eyes had gleamed when he'd seen her dark blue velvet dress. His attention made her feel special. This newest move, bringing her plain ginger ale, only proved he was the Mr. Wonderful she had dreamed of all her life.

"You okay?" Ken asked.

She pointed at the mistletoe hanging above their heads. Jo could have sworn it was four feet to the right the last time she looked. Then she forgot that problem when Ken went bright red.

"I wasn't suggesting -- not unless you want to. But I swear that thing is moving. It's in a different place, every time I see it."

"Thank you." He slumped for a moment. "I thought I was just imagining it." He gestured at her glass, which she sipped with grateful relief. "That's why I decided to go for something a little less likely to be polluted. Just in case."

"My hero." She laughed when he colored up again. From the corner of her eye, she saw Mr. Myerhausen beckoning to Ken. "It looks like the visitors from the Pittsburgh office want to talk to you." She decided to be flattered when he groaned.

He apologized and promised to hurry back before he walked away. Yes, Ken was definitely Mr. Wonderful. So nice. So strong and considerate. How could that idiot Brittney have let him go,
~~~~~

much less tossed him over in favor of Allistair?

As if on cue, Allistair appeared at the edge of her vision, slithering toward her through the crowd of chatting, nibbling, drinking employees. That was her cue to flee.

~~~~~

"When I was younger, we'd call that tactic 'cruising for a bruising,'" Mr. Myerhausen remarked as the Pittsburgh contingent moved away to refresh their drinks.

Ken turned and saw Allistair creeping through the crowd. Ahead of his nemesis, Jo beat a hasty retreat.

"You have my permission to break something vital," Mrs. Myerhausen growled. Her husband gaped at her for a moment, then burst out laughing.

Jo slipped into one of the side rooms, Allistair right behind her.

"Excuse me, sir." Ken hurried after them. Mr. Myerhausen chuckled, and it warmed him to know the old man approved.

Halfway around the perimeter of the room, a red-nailed hand latched onto his arm and pulled him off balance. Ken muffled a curse and caught himself before he swung and popped Brittney in her heavily made-up face.

Tears made her eyes seem twice as large and her bottom lip quivered. "Ken, how could you?" she wailed in her baby-doll voice.

Ken looked around. People were watching, just as he had always feared. However, the looks of disgust were cast at Brittney and the pity was aimed at him. He had always thought it would be the other way around. He laughed as he realized what an idiot he had been for so long, restrained by his fear.

"How can you laugh when you hurt me so badly?" She yanked back her hand as if burned.

"What did I do? Besides sign the divorce papers *you* filed?" He turned his back on her and continued across the room.

"I just wanted you to prove you really loved me." Her high heels clattered on the tiles as she followed him.

"Oh, yeah, that's logical," someone muttered from behind Ken.

The crowd parted before him, making him wonder what sort of expression he wore. He picked up the pace, and Brittney kept up. How did she manage to run on those toothpick heels? Those claws latched onto his arm. He turned, twisting to free it.

"Ken, honey, you have to listen to me."
~~~~~

"No, I don't. We're not married anymore." He tried to step around her. Brittney slid over, blocking his path.

"But I want you back!" She grabbed onto his arms again.

"I don't want *you* back." He jerked free.

Brittney stumbled backwards and hit the wall, only three feet away. "You'll pay for that," she snarled, all the helpless squeaks and wails gone. "I'll have you thrown in jail for beating me."

"Is that what's under all that makeup? Allistair's been beating you, but you're afraid to report him to the police?"

"Allistair adores me. He would never lay a hand on me."

Mr. Myerhausen caught up with them, with his wife right behind him. "Then why are you chasing Mr. Jenkins? Haven't you heard the old phrase, what goes around comes around?"

"You don't understand," Brittney wailed, switching back to her helpless mode.

"I understand completely. I may be old, but that helps me see far more clearly than manipulative, self-centered witches such as you give me credit for." His chuckle was cold when Brittney gasped. Her eyes widened and she went pale under her heavy makeup. "Ken, my lad, we should rescue your young lady and have these two party-crashers handled by security." He caught hold of Brittney's arm when she tried to slither past him, and gestured for Ken to lead the way.

~~~~~

"Come on, sweetheart." Allistair chuckled when Jo evaded his grip. His breath smelled like a whiskey factory. "Look, mistletoe. Company policy. Gotta kiss under it." He gestured up at the ceiling and nearly lost his balance.

Jo glared up at the mistletoe, positive now it did follow her. She almost didn't see Allistair make another lunge at her.

"Get off me, you sleazebag!" She spun and brought her knee up, just like she'd seen in a ridiculous martial arts movie last week. Despite being forty pounds heavier than the willowy heroine, she easily hit her target. Then she told herself she'd aimed for Allistair's gut, not ten inches lower.

He *oophed* and folded over with satisfying speed.

She backed away, heading for the door, and tripped over the lounge chair in a conversation grouping.

Note to self: never walk backwards when in dangerous situations.
~~~~~

"If you walk out of here without giving me what I want," Allistair wheezed, "then don't come to work on Monday."

"You don't have that kind of authority." Jo didn't sound as confident as she wanted. From the smug grin replacing the agony on Allistair's face, he'd heard it in her voice.

"Babycakes, I stole old Kenny's woman and I got his promotion. I always get what I want and nobody ever catches me. You play nice and you give me what I want, or you're canned. And I'll make sure good old Ken gets the blame for all the embezzling I've been doing the last four years." He cackled when dismay crossed her face. "That got you, didn't it? Yeah, I have to hold onto that skinny witch just to beat old Ken, but that doesn't mean I have to suffer for it."

"Witch?" Brittney squealed, and leaped across the room.

Jo darted out of her way and stumbled into another chair.

No, it wasn't a chair.

That was Ken, wrapping his arms around her.

"Are you okay?" His arms were strong and warm and his breath smelled nice and he had such gorgeous eyes, so warm and concerned.

"Yeah. Great." She knew she was grinning like a fool. It didn't matter, because Ken was grinning like a fool now, too.

Allistair and Brittney snarled and screamed at each other, oblivious to their audience, until security arrived with suspicious speed, as if they had been waiting for this moment.

"Miss August, I'm sorry to bring up office matters at a social occasion..." Mr. Myerhausen turned to watch the three security men escort Allistair and Brittney away.

"Sir?" Jo tried not to shiver. Was she going to be fired or her pay docked for being part of the scene that had just taken place?

At least Ken was safe from Allistair.

"Sorry. Mustn't drift like that. Quite a revelation, eh, Ken?"

"Yes, sir." Ken tightened his arm around Jo's waist. "Lucky for us, there wasn't much fallout."

"Fallout. Exactly. Miss August, please make a note when you come in Monday morning, I want security to meet Mr. Somerville at the front door. He is not to be alone for one second while he cleans out his desk. I want Mr. Wilberforce and Miss Spencer to supervise, so he doesn't try to take home anything that belongs to the company. I especially don't want him to have access to his computer before our IT people can get inside and backtrack his larcenous activities.

"Oh, and speaking of IT ... ah, there they are." He beckoned to a cluster of people standing on the edge of the crowd. "I regret asking them to work tonight, but they'll get double-time, of course. We need to close down his Internet access before he destroys evidence. And perhaps we'll find whoever has been helping him." A sigh. "I suspected him, but there was no proof. Well, we all heard what he said, didn't we? Good enough reason to fire him immediately."

"Yes, sir," Jo said, and Ken echoed her.

"My dear Miss August, this is a Christmas party. I recommend the two of you enjoy yourselves." He gestured up at the ceiling. "And do take advantage of the mistletoe while you can." Chuckling, he walked away, gesturing for the others who had remained in the room to follow.

"Mistletoe?" Ken tipped his head back. Sure enough, the mistletoe hung directly over their heads. Jo could have sworn it was on the other side of the room just a few minutes ago.

"Orders are orders," she whispered.

"Yes, ma'am." He kept his arm around her waist and drew her up against him.

Jo caught her breath when Ken cupped her cheek, just as he had a few days ago. Her eyes closed and she sighed as his lips brushed warm and soft across her mouth.

The old movies were right. She saw fireworks and heard bells chime. Ken laughed softly, his breath warm across her face. He came back for a second kiss, longer than the first. It stole her breath and put a fist-sized spark into the pit of her stomach.

Merry Christmas, indeed.

~~~~~

"Whew!" Maurice sank back on his heels and didn't complain when the image of Jo and Ken kissing faded from the surface of the Wishing Ball. He mimed wiping nervous sweat from his forehead and looked up at Angela. "Worked out, didn't it?"

"This time." Her expression serene, Angela continued counting out the cash register.

"This time?"
~~~~~

"That was a little heavy-handed, chasing them with the mistletoe."

"Got the job done, didn't it? They finally took the hint, didn't they?"

"Yes, they did. At the end of two years, I think you'll shape up into quite a fine matchmaker. Maybe you'll like it so much, you'll want to stay just as you are." Angela held onto her calm expression while Maurice stared at her, mouth open and eyes wide in dismay. When he let out a moan of utter horror, she burst out laughing, warm and rolling, so it brightened the lights on the Christmas tree. Maurice couldn't help but join in.

"They really do look great together, don't they?" he said, his laughter dying away as a sigh.

"You know, Maurice, I think more important than teaching you to mix some mercy into your justice, Asmondius wanted you to learn to care, to get to know the people you set out to help. You care about Jo and Ken now, don't you?"

"Yeah, they're great. You can't help getting to know folks when you spend your whole day following them around, trying to stop the creepolas from winning out over them." He turned around and took a perch on the bent leg of the dragon holding the Wishing Ball. "So, do I get time off for Christmas, or do I get a new assignment?"

"Let's call it research, rather than an assignment. I want you to get to know Holly." She paused, but Maurice just nodded. "What? No complaints that she'd be impossible to hook up with someone?"

"She's okay. You gotta like a kid like her, the way she cares about books. And I've seen her with the kids at the library." He sighed, his elbows on his knees and his chin on his fists. "The problem is, hooking her up with a guy who's good enough for her. A guy looks at the outside package first -- I know, because I'm a guy. So nobody's gonna stick around long enough to see the gold mine hiding inside that dumpy librarian look."

"So get to know her and figure out a way to make the real Holly shine." She nudged him with the tip of her index finger.

"Okay, okay, I'll think about it."

"Don't think about it. Do it." She stepped back from the counter and crossed her arms, looking down at him. "I want you to find her someone who makes her feel like the special person she is by next Christmas."

"Or else?"

"Or else...you'll be stuck trying to get dates with Barbie for the rest of your life."

~~~~~

On Saturday, Ken and Jo stopped in to buy ornaments for the tree they bought for Jo's living room. Maurice kept watch over them as they wandered the shop, exploring the treasures on Angela's shelves, choosing what would make their shared tree perfect. Maurice watched them, trying to figure out how things had worked out, so he could duplicate the success with his next assignment.

"The thing is..." He sank down on the pincushion shaped like a throne that he had confiscated as an easy chair. His "living room" was on a small table in Angela's living room. Jo and Ken had left more than an hour before, happy and glowing with their newly discovered love. "The thing is, the more I think about it, the more I feel like I didn't do anything."

"Hmm. That's a matter of opinion." Angela filled a doll's teacup the size of Maurice's head with eggnog, and put it on the dollhouse table next to his chair. She settled on her couch with a book.

"I wanted to help, but most of what I did was give that slimebag a hard time. It was fun driving him nuts, but what good did it do?"

"Besides keeping him too busy to give Ken a hard time?" She allowed a small, satisfied smile. "You still have a lot to learn."

"Yeah. A matchmaker, I'm not."

"No, but you weren't put in this world to be a vigilante, either."

"Well I ain't dressing up like Cupid and shooting love darts into a bunch of losers, if that's what you're thinking."

"You did just fine with Ken and Jo by smoothing out the road around them. You're here to help, not shove people through doors they're not ready to approach. Just help. Get to know my friends. That's all I ask."
~~~~~

Chapter Seven

Christmas Eve day, Maurice woke up on a couch in Angela's furniture room, at full size. To his relief (and embarrassment), the footed pajamas he had borrowed from a Skipper doll grew along with him, so he wasn't caught in the buff downstairs. More important, his wings were gone.

He let out a howl of jubilation and snapped his fingers to call his clothes to him. There were things he wanted to do. The howl turned to dismay: he had about as much magic as the dust bunnies underneath the couch.

When Angela came downstairs a few moments later, wrapped in a long blue quilted robe, she looked unruffled and serene. She sat on the couch with him and wrapped an arm around him. Maurice didn't feel at all embarrassed to rest his head on her shoulder. At least he didn't whimper or sob like a toddler.

"I'm sorry, Maurice. It was all I could manage." She patted his head.

"You gave me my body back?" He sniffled and tried to smile. "Well, at least I'm not stuck looking like a joke, but how am I going to manage the next twenty-three months without any magic at all?"

"Oh, you misunderstand." She nudged him to sit up, then took hold of his hands. "I tried to persuade Asmondius that you deserved to be yourself for at least one day, because you had made so much progress. From midnight until midnight at Christmas Eve, spring and fall equinox, and summer solstice, you will go among Humans as a man, but with no magic. I'm sorry." She blinked, and Maurice was disturbed to realize she fought tears.

She was sorry? For him?

"Hey, no, actually this is great. I can run around town, see things, talk to all the people you've had in the shop. It'll be fun." He stood up and posed in his footed pajamas with pink puppy dogs on them. "But Angie-baby, I gotta get me some decent clothes."

"You know where the clothes room is." Her usual humor returned to her eyes. "Get yourself dressed while I whip up a big breakfast for us. You have a lot to do today."

"Great." He rubbed his hands together, pretending anticipation. "What's on the list?"

"Anything you feel like doing." She graced him with a serene smile, just a touch of smirk, and glided out, heading back upstairs.

Maurice found jeans and a bulky black sweater, and boots in just his size. They weren't the GQ quality of clothes he was used to, but he didn't care. To walk from one room to another, up the stairs to Angela's quarters, and use normal-size dishes thrilled him.

First he went to the town square to sit in the gazebo and listen to the carolers, then watched children sledding. He helped Angela take a load of presents for the town Christmas party to Eden, the community center.

He saw Holly, dressed up as one of Santa's elves, gather up children and take them into one of the smaller rooms for storytelling. Remembering what Angela had told him about getting to know her, he followed her and listened. The children sure loved her. The littlest ones fought to get to sit on her lap during the storytelling. He helped distribute cookies to the children in the storytelling room and then pass out presents. Lanie did a stint in the main room, performing her comedy routine. Later her wheelchair basketball team did an exhibition in the smaller gym. Maurice was impressed.

He was even more impressed when walking through the lobby of Eden gave him odd vibrations through his feet. He circled the floor until he found the spot, then stood there, trying to figure out what he was feeling. While he didn't have magic, obviously he could still feel where something magical had happened.

"Maurice?" Jane paused in the doorway to Eden's office. "I don't even want to know what's going on, but ..." She gestured at the floor where he stood. "Do you feel the residue from our fight this summer?"

"What kind of fight?"

"Who're you?" a big, wheat-haired, gray-eyed guy asked, stepping into the doorway behind Jane. He rested a hand on Jane's shoulder and gave Maurice one of those challenging glances guys understood and women thought were stupid.

"This is Angela's Maurice," Jane said. "Maurice, this is Kurt."

"O -- o -- kay. Who clipped your wings?"

"Furlough for Christmas," Maurice said with a shrug.

That got a grin from both of them. When he asked about the fight Jane mentioned, Kurt said they were on a deadline. If he wanted to hear the story, maybe he wanted to help them with an errand?

Maurice went with them to drop off toys Kurt had made for the children at Neighborlee Children's Home. The pride and affection in Jane's voice when she told Maurice that made something ache inside him. Other than his parents, had anyone ever talked about him with that sound in their voices, that look in their eyes?

On the way there and back, Kurt and Jane told him about the interdimensional invader they referred to as Big Ugly, who made regular attempts to either destroy the guardians of Neighborlee or rip a hole through to Earth from another dimension. Now Maurice was even more impressed. Neighborlee was no quiet little nowhere town where he had to serve his sentence. It was a pivotal point holding closed one of the dangerous weak spots between multiple dimensions. His respect for Angela tripled.

He met a friend of Angela's at the orphanage. Jon-Tom made his living as a carpenter and had brought hand-made wooden toys for the children. Jon-Tom offered Maurice a ride back to Divine's, which was convenient because Kurt and Jane were going to Felicity and Jake's house for Christmas Eve.

Angela had a houseful of guests, including Holly, Diane, Ken and Jo. There were people at tables in four rooms, set with mismatched dishes and every chair in the shop. Everyone brought a dish to share and they set up a long buffet table in the main shop room in front of the tree.

Maurice was introduced as a distant cousin of Angela's, and welcomed as if he belonged. He didn't mind his total lack of magic as the evening passed in laughter and singing and storytelling. Until he heard the clock strike the quarter hour. He looked up to realize it was 11:15. Where had the day gone?

He hung back as everyone started making their farewells, as if the chime was a signal. It pleased him and humbled him, when almost everyone made the effort to find him and say good-bye.

"Nobody asked how long I was hanging around," he said to Angela, when she stood in her open doorway, watching the last carload of guests drive away.

"I told them you were only able to stop to visit today, but you would be back." She turned to rest a hand on his shoulder. "Did you have a good day?"

"Yeah. It was... I've never had a day like this. Thanks for the Christmas present, Angela." He inhaled sharply as he heard the first bong of the clock chiming midnight.

"Merry Christmas, Maurice." She closed her eyes, and a single tear trickled down her cheek as silver magic sparks swirled around Maurice and swept him away.

"Merry Christmas, Angie-baby," he whispered, and opened his eyes to find himself back in his apartment hutch. He wore the same clothes but shrunken down, with his wings fluttering as if frightened by being separated from him all day.

He couldn't decide if looking ahead three months to another day at normal size, without magic, was a good thing, or more depressing than words could express.

~~~~~

Maurice settled into his exile and got to know the people of Neighborlee. He rode on Lanie's shoulder to attend the wedding of Gordon and Mandy, members of her Star Trek club. She made him laugh, describing all the efforts to fool both sets of in-laws into thinking the wedding would be Star Trek-themed, to pay them back for trying to hijack the preparations.

January crept along on frozen feet, and most days he stayed indoors, observing the people who came into Divine's Emporium. He got to know the guardians, their backgrounds, and the tradition of the Lost Kids. Only Lanie, Jane, and Angela, could both see and hear him. Kurt could sense Maurice's presence, but could only see and hear him when he borrowed Jane's or Lanie's talents. Felicity could pick up a glow from his magic, and track Maurice's location, but couldn't hear him unless he landed on her shoulder or hand.

Ford Longfellow and his granddaughters could hear Maurice, but couldn't see him. London and Sherwood, the electronic beings who had been "seeded" from Doni and from her boyfriend, Cosmo, couldn't see or hear Maurice through any computers or security cameras they accessed. Kurt decided this was a challenge and promised he would come up with something that would make Maurice visible to computers and sensors. For now, the three carried on conversations through texting. They were usually short
~~~~~

because he had to jump from key to key on the computer in Angela's living room, or punch the screen of a borrowed cell phone.

Jake, Cosmo and Wallace, the "ordinary mortals" who were part of the guardians by virtue of their relationships with them, and their useful skills, had to take everyone else's word for it when Maurice was in the room. Repeating his comments became tiresome, for him and whoever acted as intermediary, so he avoided meetings of the guardians and limited himself to interacting with the people who could see and hear him.

On days when the weather was benign, he flew around the town of Neighborlee. He took shelter at Jane's spa or Lanie's newspaper office when the weather got unfriendly while he was outside and his magic levels were too low for teleporting. His wings were especially sensitive to cold. He suspected that was part of the limitation spells put on him, because he couldn't remember any mention of such sensitivity in the historical records of the Fae. His curiosity on that subject revealed another limitation: he was prohibited from accessing the Ether Lexicon, the Fae repository of all knowledge and advice and a better research source than even Athena, Cosmo and Wallace on their computers, put together.

One member of the guardians he hadn't met right away was John Stanzer, local PI, and fellow exile from another dimension. Stanzer had been away on an extended investigation, connected with tracking down some of his fellow exiles and trying to follow up on information on Lanie's missing parents. When he came back to town in mid-January, Angela suggested Maurice go visit. Stanzer didn't come to Divine's very often, because the presence of winkies created a little bit of a conflict for him.

"He has some inter-dimensional guardians. The Hounds of Hamin. Something like guardian angels, but enormous, with very sharp teeth. They don't like the winkies. We suspect it's a clash of magical resonances. So I suggest you go on a day when your magic is either very strong, to allow you to escape quickly if they decide they don't like you, or when your magic is very weak, so they don't see you as a threat."

"Hmm, maybe I'll just stay here and wait until the next meeting of the guardians." Maurice offered a cheesy grin and hoped he didn't look as sickly pale as he felt, at a sudden mental image of being caught in and shredded by those very sharp teeth. He wouldn't be able to escape them, like he could ordinary dogs.

Angela tipped her head to one side and studied him. "I'm sorry, Maurice. Are you lonely?"

"Hey, you're great company, Angie-baby, but it's kind of a relief having other people around here who can see and hear me."

"I thought you were ashamed to be seen in your current condition."

"The way I look at it... They didn't know me before, and it's a long two years to just pick on you all the time."

"True." She refrained from smirking. "So, how are things coming along with Holly?"

"Okay, I guess. It's kind of fun, helping her repair all those books she brings in, without her realizing I'm doing it. And your library is major cool, so it's no hardship hanging over her shoulder and helping her with the cataloging and all that." Maurice shrugged. "She's a smart kid. If she'd pay a little more attention to her face and her clothes, guys would get their attention hooked long enough to see what's underneath. Know what I mean?"

"Well, at least you don't think she's hopeless now," Angela muttered.

~~~~~

Late January in Ohio turned cruel. When wind howled past the shuttered windows and snow piled up nearly to the windowsills on the first floor, Maurice didn't venture out to explore, even with the protection of magic.

He was bored, with no relief in sight. He could only read for so long before the effort of turning pages exhausted him. He had to stand up to read, either with the book lying on the table or leaning against a pile of other books. Using magic to turn the pages was almost as much effort as physically grabbing the paper and dragging it after him.

Angela didn't have a television, so all the videotapes and DVDs in the book room were useless to him. His only relief in sight was movie nights with Jane and Kurt, or Lanie and her brothers. One time, Athena and Doni invited him to come with them and their boyfriends, but that had nearly ended in disaster. It had been an incredibly windy night and he had been blown away on the walk from the theater back to Wallace's car. The worst part was that no one could see him get blown away, and the girls didn't hear him
~~~~~

yell with the wind blowing and their earmuffs on, and didn't feel when he left Doni's shoulder, because of her thick coat. They didn't realize he was gone until they got into the car. Athena suggested he sit on the dashboard by the closest heater vent, and he didn't respond.

One good thing came of that near-disaster: he met Cerb. One minute he was tumbling head over heels, feeling his hands and feet going numb from the cold. The next minute, massive teeth clamped down on his coat tail. Stinging swirls of heat and cold spun around him, and he was sure he was going to be permanently fried. Had one of Stanzer's Hounds decided to come check him out, and decided he made a good snack, and he was right that second going down the gullet of an interdimensional traveler?

"Wait a second ..." he wheezed.

In that second, he hit snowy wooden boards. A sleek, angular, gold and black canine head looked down at him. A chime rang through the air, at the same moment he realized that energy still tingling in his skin was part of his exile curse. The part that kept him from slipping through dimensions, to try to escape Earth for some place a little more comfortable for a five-inches-tall Fae with reduced magic.

Light spilled over him, and Maurice looked up at Angela, standing in the doorway of Divine's, and the canine head morphed into ... that big, fluffy, shaggy, gold-and-white mongrel dog he had glimpsed trotting past the shop from time to time.

"Thank you, Cerb." Angela bent down and held out her hand.

Maurice nearly laughed at the inconvenient timing of her concern for his dignity, letting him climb into her hand instead of picking him up by his collar. He ached, and groaned, and turned over and half-crawled into her hand. Cerb followed them inside, and upstairs to Angela's quarters. Maurice half-expected to see smoke rising from his skin when he took his coat and hat off. It certainly felt like he had been sunburned on the inside. Angela confirmed what he theorized. Cerb had taken a shortcut back to Divine's through a dimensional doorway, and Maurice had been scorched.

She gave him ointment for his discomfort, and he ducked into his cabinet to change into looser clothes, after rubbing the ointment all over. It smelled of lavender with undertones of peppermint, and the taste of chamomile filled his mouth. Cerb was gone when Maurice stepped out, and gratefully found a cup of hot chocolate, heavy on the dark chocolate, waiting on his little table.

"Cerb told me what happened. I called Athena to let them know you made it home safely," she said, as she settled on her couch with her own cup.

"Thanks." He sighed and settled gingerly into the pincushion throne. "Wow, that stuff works fast. Double thanks." He reached for the cup. "That'll teach me not to be a third -- correction, a fifth wheel, with dating couples."

"Oh, Maurice ..." She sighed.

"What's with presto-change-o hound dog?"

"That's what I wanted to know. We thought we would have a longer reprieve when the Rivals got themselves sucked into that dimensional dungeon. Cerb claims he's just doing regular check-ups, but ..." She shook her head, her gaze going distant.

Maurice sipped his chocolate and let the old-fashioned magic healing properties of dark chocolate go to work on his Fae bio-chemistry, while Angela told him more about the threats they had faced last year. Cerb had come from his dimension, taking on his current shape, to help guard Lanie from a pointed attack by the Rivals.

"All he admits is that he likes our dimension, he likes the shape he wears while he's here, and likes some of the more regularly assigned guardians he has met." Angela's eyes widened and she sat up a little straighter. Then her lips quirked up in a smile and Maurice swore she muffled a giggle by taking a sip of chocolate.

"What? Something good?"

"It's rare, but not unheard of ... what if Cerb ... fell in love?"

"What, like with another interdimensional visitor?" Maurice shrugged, then the implications seemed to rise up in his brain like something dredged up from the level of the Titanic. "Oh, like someone whose home dimension is different from his, so they aren't the same species?"

"Except when they're here, on Earth," she murmured, nodding.

"Wow. And I thought I had it rough."

"Maurice ..." She shook her head, but her smile brightened.

~~~~~

He explored Divine's on a regular circuit because the contents
~~~~~

did change without warning. He liked going into a room and discovering that it was a foot wider than the day before, or the winkies had lowered the ceiling to make it easier for Angela to clean the lights or the ceiling fan. However, there were places Maurice did not go after the first exploration.

There were paintings stored in the attic of Divine's Emporium. Even with three floors between him and them, Maurice sensed the magic filling them, making some prisons and others portals to other worlds. The presence of those paintings was torment to him, because it was useless to even ask if he could go into one for some diversion. He already had strong proof the spells controlling his exile wouldn't let him leave Earth, even if technically the painting stayed in Neighborlee. Besides, common sense said he wouldn't be able to handle whatever magical dangers those paintings held.

The winter winds and snow also hindered his exploration of the trails of magic that spilled from Divine's Emporium and streaked through the park. On clear, slightly warmer days, he managed to venture down the hill and hitch rides with the deer that came to eat the grain and lick the salt that Angela put out for them. Unfortunately, his sense for weather was also shrunken, sometimes leading to disasters or close calls. Cerb showed up from time to time, but whatever his reasons for coming back to Neighborlee, they kept him busy, so sometimes Maurice had to rescue himself.

One Sunday afternoon in mid-February, an icy wet snow struck while he was down in the park. The worst of the snowfall had passed by the time he got to the back door, but his wings were coated with ice. They hadn't defrosted enough for him to fly until he had walked from the back door to the stairs. He was still dripping icy water when he fluttered into Angela's apartment. She was curled up under a quilt on her sofa, reading.

Fluttering up onto the table, he settled down on the edge of a big pillar candle, warming his hands over the flame. He shook his wings, getting a last few drops off them.

"It's brutal out there." He snapped his wings shut, irritated when Angela barely glanced up from her book, that soft smirk catching up one corner of her mouth. "Go ahead and say it."

"Say what?" She turned the page.

"You warned me not to go outside. But Angie-baby, there's nothing to do in here."

"I thought you liked to read. I gave you freedom of all the book rooms, including the magical library."

"Yeah, but all those books are bigger than me. It's real hard to hold a story in your head when it takes minutes to turn a page."

"Hmm, yes, I didn't think about that. Sorry." She turned another page. "You could study people."

"You're the only 'people' in the shop." Maybe, he thought, he would take a chance on going through a painting after all.

"The Wishing Ball will let you see people." Angela glanced up from her book. "Why not start with Holly?"

"Who?" He actually forgot who Holly was for a moment, trying to wrap his brain around the revelation that the Wishing Ball could do more than grant wishes. Then his brain caught up with her words. "Oh. The librarian. How exciting can she be?"

"Just think of all the stories she has tucked away in her mind."

"Huh?" He wondered if his brain had iced up.

"The Wishing Ball will let you visit her dreams. ***If*** you truly want to get to know her and be her friend."

"There's always a catch." His brain locked on the idea of visiting the dreams of a librarian. Holly had good taste in books. "Okay, why not? Might be fun at that. A chick who loves books can't be all bad, right?"

"I'm biased. Holly is one of my dearest friends."

"Well, that's a subtle warning." He settled back against the pillar candle and slid down to sit on the tabletop. His wings scraped the candle, creating little curls of wax that stuck to his clothes.

"Maurice, will you please leave me in peace to read my book?"

"I'm going, I'm going!" He leaped high, snapped off a salute, and zoomed out of the room.

Downstairs in the main room, he made a bumpy landing on the counter. His wings were still damp. The thought of visiting Holly's dreams didn't exactly fill him with anticipation. More like mild curiosity. He had watched her at work, surrounded by hordes of kids with runny noses and screechy voices during afternoon story hour. What if her dreams were nightmares of being stampeded by kids?

"Okay, buster, gimme what you got." He tapped on the side of the Wishing Ball.

The dark, rainbow-streaked, metallic surface immediately

grew misty. Good sign. He had feared he would have to dredge up what little magic remained after keeping himself from turning into a Fae-cicle, to activate it.

The mist glowed, then settled into a flowing expanse of white, the focus sharpening. He looked at an outdoor scene with falling snow all around Holly.

What was she doing outside? Had the weather gotten worse, and she was lost, walking home from the library? The fear on her behalf startled him, so he backed off from the Wishing Ball. The glow died and the image faded.

"Get a hold on yourself, boy." He wondered if his scheming ability and common sense had been shrunk, along with his size and his magic. If Holly was lost, he could use the Wishing Ball to find her, and tell Angela, who would send help.

He stepped up to the Wishing Ball again and asked it to show him Holly. The image returned, gaining more resolution, until he looked at the back porch of a house not far from Divine's Emporium, sitting level with the park, instead of on a hill above. It was a little crackerbox house, with light spilling from the open back door. The woods were maybe fifteen yards away. A dusting of snow on a gentle breeze made it a Christmas postcard scene.

Holly slowly walked across her backyard toward the trees. She wore a parka with the hood down, unzipped, and held pieces of bread in one bare hand and a sectioned apple in the other. The falling snow caught on her hair and her eyelashes, sparkling in the light spilling out of the open door. She stopped halfway across the backyard and stood so still Maurice thought she might eventually end up a snow statue. Her breath escaped in slow tendrils of mist.

One doe, then a second, then a third, appeared from the shadows of the trees and crept across the snowy yard toward Holly. Maurice held his breath, waiting, anticipating the moment when they would eat from her hands. Bits of melting snow dusted her hair and face with diamond sparkles, and the cold brought roses to her cheeks. Her eyes glowed as the deer nibbled at the bread and apples and then nuzzled at her hands.

Maurice barely restrained himself from cheering when one doe licked Holly's cheek, as if in farewell, before she turned to go back into the woods.

"That's pretty cool." He watched the does meander back the

way they had come. Something ached inside him when Holly's delighted glow vanished with the deer. She turned and trudged back into the warmth of her little house.

She shed her coat, leaving it on a hook by the back door. The Wishing Ball's images changed, following her through the house as she checked doors and windows and turned off lights. In the kitchen she made herself a big mug of hot chocolate, rinsed out the pan, then turned off the light and headed upstairs.

He liked it that she made hot chocolate the old-fashioned way, with real milk and cocoa and sugar. He watched until she went into her bedroom, put the mug on her nightstand, and snagged a dark blue flannel nightgown off a hook on the back of her bedroom door.

"Gonna be here a while," he muttered, for the sake of whoever might be watching him. The last thing he wanted was to be accused of being a Peeping Tom.

When Holly stepped into her bathroom, he scurried away from the Wishing Ball. He scrounged in the shelves under the cash register until he found a couple pads of paper and a quilted book cover that needed mending. With his back to the Wishing Ball and whatever Holly was doing, he dragged them back and set up a couch to sit in comfort. By the time he had everything to his satisfaction, Holly was safely in her nightgown and padding back to her bedroom, barefoot.

Maurice sighed relief and settled down on the makeshift couch. Holly climbed into bed, plumped her pillows against the headboard, and pulled the covers up past her waist. That glow returned to her face as she reached for the book, three inches thick, at the very least, sitting on her nightstand.

In the glow of the lamp, Maurice could read the age-darkened spine. "Robin Hood, huh? And the really old stories, too," he muttered. "Okay, good choice. But watching you read a good book isn't my idea of quality entertainment, y'know?"

Holly turned three pages, before he decided this was even less thrilling than watching paint dry. His wings were dry and warm again, so he flew upstairs to check in with Angela. Maybe she was done with her book, and he could talk her into playing poker.

Chapter Eight

"You might find it interesting to visit Holly's dreams," Angela said, before Maurice could even land on the table next to the sofa.

"How?" He tried not to whine.

"Put your mind to it." She raised the book a little higher, hiding her face. She shouldn't have seen him stick his tongue out, but he heard a muffled chuckle as he headed downstairs again.

He detoured to the candy jars and helped himself to a dark chocolate kiss. One benefit of his reduced size: a piece of candy that normally would last less than a minute now could last him for an entire evening. Dark chocolate to the Fae was like medicine and energy rations and ambrosia, all mixed together. He would need it if he was going to be stuck watching Holly read for the next hour.

And if things got bad, he might just beg Angela to get him a six-pack of diet cherry cola the next time she went grocery shopping. While normal Humans got nothing but a caffeine buzz, the chemicals and artificial sweeteners combined to affect the Fae in ways that alcohol never could. And no hangover.

Maurice muffled a chuckle at the thought of how sloshed he could get on half a can, in his current size. Normally it would take him two cans to get a happy tingle. He settled down on his couch again with the foil peeled back from the chocolate kiss.

Holly had finished her hot chocolate and was rubbing her eyes, visibly fighting to stay awake. Did she get that tired just from helping kids find books and shushing people? Maybe being a librarian was a rougher job than he thought.

"That's it," he said. "Close those sleepy weepy wittle eyes, before I die of boredom."

He broke the tip off the chocolate kiss and crammed it into his mouth as Holly struggled through one more page. He had been considering Angela's vague directions, so he thought he knew what to do when Holly turned onto her side, clutching the open book, and her eyes slid closed.

He got up and pressed his hands to the image of Holly in the Wishing Ball. A slight buzzing grew in his palms. A sensation of falling forward, into the Wishing Ball, enfolded him. He sank through a thick, gelatinous substance that tingled against his skin, through his clothes -- like diving headfirst into a vat of diet cherry cola. He closed his eyes as lights burst all around him.

He stumbled. He opened his eyes and stood on a forest path, dressed like someone in the Errol Flynn version of *Robin Hood*. He chuckled and looked around, turning slowly. The forest looked like the stylized period of Hollywood.

Holly raced down the path toward him. She was dressed as one of the Merry Men, still plump, but agile and full of life, with that delightful glow surrounding her. She grabbed his hand as she raced past. "Run for your life!"

Maurice let her drag him along. After all, it was her dream. She would know if they really needed to run, wouldn't she?

"What happened?" He tried to look behind them without tripping over his feet. How did Robin Hood run in pointy-toed boots, anyway?

"The Sheriff is after us."

"What Sheriff?"

"Of Nottingham!" She laughed, even as she looked behind them and let out a shriek that was half excitement.

A troop of men came tearing around a bend in the forest trail, gaining on them with every thud of the hooves of their over-dressed horses.

Maurice decided this was fun. He let Holly lead the way, down a winding forest trail with the Sheriff's men close on their heels. They came out onto a riverbank. Ropes conveniently appeared from the trees overhead. Holly leaped, grabbed a rope, and swung across with a style that earned a whistle of appreciation from Maurice. He hesitated just long enough for her to reach the apex of the swing and let go. Then he leaped, snatching at the next rope, and followed.

They landed on the opposite bank without stumbling and ran. He looked back in time to see the horses come to an abrupt stop, physically impossible in the real world, and send the Sheriff's men tumbling over their heads, into the river.

"You're one nasty kid. I think I like you," he said, as they ran around a bend in the forest trail.

"Thank you so much, kind sir." Holly slowed enough to curtsey without tripping over her feet. Her clothing transformed into Maid Marion's outfit from the beginning of the movie.

They slowed to a walk when the trail brought them out onto the riverbank again. Maurice reached up and discovered he had a hat with a long feather in it. He tipped it grandly to her, then offered her his arm. Holly curtsied again and linked her arm through his, and they settled into a leisurely stroll along the water's edge.

"So, does this kind of thing happen a lot around here?" He would visit her dreams every night, if this was her pattern.

"It depends." She shrugged and reached up in the air. A butterfly appeared from thin air and landed on her finger, slowly fluttering its jewel-toned wings.

"On what?"

"How rotten the real world is and how much I need to bash somebody before I turn into an ax murderer in real life." She blew a kiss to the butterfly and it fluttered off her finger and away into the sunshine and shadows.

"Wait a minute! You know you're dreaming?"

"Is this a dream?" She tugged her arm free and darted away, laughing. She immediately vanished into a hedge maze that sprang up from the ground faster than a lightning flash.

Maurice grinned and dashed into the maze after her. "Hey, Holly, where are you?"

"Over here!" Her voice came through the greenery from straight ahead.

"Oh, yeah, that's a big help," he muttered.

He stumbled around five corners with no results before he got fed up. He raised his hands experimentally, because this wasn't *his* dream. Magic swirled thick and hot, buzzing around his fingertips. He snapped his fingers at the hedge wall in front of him. It vanished in a blue flash of light.

"That's more like it. I don't care if it's only a dream. It feels good to be up to full power again." He blasted the next hedge wall, then a third. He stumbled out into a rose arbor.

Holly sat on bench and Robin Hood knelt at her feet, trying to get hold of her hand. Not Errol Flynn, Kevin Costner or Cary Elwes, but suspiciously like the guy from the BBC version where Paul Darrow from *Blake's 7* played the Sheriff. That just proved her very good taste. When Maurice walked through the sparkling hole in the hedge, she stopped resisting. Robin Hood got hold of her hand and raised it to his lips.

"Oh, please. This is getting really old." Mischief sparkled in her eyes as she watched Maurice approach.

He got a funny, hollow sensation in the pit of his stomach. How long had it been since someone was glad to see him?

"But, my darling..." Robin Hood whined.

"Aren't you forgetting somebody?" Maurice had to ask. For the fun of it, he swept off his cap again and bowed to Holly.

"Who are you?" Robin Hood barely glanced over his shoulder. "Begone. My lady and I wish to be alone."

"I'm not your lady." Holly yanked her hand free and stood up.

Robin Hood followed her as she circled the bench.

"The lady wants you to scram, so scram." Maurice stepped between them.

"I know not who you are," Robin Hood rested a hand on the hilt of his sword, "but you would be wise--"

"Yeah, that's me. The wise guy. That's how I got in this mess in the first place." He grabbed Robin by his shoulders and gave him a heave-ho though the closest hedge wall.

Holly laughed and applauded. "You have no idea what a nuisance he can be. If I don't get rid of him fast enough, Maid Marion shows up, and she fights dirty."

"But--" For a moment, he felt dizzy with the contradictions and questions colliding in his brain. "If you know this is a dream... You know you're in charge here, don't you?"

"I know, but if I use the power too much, all the magic goes away. It's more fun to follow the rules, you know? Figure things out the hard way. And I need all the magic I can get my hands on."

"Yeah, you and me both, kid." He bowed and offered her his bent arm again. "Shall we?"

"Thank you, kind sir."

They wandered for hours, in and out of various landscapes that reminded Maurice of old books he loved. He and Holly made each other laugh, coming up with their favorite lines from the books that fit in each landscape. He stayed aware of the passage of real time, and it amazed him how quickly the night passed.

Somewhere between 3 and 4 in the morning, they came to a castle straight out of a Disney movie, with white stones and gold edging on all the roofs, and dozens of turrets and towers, all with pennants flying. He braced himself for an onslaught of servants and courtiers and an evil prince, or worse, a too-good-to-be-true prince, who would try to steal Holly away from him.

To his surprise, the castle was empty of all inhabitants. He and Holly wandered, exploring the treasure room, the massive library, the throne room, the armory. They said less and less as time passed. He had never been so content with silence before. Every time he looked down at Holly, she was looking up at him, smiling. He couldn't help smiling back at her.

They ended up in the great hall of the castle. It was set up for a ball, with trestle tables groaning under a feast. There were instruments in the musicians' gallery, but no musicians. Yet music played. He heard the whisper of shoes on the flagstone floor and ball gowns rustling, swirling around dancers' legs, yet there were no people. Maurice kept hold of Holly's hand as he bowed.

"My lady, will you do me the honor of this dance?"

She curtseyed. "I am honored, kind sir." Then she slid into his arms and they spun across the floor, in and out and around the invisible dancers. And the music played on and on.

Faintly, in the distance, Maurice heard a scraping, grinding noise. He knew it didn't come from inside the dream, but he was at a loss to identify it. Then it occurred to him that it was the familiar sound of snowplows scraping the streets clean. Why was he hearing that, in the middle of Holly's dream?

Even as he asked himself the question, Holly slipped out of his arms. She looked around the castle hall with real sadness on her face, and he felt as if someone had punched him right under his ribs, stealing his breath.

"Hey, don't stop the fun now." He reached for her hands.

Holly stepped away, out of his reach. "It's almost morning. Will you be back tomorrow night?"

"It's your dream, remember. You make the rules."

"Not all the time." She smiled, but it was the saddest smile he had ever seen.

"Princess Holly." He went down on one knee and caught hold of her hand. "Ruler of this wondrous kingdom, will you grant this lost soul permission to return to your kingdom?"

"Most gladly, sir. I'm sorry, what did you say your name was?"

"I'm--" His voice caught.

Holly vanished. The world around him faded to gray.

And then even that vanished.

"...Maurice."

On the counter in Divine's Emporium, Maurice staggered back from the Wishing Ball and sat down on his makeshift couch, watching Holly turn over in her bed and slap blindly at her alarm clock. Then she opened her eyes, looked around, and smiled, glowing just like she had during their adventure. He raised a hand to trace the curve of Holly's cheek. Before his fingertips touched the cool surface of the Wishing Ball, she vanished.

"See you tonight, kid," he whispered. "Read something really cool today, and dream about it, okay?"

Over breakfast, he reported to Angela what he had seen and done. He'd decided it was the honorable thing to do. Holly was Angela's friend, after all.

He was sitting at the doll table across from Angela. "So, are you gonna let me go back?" he said, while he sipped at his hot chocolate. He must have done something right, because she usually didn't make hot chocolate for breakfast.

"You like Holly, don't you?"

"There's a whole lot more to her than anybody'd guess, just looking at the outside package. I like how she thinks."

"Yes, I thought you might." Her little smirk, just before she took a bite of bagel, sent a shiver up his back. His wings thrummed.

"What's that supposed to mean?"

"The two of you have a lot in common."

"You mean besides being trapped in bodies we don't want?" He reached back and yanked on one of his wings, which made him lose his balance and fall out of his chair.

"You both have a keen sense of justice, for one thing. I'm pleased that you see Holly as she really is, inside. Not many people are brave enough to do that."

"Gee, Angie-baby, somebody'd think you're starting to like me." Maurice couldn't explain the warm glow filling him.

"Stranger things have happened." She serenely sipped at her hot chocolate.

~~~~~

Valentine's Day was coming up. Maurice hoped to get some
~~~~~

points with Angela and the Fae Disciplinary Council if he could match up another couple. For Jo and Ken, Angela gave him little credit for getting them together, other than running interference. So he felt a little desperate as time inched through snowy days of gloom and chill.

His only fun time seemed to be the nights when he visited Holly's dreams. He frustrated himself for more than a week, trying to influence them by whispering to her whenever she visited Divine's. He was positive she sensed something when he called her name or rode on her shoulder. But that was the extent of their interaction outside of dreams.

Diane, Angela's clerk, was a little better. She paused often and looked around when he spoke to her, but no matter how many times he hovered in front of her nose, she never seemed to see him or feel the breeze from his frantically fanning wings.

"So what's her story?" he asked Angela one evening.

"Diane?" She slipped the embroidered silk bookmark between the pages of her book, and closed it. "Diane is a rebel."

"You could have fooled me. She's a good, quiet kid. Sensible clothes. Works hard. Likes her classes at WB. She volunteers over at Eden, right? I've heard her talking to some of the kids about the basketball team and other stuff." He settled on the arm of the sofa where Angela lay and got comfortable for a long talk.

"That's why she's a rebel. Against her upbringing, that is. Diane's parents are very rich, very powerful, and very ruthless when it comes to their business dealings. Social climbing is only a tool for them, in comparison to other old, wealthy families who believe that social status is the be-all of existence."

"Uh huh. So Diane got tossed on her kiester when she didn't want to go to the debutante's ball?" He knew Diane was a straight-shooter and had a level head on her shoulders, but he thought her taste for second-hand clothes and used books was because she was the proverbial penniless, perpetual college student, not because she had been disowned by her rich family.

"She could go back to her family any time she wants, on her terms. The last I knew, she still has access to her trust fund and her shares in the family's empire."

"So why's she here instead of using the family's bucks to make the world a nicer place?"

"She made her choice a long time ago and has stuck with it. Diane likes small towns and quiet living. If she prefers denim over silk, it's none of your business why. Got it?"

"Got it." He sighed. "So it's just her style, huh? The spoiled rich girl didn't have to get whacked upside the head to make her see what's important in life. No hard lessons. No having to choose between Mumsy and Daddy or doing the right thing."

"Maurice, you are a snob." Angela tipped her head back onto the arm of the sofa and laughed softly.

Outraged, he stared at her.

"You are, you definitely are a snob. You think you're better than she is because you're learning some hard lessons," she said between chuckles. "You think you're better because you are being forced to reform, while Diane just chose her simple life because she likes it."

"Me? A snob?" Maurice felt a little dizzy. He teetered between fury and laughter as her face got rosy and laughter tears gathered in the corners of her eyes.

He chose laughter, because a flicker of fear remained that he would get squashed or get sent to a really nasty probation officer if he ticked off Angela.

~~~~~

Valentine's Day passed, with all its attendant fuss and hoopla over romance. A few slightly warmer days peeked through the usual February gloom and sleet. Maurice got permission from Angela and rode on Diane's backpack to Willis-Brooks College to investigate her classes, and then went to Eden to watch her work with the children of Neighborlee. He stayed safely deep in Diane's backpack when she went into the smaller gym to coach the peewee basketball team with Lanie Zephyr.

"Something about that place freaks me out, big-time," he reported to Angela, when Diane came to work the next morning and he climbed out of the backpack again. "It's worse when I'm peewee size. Tell me more about Big Ugly? Just in case he acts up while I'm around? Not that I can do much, but ..." He shrugged.

"Wise." Angela rested her elbows on the counter and stared at a spot somewhere down the first aisle, and yet a million miles away from the shop. "Last winter was truly the worst, most brutal attempt by the intruder to break through." She shuddered and
~~~~~

closed her eyes for a few heartbeats.

Maurice lost his breath, seeing that moment of fear in her. It gave her a sense of great age, and fragility.

"We were blessed to catch the warning signs, and to prepare." She went on to describe in more detail the events of New Year's Eve, and the day after, when the Rivals had nearly succeeded in bringing Big Ugly through the barrier into Neighborlee.

"So it's gone?" His wings shuddered and he didn't care how it made him look. There was nothing wimpy about being afraid of something that was big and nasty and could devour Fae without even opening its mouth.

"Technically ..." Her normal mischievous twinkle returned, and he was relieved. "Technically, Big Ugly was never here. It or he or they have never managed to break through, but the enemy threatens, attempts, is defeated, and retreats to lick its wounds and regain its strength. Our task is to be alert and be ready ... and be willing to sacrifice all to defend our town, and our world." She took a deep breath and stood up straight. "I'm pleased you're able to sense where the barrier was pierced and reinforced."

"And left pretty slimy and stinky, if you ask me." He felt better when Angela laughed softly.

"You're becoming attuned to the music of Neighborlee, if you sense that discord. I would be grateful if you added your sensitivity to our effort. You don't have to do anything except listen."

"For now, anyway," he said softly, and was rewarded by a slow nod and a warming of Angela's smile.

~~~~~

Maurice took on sentinel duty whenever Angela left the shop on errands. He made up a place for himself in the shelving directly behind the cash register where he could see the front door and the stairs, and keep watch on whoever was tending the register.

Angela employed several high school girls from the orphanage in the afternoons and on weekends. Maurice decided early on that she wouldn't have done that unless there was something special about the girls, more than met the eye. Just as there was more to Diane and Holly.

On March 1, the store was quiet. School hadn't let out for the day. It was just him and Diane in the shop. Angela was down in the park. Maurice settled into his nest behind the counter and
~~~~~

daydreamed about his latest dream visit with Holly.

Last night he'd stepped into Holly's dream as she stood on the edge of a dark, churning river. Its chill reached through the air and formed fog along the ground. He hadn't particularly cared for the Renaissance-style clothes Holly had chosen for them, but he'd supposed he didn't look any more ridiculous than anybody else who might drop into the dream...

A long boat like a glorified gondola slid up to the riverbank, emerging from the mists. Maurice helped Holly climb in. They worked together in silent harmony, pushing off from the shore with long poles. Everything was shrouded in mist. Vague man-shapes filled the water. Pale, skeletal hands tried to grab hold of the boat's sides. Maurice nearly rapped at the hands to drive them away, but Holly ignored them and didn't seem afraid the boat would be overturned, tossing them into the churning water.

"So, where are we?" he said, after the boat slid out into deeper water and the grasping hands grew less insistent and numerous.

"This is the River of Death." Holly tugged the hood of her cloak a little higher on her head. "Those are the lost souls trying to climb on board and escape their eternal fate."

"Have I mentioned what a really morbid imagination you have?"

"A few times." She nodded calmly. "But you'll protect me if anything goes wrong, won't you?" She fluttered her eyelashes at him.

"You better believe it." Maurice had been almost disappointed when no monsters beyond those grasping hands showed up to threaten them, so he could step up and be Holly's hero.

A vibration moved against the magic protecting the shop, like talons scraping on a chalkboard. Maurice leaped from his little nest and soared over Diane's head. She leaned on the counter, reading her world history textbook for mid-term exams. He felt somehow betrayed when she didn't react. Something threatened the net of protective spells around the shop. Why couldn't she feel it?

The sense of pressure increased. Soon he heard and felt the splitting of the net. He muffled a yelp as something like big, icy, electrically charged hands grabbed his wings and pulled in opposite directions. The sensation vanished a second later.

The bells over the door jangled. Soft footsteps approached.

Maurice fluttered his wings. He'd never felt so relieved to have them there, still attached to his back.

Diane looked up and smiled at the square-featured man who stepped into the main room. "Can I help you?"

Maurice felt like slapping her for being so pleasant.

Okay, so the guy looked like a poster child for Hollywood heroes. Hadn't Diane ever heard the warning not to judge a book by its cover? The Marlboro man was a decrepit, broken-down rodeo clown in contrast to him, elegant despite his worn jeans and leather jacket and those scuffed brown boots. Maurice peered through the front window and saw a Lexus out front. Nobody drove expensive cars in Neighborlee, except the Grandstones. Who was this guy?

"I know you, don't I?" the guy said.

Maurice hated him even more for his smooth baritone and that friendly, perfect, pearly white smile.

"I got it. Eden. You coach the girls' basketball team."

"With Lanie," Diane hurried to say. She blushed.

Bad sign. Who was this guy, and what did Diane know about him, to make her so flustered?

"Hold tight, baby," he growled, and flew over to perch on her shoulder. Passing the stranger, that sense of inimical magic grew strong, making all the hairs stand up on his wings. He hadn't known he had hairs on his wings until that moment. "Don't let hormones turn off your brain."

"Can I help you find something?" Diane said.

"I'm interested in some rare books. I heard Angela has a room where she keeps some first editions and hard-to-find volumes." His smile widened. Yet at the same time it grew tense, and something like fear glittered in his eyes. "Could you let me look around?"

"Sorry. Angela is the only one who can let people look at those books. She's been given some on commission, and she's extremely careful with them." Diane shrugged. "If you want to wait, or come back in about an hour, she can help you."

"Ah, thanks. I have to get on the highway in about twenty minutes for a meeting downtown, but I thought I'd at least make a start..." He looked around the shop and jangled the keys in his pocket. "I'll check back later, if that's okay?"

"We're open until 6, Monday through Wednesday, and until 9 Thursday through Saturday, and we're closed most Sundays."

"Most Sundays?" His smile faded after a moment, going crooked and uncertain.

"When Angela thinks someone needs to be here, she'll open early or late or on Sundays." She shrugged. "You know Angela."

"Actually, I don't. I've been meaning to rectify that, but..." He looked around again. "I'll check back tomorrow. Maybe both of you will be here then. Thanks." He turned to head for the door.

"You're welcome." Diane watched him go out the door, then she slumped over her book again.

"What's with this guy?" Maurice asked, knowing she couldn't hear or answer him. "It's not like you to get swayed by a pretty face." Or was that part of the magic he had wrapped around him? "Angie-baby, get back here!"

Angela walked in twenty tense minutes later. Maurice heard the back door open and he leaped from his nest on the top shelf to fly to her. He nearly ran into Diane, who had scooted around the counter and ran to the back room to meet Angela.

"You are never going to guess who came in here! Troy Richards," she said, before Angela could even take her coat off.

"What did he want?" Angela paused, her hand on the doorframe.

Maurice saw a flare of magic in the frame and caught the instantaneous burst throughout the whole house. It was more sensed than seen, like the after-image of a lightning strike.

Angela turned to him, her eyes wide with questions, her mouth flat in concern.

"Yeah, you still feel it, don't you?" Maurice settled on her shoulder, chilled from the breeze that impeded the melting of the snow in the sunshine. "Who's this Troy Richards guy, anyway? Diane sure looked happy to see him. Not a friend of yours, is he?"

Troy has never come into the shop, but I've met him around town at various events, Angela responded, her mouth still a flattened line. She took off her coat and gloves and hung them up by the door. *He's a good man, a self-made millionaire, involved in several charities. Now hush so I can talk to Diane. I can't carry on two conversations at the same time.*

Chapter Nine

Maurice shut up, mostly because he was surprised at Angela's response. Whatever she sensed, whatever vibrations from the inimical magic Troy had brought into the shop, it had unsettled her.

"He was looking for a book." Diane led the way back to the main room. "A rare book. He asked about your special room."

"Not the special, special room, I hope," Maurice muttered.

There were several book rooms at Divine's Emporium. One was downstairs, where people could come in and browse through old and used books. The second was on the third floor. Angela kept it locked and only let people in by appointment, with supervision. The third was on the fourth floor, between the attic that held the magical paintings and a room holding objects that were benign in their own right, but dangerous if they fell into the wrong hands. The fourth-floor books were magic, in and of themselves. Some had been given into Angela's custodianship, to preserve and protect them. Some were there to protect the world from their contents.

"When is he coming back?" Angela settled down at the bistro table in the main room. She let Diane fuss with the cappuccino maker under the counter, and frowned at that invisible spot in mid-air, thinking so hard Maurice could almost hear the whirring and buzzing inside her head.

"Probably tomorrow. I gave him our open schedule." Diane shrugged and settled down with two frothy mugs.

"Any clue what kind of book he was looking for?"

"No." She frowned and paused on the verge of sipping.

Maurice? Did he do anything to her?

"Not a thing. If he had, I would have gone after him. Hey, he should have known I was there, if he was working magic. That means all the magic was just..." He came in for a landing on the hanging basket planted with spearmint that hung on the wall over the bistro table. "The protection magic must have reacted to magic he was carrying. Like if I was carrying a charm and it set off an alarm, know what I mean?"

Yes. Angela sipped at her cup. *So he was carrying something that had negative magic attached to it, but he wasn't using it. The question is therefore what the magic was meant to do, if it was controlling him, or if he was merely being used to carry that magic in here, past my defenses.*

"Don't think much of those defenses if they let him through."

If Troy was an innocent courier, the magic would tone down to avoid hurting him. Which means... Well, if I have enemies, they must know how to get around my defenses.

"And that makes the problem doubly bad trouble," Maurice snarled. "Don't you worry, Angie-baby. I'll watch out for Diane. You concentrate on zapping the creep."

Angela smiled slightly as she sipped at her cappuccino.

~~~~~

The next day, Maurice felt the straining of the net protecting the house when Troy returned. Angela was in the clothing room, advising Jo on clothes for a business trip. Choosing the right clothes for meetings and formal dinners was probably a big thing, but couldn't Angela feel the house's reaction to the inimical magic Troy brought in with him? Diane, helping a gaggle of girls pick out enough candy to make Willy Wonka sick, wouldn't sense anything.

"Well, duh, why should she worry when I'm here?" Maurice snarled, and zipped down the stairs to the entryway. It pleased him a little when Troy rubbed at his temples and looked around as if slightly dazed. Maybe the house did resist his entrance, despite the fact the guy was an innocent dupe.

Sometimes being ignorant and innocent wasn't a valid defense.

"How come you're carrying magic? Where is it?" Maurice reasoned the best way to keep track of the intruder was to stick with him as close as possible. He aimed to land on Troy's shoulder.

The next thing he knew, his entire body tingled and his wings felt slightly singed, like he had flown too close to a flame. He blinked and tried to focus his blurry eyes.

What had happened? What was he doing a second ago? He lifted his head, and it immediately throbbed like he had tried to pump boiling oil into his skull through his ears. Moaning, he felt his ears, afraid he would find the points singed off. His eyes regained focus. He saw Troy going up the stairs, but upside down. What the heck?

No, Maurice realized. *He* was upside down. Hanging upside down in the chamomile plant Angela kept by the door to purify the
~~~~~

air. Something had zapped him and flung him off Troy's shoulder.

Troy headed upstairs and nobody knew. Groaning, Maurice rolled over, scrambling to grab hold of the chamomile leaves before he slid off. If his wings were singed useless, he was in big trouble. He doubted he had enough magic to teleport himself upstairs.

"Thank you," he muttered, breathing out a sigh of relief when a test flap revealed his wings still worked. They just felt stiff and prickly like sunburned skin. "Don't fail me now." He took a deep breath and launched himself from the hanging pot. One thing in his favor: he didn't have to take each step and turn of the switchback stairs going up through the center of the house. He could go straight up.

He caught up with Troy on the third-floor landing. He settled down on the newel post and watched. Okay, so how come the guy just stood there, staring at the wallpaper?

Suddenly Troy staggered forward and went to his knees.

"Whoopsie daisy!" Maurice almost reached out to try to help him, but he had learned his lesson. "What's wrong, fella? Maybe whatever zapped me got you in the backwash?" He was in no mood for sympathy if Troy suffered from whatever had scorched him.

Troy turned around and half-crawled, half-staggered to the newel post where Maurice perched. He rubbed his eyes, hauled himself upright and looked around. One foot swung out like a pendulum, aiming for the stairs to the fourth floor, but Troy didn't move. He swayed a second time and grappled at the banister when it looked like he would pitch headfirst down the stairs.

"Interesting." Maurice grinned. *Hey, Angie-baby, are you up to playing Miss Marple?* Shouting was useless. He couldn't project enough to reach Angela in the clothing room.

I prefer Kinsey Milhone or Eve Dallas, she responded after a moment. *I assume Troy is here? Where is he?*

About ready to pass out on the third floor. I landed on him and whatever did a bug zapper routine on me drained him, too. I got the feeling there's some magic guiding him, but it isn't strong enough anymore. Okay, there he goes. Time for a strategic retreat, I guess. Discretion is the better part of valor and all that claptrap.

Maurice followed Troy down the stairs, his wings spread for gliding. He used the faint air currents in the stairwell, floating in lazy circles and keeping his eye on the staggering intruder.

As he followed Troy past the doorway to the main room, he saw Angela guide Jo to the counter and keep her and Diane busy. Troy nearly sideswiped a wooden display rack on his way out the front door. Maurice perched on the friendly chamomile plant and watched through the sidelight window as he stumbled to his Lexus. The house's defense net barely reacted as Troy passed through the second time.

"Who weaves a spell so badly that it drains you when it zaps your enemies?" Maurice groused as he fluttered into the main room. He twisted to the side at the last minute as Jo swept toward the door, accompanied by Diane. They were talking about Ken and the business trip. Jo's smile was nearly as bright as her eyes.

It had to be pretty nice to be in love. Maybe in another fifty years, he would see about courtship. The problem was that most of the girls he grew up with in the Fae enclaves hadn't focused on him when puberty hit them. Or the ones who had targeted him as potential husband material had been downright scary.

He agreed in principle with Need: the emotional, mental, and physical binding between two Fae when they paired up. It guaranteed that, with a little attention and effort, that romantic zing lasted forever and kept both the husband and the wife happy to be shackled together. He just wasn't ready to take the plunge and have it happen to him, personally.

"Someone who weaves badly doesn't care about his minions." Angela leaned against the counter and stared at the front of the shop as if she could see through the walls and watch Troy leave. "Or, he doesn't know what he's doing in the first place. Which might give us a clue as to the type of book Troy is looking for."

She finally tore her gaze from whatever she saw that had nothing to do with the physical world. Her mouth tightened and she nodded once, sharply. "Next time Troy comes in, let him go wherever he wants. Don't stop him. Let's see what he's after. Or what his master is after."

"Okay, sounds like a plan. Just one question. What if he finds what he's looking for? And what if that magic that's guiding him around has the ability to teleport him, even leapfrog dimensions, and take the book out of here, without having to go past us? We'll be right outside the door, waiting to see what he grabs, right?"

"Oh, very right. And the answer is that I will adjust the net protecting the house. It will let in Troy and the magic he carries, but it will let no one and nothing out again unless I give permission."

~~~~~

Angela announced she was going to the Friday night performance of *Hark, the Ark,* at Lanie and Jane's church. While Maurice thought it might be fun to see a comedy version of the story of Noah, he couldn't get excited about theater right now, with the threat to the shop. Stepping out of her usual routine would probably lure Troy and whatever magic controlled him into visiting the shop after hours. Maurice was all for getting this problem solved ASAP. After all, he didn't want to miss next Friday's meeting of the Star Trek club. Lanie had promised to come get him.

"You're sure this is okay?" he said, as Angela closed up the shop two hours earlier than usual. Lanie would be there soon to pick her up.

"The shop isn't unguarded." Angela gave him a serene smile and swung her cape around her shoulders. "You're here."

"Thanks for the vote of confidence, but I've been getting a taste lately of just how limited my magic is." Maurice followed her out the front door. The sound of the door closing of its own accord, and the locks clicking into place without Angela touching anything, made him leap high enough to brush his head against the lamp hanging from the porch roof. Okay, he was officially nervous.

"You're fully recovered from that magic zapping you, and you haven't done any magic for quite a while. All I want you to do is watch. And call me when Troy shows up."

"Yeah? How?"

"Use my pager."

"You don't have --" Maurice stopped short and shook his head in disbelief when Angela pulled a small pager from her purse and showed it to him. He didn't doubt that the twin to it, with Angela's number already entered in it, waited on the counter by the Wishing Ball. "Okay, boss. Have a good time."

Angela chuckled and waved to him as Lanie's Jeep turned the corner and headed toward the house. He flew around the back of the shop and tapped a window that constantly sparkled with the presence of a magical slit in reality. The glass evaporated and he flew into the back room of the shop. A heartbeat later, the glass reconstituted.
~~~~~

What was Holly doing tonight? He hadn't visited her dreams in more than a week, and he felt as if he had broken a date and abandoned her. When Angela came back, he would check in on Holly's latest dream. In the meanwhile, he could at least watch what she was doing tonight through the Wishing Ball.

Twenty minutes later, Maurice had assembled his sofa, brought in a thimble full of diet cherry cola, a dark chocolate kiss to counter the intoxication, and for dinner, two sandwiches made with oyster crackers, pimento cheese spread and tuna salad.

"Dinner and a movie," he muttered, as he tapped the Wishing Ball and focused his thoughts on Holly. "How about we make a date for dinner out when I'm a free man? Does that sound good to you, kid?" Holly's smiling face appeared in the curved surface of the Wishing Ball, nodding in response to something a little pigtailed, red-haired girl said to her.

Maurice finished his sandwiches and his first thimble of diet cherry cola while he watched Holly close up the library for the night and get in her car.

Now was a good time to get a refill. He flew upstairs to Angela's kitchen. She had found a tiny tap, like someone would insert in a beer keg, that he poked into his cans of diet cherry cola. It let him fill his drinking thimble and preserve the carbonation. By limiting himself to two thimbles of the intoxicating liquid each day, Maurice could make a can last almost a week.

"Yep, I'm definitely a cheap date," he announced as he flew back to his seat in front of the Wishing Ball and set his thimble on the counter in front of him.

The protective net around the house flared. Maurice hissed, feeling as if something fragile had been ripped down the middle. The feeling vanished, but he knew better than to assume whatever had disturbed the net had gone away. He glanced at the grandfather clock in the corner of the main room. Not even 8pm. Troy hadn't waited long to take advantage of Angela leaving the shop unguarded. Then again, he could have no idea what time she planned on returning, so he had to act fast.

A faint, reddish glow appeared in the far wall. Maurice's mouth dropped open as a door appeared. Smoke flickered around the edges, as if the opening had been scorched just like he had been.

The door swung open and Troy Richards lurched into the

room. He barely got all the way inside before the door slammed shut and vanished. The burned smell and wisps of smoke hung in the air, mute evidence to what had happened. Troy didn't look around, but staggered through the room, heading for the stairs.

"Pager, pager, pager," Maurice muttered, searching the counter. He was positive he had seen it before he made dinner. "There you are!" He pounced on it, slamming the power button with both hands. He looked at the readout screen. "Okay, how the heck do I tell Angela what's going on?"

~~~~~

Diane had left her winter coat at Divine's. She had been able to get by on just her sweater and a light jacket, but the forecast was for another freak snowfall tonight. She knew she would regret it in the morning if she didn't get her coat tonight.

She unlocked the back door of the shop. Inside, the smells of scented candles, chocolate, and dusty old books surrounded her. The crackling tension that had been building up in her all evening oozed away and she smiled.

A thud came from the attic. She ignored it. Divine's always made strange noises. She reached for her coat, hanging on the eagle-headed hook. A man swore in the attic.

Angela was going out tonight. The shop wasn't open, so that wasn't a customer in the attic. Diane grabbed the black rubber-encased nightstick flashlight and started up the steps. What use were all those kickboxing and gymnastic lessons at Eden if she didn't use them to defend her friends and their property?

Divine's Emporium and Neighborlee were more home to her than the family mansion. The friends she had made in this college town meant more to her than her snooty relatives; most of whom hadn't spoken to her in eight years. Angela was mother figure and employer, even if Diane didn't need the money she earned as a part-time clerk.

She knew where to put her feet so three flights of stairs didn't creak and betray her. Light seeped from under the door of the book room when she got to the attic. She paused to catch her breath and plan her attack. She hefted the flashlight and imagined swinging it like a Major League slugger getting a grand slam. Biting her lip, she silently scolded herself to either get a grip or call the police.

Diane paused with her hand on the doorknob. Angela had
~~~~~

asked her never to go into these attic rooms. Priceless, rare items were protected here, for special customers. Even more reason to get the intruder out. She took a deep breath, turned the doorknob, and pushed the door open.

The lights were on, the shades down. Troy Richards, her hero, stood by the floor-to-ceiling shelves in the corner.

"What are you doing here?" She lowered the flashlight.

Troy tucked the ragged, leather-covered book under his arm like a football and dove at her as if going for a touchdown.

Diane squawked and flattened herself against the wall. Instead of making like a batter, she stuck her foot out.

Troy's foot caught. He let out a yelp and pitched headfirst out the door. He curled himself around the book and protected his head with his arms. He turned a partial somersault and uncurled when his back hit the newel post, before she could get through the door with the flashlight in her upraised hand. He staggered to his feet and stumbled backward against the door of the painting room. It opened and he fell through.

"Don't go in there!" She charged after him.

Silence met her when she slammed up against the doorframe. Diane peered into the gloom and heard cloth rustling off to the right. For a second, she thought she heard a high-pitched voice shrieking at her. Flickering lights swarmed in front of her eyes. She waved them away. She had seen and heard and sensed many strange things in Divine's Emporium over the years, and longed for Angela's tales of other beings and worlds to be true. However, faeries were not going to show up and save the day. She was here, so it was up to her to defend her friend's home and business.

The stairway lights shone behind her, putting her at a disadvantage. Time to level the playing field. She reached inside the room to the right of the doorway and hit the light switch.

Troy stood behind a stack of crates in the middle of the room, with paintings leaning against it on both sides. He covered his eyes with one hand, still clutching that ragged old book to his chest. "Don't you know better than to come here after dark?" he snarled.

"I work here. You're the crook!" Diane lunged at him.

Troy's shoulders hit the frame of an enormous landscape painting, full of bloody sunsets, cliffs, and waterfalls. He twisted and heaved her over his head.

Diane shrieked, imagining her shoulder going into that painting and breaking the antique canvas.

Nothing stopped her. She kept turning. Her knees hit the frame. Her head went down. For an eternal heartbeat, she hung over the landscape, but now it swam before her eyes, turned to three dimensions. She smelled grass and water and the mineral tang of bare stone, warmed by the sun.

The frame shifted under her legs and she fell, headfirst, toward those cliffs and the water and the grass.

~~~~~

"Diane!" Maurice stared, aghast, as Diane became part of the painting, her arms and legs spread in helpless, twisting flight. She hung there, wide-eyed in shock.

For a moment he had the distinct impression she could see him. "Here, grab my hand!" He lunged at the painting, but bounced off the canvas and banged against the opposite wall.

Now was not the time for the rules governing his exile to get in the way. He wasn't trying to escape. He was trying to help Diane. Didn't that count for anything?

Troy groaned as he twisted around to get back onto his feet. He braced himself against the frame. His mouth dropped open when he saw Diane in the painting, inches from his nose.

"You scum-sucking dog!" Maurice launched himself at Troy, gathering up all the magic he could summon. He hit Troy's shoulder and the inimical magic flared. Maurice clearly saw the source, outlined against the flash, like an x-ray -- something round tucked into Troy's jeans pocket. He smelled the burned-hair stink of the smoke from his wings as he slammed into the wall.

For a long moment he couldn't see, couldn't hear, couldn't move, couldn't breathe.

Then he hit the frame of a painting on the floor below him. Troy tumbled headfirst into the painting that took Diane. The painting's magic flashed, battling with the magic in his pocket. Then the intruder magic was swallowed up and so was Troy.

"I am so dead," Maurice moaned. He should go downstairs and page Angela again. Unfortunately, he felt like he had broken every bone in his body and whatever passed for bones in his wings. He barely had the energy to breathe, let alone move.

~~~~~

Diane waved her arms, a futile effort to fly. She took a breath to shriek again, and something big and warm and heavy slammed into her from behind, sending her tumbling toes over nose through the air. It grabbed her.

"Get off me!" she snarled, even before she twisted around enough to see Troy, wide-eyed, his mouth a silent 'O' of terrified astonishment.

Then the trees snatched them out of mid-air. For three heart-stopping seconds, Diane clung to Troy, and he held her tight as the trees played a crazy game of catch. Or maybe it was keep-away? Trees and ground vs. the sky?

Branches and leaves slapped at her face and the ground spun around her. The ground won the game, slamming her up against Troy. Diane felt the hard flatness of the stolen book pressed between her ribs and Troy's, but she didn't dare let go of him long enough to try to take it back. Grass rustled and branches snapped. Diane prayed those popping and snapping and rattling sounds weren't her bones.

They jolted to a stop. Diane lay atop him, her nose pressed into Troy's washboard chest. His Cleveland Browns sweatshirt and scuffed brown leather jacket smelled faintly of Old Spice. She took one more deep breath, scrambled backward, landed on her rear, and kept going for a few more steps. She stared at the forest in front of her. She turned to look back at the stair-step cliffs she and Troy had tumbled down. They couldn't have fallen that far, could they? Not without some serious damage.

Troy groaned and sat up. He checked the book, sticking out from his partially unzipped leather jacket. Then he tipped his head back to study the landscape behind and before them.

"Baby, we aren't in Kansas anymore."

"What happened?"

"You work at Divine's and you don't know what it can do?"

"I stay downstairs," she snarled.

He met her glare with a roll of the eyes and a lopsided grin.

They sat in silence until she gave in with a sigh. "What about Divine's?"

"It's ... bigger inside than it is outside. Magic isn't the right word. Quantum physics?" He shrugged. "I was warned not to touch anything. Like Aladdin in the treasure cave, y'know? Get what you're sent for and get out. As fast as you can."

"So you're telling me you didn't steal that book for yourself? Somebody sent you?" The relief she felt was overwhelming.

Troy Richards was the proverbial self-made man. He had developed four patented processes for handling hazardous material and he served on the board of a non-profit that reclaimed wilderness and protected endangered species. He was a hero in Neighborlee, even though he lived just over the border in Darbyville. The thought of him as a thief made her ill. Then again, comparing her previous dilettante existence to his worthwhile life made her ill.

He lowered the book to rest on his lap. His lip curled as if he tasted something foul. "I only know I have to get this book, or Meggie's life is ruined."

"Meggie?"

"My kid sister."

"What'd she do?"

"Nothing!" His glare devolved to weariness. "I'm a pain in the butt for some big-time industrial polluters. She got framed for a bunch of bad things she didn't do. These people have the power to make lies appear to be truth. They have evidence I can't fight. They told me if I got this book, they'd give me the evidence and will leave us both alone. And Meggie won't go to prison."

"Why didn't you go to the police? You have the kind of reputation they'd have to believe you, despite the manufactured evidence. Or at least help you get evidence against these guys."

"Do you believe in magic?"

Diane was about to say, *No, of course not.* Then she looked around at the where they had landed. Just fifteen minutes ago, she had been climbing the stairs to the attic to face down an intruder. She had always believed there was more to Divine's Emporium than what she saw on the surface. The sensation that Angela could do things and knew things ordinary Humans couldn't, just made the sense of wonder and adventure stronger.

Time to face reality, to shrug off the blinders of being an adult.

"I guess I have to."

"Well, these guys blackmailing Meggie and me, they have magic. And there's magic wrapped around Divine's, and it doesn't like the blackmailers' magic. They can't get in, so they sent me."

Troy shuddered. "They demonstrated their magic. It's ... not like they show you in the movies. Let's just leave it at that, okay?"

"Okay." Her stomach twisted with nausea at the momentary bleakness in his eyes. "Really strong, nasty magic, but they can't stand up to Angela's. So they made you come steal something, because you can go where they can't. And if you fought them, if you could refute the evidence against your sister, they'd still have the magic to do nasty things to punish you?"

"That's the simple way of putting it." He rubbed at his face. With a deep breath, he squared his shoulders, and looked around. He pointed to a glimmer of light at the top of the cliffs. "Is that the painting frame up there?"

"Like a window into our world," Diane murmured.

"We are taking this way too calmly."

"I panic after the dust settles." She offered him a grin. Something fluttered in her chest when he grinned back. "I guess we both read the right books when we were kids."

"Aslan isn't safe, but he's good." Troy nodded and stood up. He tucked the book inside his jacket. "The only way we'll get home is to climb. You coming?"

She stood, surprised to find she could move despite all the banging she'd taken. Somehow her catch-all purse had landed with her. She hooked the strap over her chest like a bandolier and followed him. That glimmer of light above them had to be the painting frame, or she was sunk.

The first fifty yards or so were relatively easy to climb. Then the steps got higher, and she had to use her arms to get up to the next level. Troy reached down and took her hand. A buzz, like she'd touched a live wire, raced through her.

"So, what do these creeps say your sister did?" She wanted to re-direct her thoughts before she got into trouble.

"You know that raid at Slamming Joe's in the Flats?"

"They said she was there?" Diane shuddered. If only half the stories were true, high school girls had been drugged and 'sold' for a night of really kinky sport. "They say she went along willingly with all that dirt? I bet they have pictures suitable for framing."

Chapter Ten

"Worse. They have proof she lured the girls there." Troy glared at the slope ahead.

"She wasn't there, but you can't prove it?"

"She was with me, getting evidence against Royal Deutsch Allegiance. If I prove she was with me that night, then I destroy months of work by the Feds. I can protect my kid sister, but doing so will warn some major polluters who export illegal firearms. They'll be able to shut down their operations before all the evidence is gathered. Or, I can keep quiet until the Feds wrap up the case. I don't produce the evidence to prove Meggie is innocent, and I let her go to prison. I don't like either choice. I'd rather risk my neck, facing down magic I didn't even know existed until a week ago, and protect Meggie and the Feds' case."

"What would Meggie say?" Diane thought of her own sister. Alexandra would immediately put her own safety first, no matter who suffered. Somehow, she was sure Meggie Richards, whom she had never met, would sacrifice herself for the greater good. With a brother like Troy, how could she be any other way?

"I didn't tell her about the blackmail."

"So she doesn't have a chance to tell you to sacrifice her?" She smiled when he had the grace to color and look away.

Stop! She mentally slapped herself. Troy was Mr. Wonderful, but she had no business falling for him. Once they got back to Divine's, and she put that book back in the attic, they would never see each other again. He saved the world and she was a perpetual student. They didn't run in the same circles. This trip through the picture frame was all the adventure she could handle.

How long until it was over, anyway? Then she got a new thought. Diane stopped and stared at her wristwatch. "Oh, heck."

"What's wrong?" Troy grabbed her arm. "Are you hurt?"

"How long have we been climbing?"

"Maybe half an hour."

"My watch hasn't changed." The glowing blue numbers read 8:25. She had come back to the shop just after 8. The colon pulsed, but when Diane silently counted to sixty, then another sixty, then another, the numbers didn't change. "Magic?" she whispered.

"What I could do with some magic of my own," Troy muttered.

"To deal with the blackmailers."

Troy shrugged and tipped his head back to look up to their goal. The tiny blot of light from Divine's seemed just as far away.

After a moment, they continued upward.

"Why do they want the book?" she said, after they'd put another hundred yards behind them. "Is it magic?"

"Heck if I know. There are no words in it."

"How do you know you got the right one?"

"They sent me drawings, symbols and signs to look for."

"Why did they pick you, in particular? I mean, couldn't they have just grabbed anyone off the street and magicked them to come in and try to steal? Why you, in particular?"

"All I know of magic is what I've seen in movies." His chuckle warmed her. "But I've been doing a lot of heavy-duty thinking since those creeps contacted me. If there's magic, then there are rules. Angela has protective magic. This was upstairs in a room I couldn't even find until the coin they gave me showed me how to find it. Maybe the book can only be taken by someone who really wants to find it, but doesn't want it for himself."

"Or who wants it for a good purpose, instead of a selfish one." She offered a smile when Troy glanced at her. "Protecting your sister is a good reason."

"Looks rough up ahead." He hooked his arm through hers.

Diane stumbled, her knees turned to mush by his touch. She knew Troy wasn't being nice to *her* in particular, that was just his way. He would help anyone who needed it. Even her, the runaway misfit of a rich, powerful family. Maybe his easy trust in her showed just how great a guy he was. After all, their current situation was mostly her fault. If she hadn't tackled him, they wouldn't have fallen into the picture.

She divided her attention between climbing and gnawing at Troy's situation, applying all the sleuthing acumen she had gained in hundreds of hours reading Grafton, Peters, Robb, and Christie. Not that she had much faith in her ability. She couldn't answer her own my-purpose-in-life question, so how could she help him with something far more serious?

But she wanted to help him. He had been her hero since she moved to Neighborlee, when she had never hoped to meet him. He did something that mattered in the world.

Someone wanted to stop him from doing something good.

"They know you can blow them out of the water," she said.

"What?"

"The blackmailers know you were getting proof against Allegiance that particular night. Why else would they choose that specific date for their blackmail against Meggie? Maybe they were hoping you would speak up and ruin things and reveal what you were doing that specific night, especially if you couldn't get into Divine's and take the book. This is the only way they can stop you. Maybe they were counting on whatever protects Divine's to stop you or destroy you or whatever." She shuddered. "I always wondered why nobody ever steals from Angela."

"Easy to get in, but not get out?" Troy's expression didn't change, but she noticed he'd clenched his fists.

"My fault. I shouldn't have tackled you like that."

He offered a lopsided smile that tugged at her heart. "You ever play football with your brothers?"

"They prefer cutthroat sports. Like swallowing up the competition." She shivered as a detail she had been trying to ignore leaped to the front of her thoughts.

Several of her relatives held the reins for Allegiance. Had they given the order to stop Troy Richards? She still heard from some of those relatives at Christmas, her birthday, and when they wanted her to vote on a particular issue during stockholder meetings.

What could she do to influence her relatives, to help Troy?

More important: What would Troy do or say if he found out her relatives had threatened his sister?

Diane nearly stumbled again when she realized where her thoughts were leading. Falling through an enchanted picture together wasn't exactly a recommendation for friendship. But she thought she knew Troy Richards well enough, just by reputation, to want him to think well of her.

She wanted to help him. If she could. She was tired of feeling useless and helpless. She wanted to work with Troy, but if he knew who her relatives were, would he allow her?

Sunset caught up with them on a long plateau filled with fruit trees. She and Troy hadn't bumped and bounced through these trees on their way down.

Maybe the landscape changed without notice?

Moss and ferns near the stream made comfortable beds that smelled heavenly. The water was clean and sweet and they had apples and peaches they had gathered along the way for dinner, along with two cereal bars she found in her purse.

Troy made her laugh as he praised her for being prepared for their hike. "What I wouldn't give for a lighter," he muttered through a mouthful of fruit, as darkness enclosed them.

"Lighter?"

"For a fire."

"It's plenty warm without it."

"And if there are any nasties out there, we don't want to draw them to us." He sighed and the ferns rustled as he lay down in his fragrant pile of bedding. "I'd like to cook those fish I saw in the stream. But a fire would be useless, I guess, since I don't know the first thing about fishing."

Diane thought about that until she fell asleep, and then while they continued walking up the stair of plateaus the next morning. When they weren't talking about books and movies and sports teams, they speculated together about what people would think or do when they discovered Troy and Diane had vanished. Or if anyone would even realize they had vanished. If their watches had stopped, maybe no time at all was passing outside the painting.

But what if they never got out of the painting? What did that mean for the real world?

They stopped to rest and eat some of the apples Troy carried in his coat pockets. Diane dug in her purse for the pocketknife that had slid into the lining through a hole in the zipper pocket. With it she cut branches off a nearby tree, and sharpened the tips.

"That purse is like Mary Poppins' carpetbag." Troy's chuckle made her insides flutter. "What are the sticks for?"

"Spear fishing. If we find a stream with fish tonight."

"You think we'll be here that long?" He didn't sound as depressed as he could have. When she turned to look at him, he smiled at her.

Diane knew better than to hope her company made this magical exile ... well, magical for him. "Who knows?"

"Got a lighter in that purse so we can make a fire?"

"You spear the fish and leave the fire to me."

"Baby, you can light my fire any time you want," he said, twisting his voice into a lazy drawl.

Diane laughed with him. Even knowing he was joking, she felt a funny twinge of longing.

While they walked, she occasionally paused to test the rocks peeking through the thin layer of soil or moss carpeting their stair-step pathway up the mountainside. Troy assured her she wasn't mistaken when she found what she thought was flint.

That night in camp, she scraped the flint with the nail file extension of her pocketknife, producing sparks. Her fire had burned down to coals perfect for cooking by the time Troy had speared and seriously mauled five fish. They burned their fingers and got bones in their tongues, but Diane had never tasted anything so wonderful in years of gourmet meals.

Troy's voice kept her warm through the fire-lit darkness. He told her about the bits of wilderness his organization had helped to save, until she fell asleep. The next day as they walked, she shared with him the pieces of her childhood she had actually enjoyed. For dinner that night, their third inside the painting, they ate apples and wild potatoes Troy had found, which they roasted in the coals of Diane's second successful fire. He mesmerized her as he told about working his way through college. They talked about Meggie, too, and what she could study once she graduated high school, and if she attended Willis-Brooks.

Troy seriously wanted her opinion. Diane liked the feeling of being useful.

They climbed higher, talking and walking and working together to live off the land for two more days. Troy's admiration for her woodsman skills was intoxicating, so she actually admitted she had learned to live off the land to spite her ultra-elegant mother. Somehow all the sordid details of her childhood and her sophisticated, never-satisfied family came out. Troy just nodded and made encouraging sounds.

He listened, and she sensed he actually heard what she wanted him to hear. He was nothing like the guys she had dated, who only wanted her family connections.

She told him about the time her cousins almost succeeded in

selling her into marriage, at age sixteen, for the sake of a business merger. When Troy called her "Poor little rich girl," she knew he wasn't teasing, but he understood. He didn't mock the guilt she felt for her easy childhood, or her helplessness at figuring out what to do with her life.

"The thing you gotta do is find out what pulls at your heart. What makes you happy and angry? Follow your passion," he said.

"What if it's something I'm no good at?"

She wasn't about to admit she felt passionate about learning how he did what he did, and how to become strong and brave like him. All right, so she had faced a thief in Divine's, but stopping petty burglary wasn't the same as saving the world.

"Then you learn. You need any help, just come to me."

What she wanted, Diane decided as she drifted off to sleep that night, was to work side-by-side with Troy and save the world.

On their sixth morning inside the picture, the frame looked as far away as it had the previous mornings. While Troy washed in the little stream that spilled down the face of the mountainside, Diane decided she didn't care how long it took to get back to Divine's. And not just because her watch said no time had passed. She liked being with Troy. Except for a change of clothes and a long, hot soak in the claw-foot tub in the house she rented, she couldn't think of anything better than spending the day with him.

"All set?" He bowed, pretending to sweep a hat off his head, and offered her his bent arm.

Diane laughed, slipped her arm through his, and started forward.

They hadn't walked more than fifty yards before the angle of the light and shadows spun around them like a movie time-lapse of a sundial. Diane shivered as crimson and gold streaks of sunset spilled across the meadow.

"We made it," Troy whispered, and stopped short.

Diane saw the frame above them. She saw other paintings against the opposite wall, facing the one they had fallen into.

"Problem," she said.

The painting frame, the way back to Divine's Emporium and Neighborlee, hung ten feet off the ground.

"No problem." Troy grabbed hold of her waist.

Diane tried not to scream as he lifted her up over his head and settled her, kneeling, on his shoulders. She clutched for a handhold before she fell and yanked on his hair. He grunted.

"Sorry, but what are you doing?"

"Didn't you ever climb on your brothers' shoulders to get through a window?"

"They only climb over their enemies' bodies."

"You missed out on a lot of fun." He patted her leg, which sent funny tingles through her body. "Stand up on my shoulders. You ought to be tall enough to chin yourself up over the frame."

"What about you?"

"There has to be rope or a ladder at Divine's. Angela has everything, right? You'll come back for me. I trust you to save me, just like you've been doing all along."

"Ah... Right. No problem." Diane couldn't think of any other plan to offer, so she struggled to stand on his shoulders.

He helped her balance, gripping her legs, until she managed to grab the frame and pull herself up to hang across it, just at the bottom of her ribs. She shrieked when he grabbed the bottoms of her feet and shoved her upward.

She went up and over, hit the floor and rolled. She fought the overwhelming need to curl up, close her eyes, and hope that when she opened them, everything would turn out to be just a bad dream. Troy was waiting, and that meant she couldn't waste time. She got up and turned back to look at the painting.

Troy stood still, a part of the painting, frozen in time. That scared her.

She ran to look for a rope. Why didn't Angela have rope up here? If she had people-eating paintings, wouldn't it make sense to have a rope handy to pull them out? Diane ran down the stairs, nearly falling three times before she reached the back door. If there wasn't rope here, then she would check the shed where Angela kept her gardening supplies.

"Forget your coat again?" Angela stood in the doorway of the back room. She flipped on the lights, the keys jangling in her hand. She must have just returned from the play. If time hadn't moved on, here in the real world. But who could be certain of anything? "What's wrong, Di?"

"Do we have a rope ladder around here?"

A few minutes later, Diane explained as she climbed the stairs with the Army-surplus chain ladder tucked under her arm.

Angela didn't seem at all surprised by anything she said. Yet why, if things like this happened regularly, had she missed seeing or noticing anything unusual?

The worst part came when they reached the attic and stepped into the painting room. She bent to hook the ladder on the frame and throw it down to Troy and got stopped by the canvas. Diane shrieked, terrified for one paralyzing moment she would tear the canvas. But it held firm, more resilient than sheet metal.

"How am I going to get him out of there?" Diane dropped to her knees, clutching the bundle of ladder. Now was not the time to fall apart. Troy needed her!

Or did he? She could have sworn he was still in the same position she'd left him in. What was wrong with time? Shouldn't it have sped by on Troy's side of the frame?

"What day is it?" she demanded, and nearly reached to grab hold of Angela and shake the answer out of her.

"Friday night. Considering that you probably came straight from school to get your coat, and how long it must have taken to get up here the first time, then back downstairs to look for the ladder..." Angela half-closed her eyes and tipped her head to one side, visibly calculating. "Less than fifteen minutes since you fell into the painting."

"So is Troy going to be stuck there forever? Can he see us? How come time flew by while we were in there, but now he's frozen? It doesn't make sense!"

Despite the tone of her voice, Diane thought she was taking this all rather calmly. Considering the fact she hadn't really believed in magic up until tonight.

"How did he get in there?" Angela stood back and studied the painting calmly, arms crossed.

"I told you. And I am not going to bump and slide all the way to the bottom of the mountain again, and take six more days to climb up."

"Well, if the ladder was anchored to something and you held onto it when you jumped through the frame..." That sly, teasing little smile of Angela's banished all the shadows.

Diane knew if she thought about it, she would lose her nerve. She hooked the end of the ladder over the frame of the painting hanging on the opposite wall and made sure it was secure. Then she looped her arm through the bottom rung, and dove into the frame.

Troy caught her, and that made the leap and the risk more than worth it. He hugged her hard and close before putting her on her feet. Diane clung to him, feeling giddy.

~~~~~

"I'm sorry. I don't know how many times I can say that." Troy put down his cup and leaned back in the creaky old chair at Angela's kitchen table.

Angela had led them to her apartment on the second floor. She'd made an enormous pot of spiced tea with plenty of cream and honey and brought out shortbread. They had drained the entire pot and left nothing but crumbs on the plate by the time Troy and Diane finished telling their story.

"I think you learned an important lesson," Angela said slowly. That cat-in-the-cream smile spread across her face. "Maybe you should teach your enemies a lesson, too."

"How?" Diane said. "Short of giving them the wrong book without them finding out, I mean."

"That's an idea. That cover comes off. It's only there to protect the journal inside." Angela stood up and left the room.

Diane listened to the soft footsteps going up the stairs to the fourth floor. She shivered. The next moment she blushed when Troy caught her hand between both of his.

"It's going to be all right," he said, rubbing her hand.

"Yeah, Di, don't you worry about it." A little man with obnoxiously sparkly wings swooped down from the china hutch and landed on the table. He picked up a big crumb of shortbread cookie and took a bite. "If you survived that trip you two took --" He froze a moment, before looking back and forth between them. "Umm, you two are acting like you can see me."

"Can you see him?" Troy's voice cracked.

"Uh huh." Diane swallowed hard. "Can you hear him?"

"Oh, maaaan," the little man groaned. He sank down on the lid of the sugar bowl and stuffed the rest of the shortbread crumb into his mouth.

All three studied one another while he chewed and swallowed.

"Okay, here's my theory. You two got thoroughly soaked in
~~~~~

magic, all that time you spent in the painting. That makes you sensitive to magic working. Don't know how long it lasts, but it means you can see and hear lots of things you normally couldn't." He looked past them. "Hey, Angie-baby, how long do you think the change will last?"

"I should think as long as they want it to last." Angela came back into the room. "I see you two have met Maurice. Let me assure you, he is not normally five inches tall and does not normally have wings. He was very...mischievous, and his punishment is to spend two years here, assisting me, and looking--"

"Like an escapee from a Disney cartoon." Maurice grinned cheekily, and then his grin faded. "Look, guys, I'm really sorry. It's my fault. Well, half my fault. Troy shoved you into the painting, and I got so pissed, I pushed him in after you."

"You pushed me?" Troy let go of Diane's hand and reached back to rub his shoulder. "I thought something felt odd, but with all the banging and rolling we did..." He sighed. "It's okay. I wouldn't have wanted Diane alone in there. You were protecting her."

"Didn't do much of a job of it." He scooped up a few more cookie crumbs. "Sorry, Di. Really." He brightened, his left cheek bulging. "But hey, we can talk to each other, now. That's a plus. Take some pressure off Angela."

"How long have you been here?" Diane scrambled back through her memories for times when she had suspected someone was watching her or talking to her, when she worked in the shop. There were too many times to count.

"Since the decorating party." Angela sat down and showed them the sour-smelling, hand-written journal she had brought downstairs with her. "Back to business." She took the journal Troy had stolen, removed the cover, and slipped the cover over the new book.

"Is it full of magic spells?" Troy said quietly.

Diane thought maybe he was as relieved as she felt, to sidestep the subject of a five-inch-tall man with wings who had been invisible up until that evening.

Chapter Eleven

"Maybe. Maybe not," Angela said, with her usual serene smile.

Diane supposed someone who could handle all sorts of magic would be serene when faced with most problems.

"One should never judge a book by its cover. Especially when it's in a different language." She stroked the book before handing it to Troy. "Your fall into the painting totally disrupted the link between your enemies and the talisman in your pocket. They will be justifiably worried, and I fear they will come looking for you soon. I suggest you take care of the exchange as soon as possible."

"If there's ever anything I can do to help you," Troy vowed, as he stood up, "just ask."

"I know you have a great deal of pull with conservation efforts," Angela said. "There's talk about reducing the park boundaries and letting developers bid on the land at the bottom of the hill on this side of town. I do love the view out my back window, all the deer grazing there in the morning dew..."

"I would have fought that decision without you asking."

"Then let's save the favor for the future."

He turned to Diane. "I owe you even more." His voice was husky.

"Friends don't owe friends," she nearly whispered.

"After all we went through, I hope we're more than friends."

Diane's cell phone went off before she could answer. She was too well-trained to turn it off, but she wanted to snarl when she saw her dizzy cousin Marielle's number on the phone's screen.

Cousin Marielle, whose father was Chairman of the Board for the conglomerate that *owned* Allegiance.

"Excuse me," she said, and stepped into the next room, flipping her phone open. "Mari, honey, what can I do for you?"

It was something so inconsequential, Diane forgot what her cousin wanted to chatter about almost as soon as the words passed through her ears. The nice thing about dizzy Cousin Marielle was that she was one of the decent relatives who enjoyed charitable functions and worthwhile causes, thus effectively balancing out some of the vicious, profit-oriented things her brothers did.

Even better, Marielle never interrupted, and she could be persuaded to support a good cause. Diane started talking as soon as Marielle paused to take a breath. She had no idea she could speak so fast. When she got off the phone, Marielle was incensed over what had been done to Troy and promised her father would send heads rolling. She might have been a ditz, but she had her father, two uncles and half the board wrapped around her pinky finger.

"Where's Troy?" Diane wailed, when she stepped back into the room with her good news and found only Angela there.

"He had a call to make. He'll wait for you outside. I suggest you hurry." Angela picked up the teapot. "Important phone call?"

"Very." Diane slung her purse over her shoulder and headed for the stairs. "Thanks, Angela. You're the best."

"That's all we can try to be. Oh, Di? Don't forget your coat this time." Her eyes sparkled. "And maybe take the weekend off?"

Diane's face burned with blush as she ran down the stairs. She hesitated a moment when she reached the ground floor. Which door?

"He went thataway." Maurice fluttered down to hover a few feet in front of her. He pointed at the front door.

"Thanks." She paused with her hand on the doorknob. "I hope I can still see you on Monday, Maurice."

"Me, too, kid," he said with a chuckle. "Don't worry about the door. I'll lock up behind you."

"Hey, partner." Troy snapped his cell phone closed as she stepped out on the front porch. He wrapped an arm around her shoulders and they fell into step as they started down the long, moonlit street toward the center of town. During their journey up the mountainside, he had mentioned he had parked his car several blocks away, so no one would know he was trying to break in.

"Partner?" She felt ready to float to the stars. Then it occurred to her that after six days of hiking up a mountainside, they should both be grimy and aromatic. Both she and Troy smelled and looked as fresh as they had been when they first fell through the painting. There were definitely some benefits to magic at work.

"Wouldn't have made it out of there without you. I might be able to save the environment, but I need you to save me. Feel like taking on the job?"

Diane could only grin, her heart in her throat making her mute. Troy understood. He always seemed to understand. He laughed and bent his head and brushed a kiss across her cheek.

And they kept walking.

~~~~~

"So, think they're going to be okay?" Maurice glided through the door into Angela's quarters. He settled down on the edge of the plate and picked up a few more cookie crumbs.

He shuddered, reliving that moment when he realized Diane and Troy could see him.

The blast of magic when he'd shoved Troy into the painting had stunned him. He could only lie there and stare at the picture Diane and Troy had fallen into, and watch when Diane emerged just minutes later. When Angela and Diane had come upstairs with the ladder, he was still dazed. Angela had picked him up, carried him downstairs in her pocket, and tucked him into bed. He'd have stayed there until morning, but he was starving. He wouldn't have ventured out if he'd known they'd be able to see him.

"I think when Troy's enemies open up that book, they'll be too busy defending themselves to try to do him any harm." Angela poured the last of the tea into her cup and added an equal amount of cream.

"What did you do? Set up a trap? You're one sneaky chick." He chuckled and walked over to lean on the handle of the creamer and look up at her. "I'm proud to know you."

"I think it's more that you're rubbing off on me." She sipped her tea, and the amusement in her eyes faded.

"Hey, what's wrong?"

"Maurice... I shouldn't have left you alone. I should have had a clearer idea of what we were up against."

"No, it's okay. You came right away. No harm, no foul." He fluttered over to her hand lying on the table and patted it.

"You have no idea how badly hurt you were."

"Yeah, I do. And I didn't realize how fast four centuries of life can flash in front of your eyes when you haven't done much good with it." He shrugged and tried to smile for her sake. "I'm okay now. Diane and Troy are okay too, and it looks like they're together, so that's a good thing, right? Once that talisman got zapped, it turns out he really is a good guy, right? Good enough for her?"
~~~~~

"Oh, I think Troy and Diane will be very good for each other."

"Think old Asmondius will count that as another matchmaking job on my part? I mean, yeah, I was pissed when I pushed him into the painting, but he said it was good because then Diane wasn't alone. So I did good, when you think about it. Right?" He fluttered his eyelashes in time with his wings.

Angela gave him an exasperated look that immediately softened into a smile, and shook her head.

~~~~~

The cold, heavy feeling seeping through the air wrapped around Troy as he pulled up in front of the Darbyville townhouse he shared with Meggie. He and Diane were both too wound up from their adventures to just go to their separate homes and go to bed. And honestly, he didn't want to let her out of his sight.

Diane reached across the console to clutch his hand where it rested on the gearshift. "Meggie! She's in there alone."

"You sense it too?" He felt as if icy fingers scrabbled up his spine. The sensation caused by his enemies' approach was twice as bad, because Diane also felt it. That overrode the curiously warm pleasure of knowing she had thought of his sister, too.

"Like Angela and Maurice said, we've been soaking in magic for the last six days, so it's going to stay with us for a while." She frowned thoughtfully and gnawed on her bottom lip as she looked up at his townhouse. She'd gotten that look every time she came up with something clever during that long hike up the mountainside.

"Have you got a plan?"

"We can sense those creeps, but they don't know it. We can use it. And Angela said that book would work against them, and they wouldn't even know they had the wrong book." She shook her head. "I wouldn't dare try to work magic, but I think we're going to be safe, just because they don't know what we know. Does that make sense?"

"I think we're both tired, because yeah, that does." He patted the journal he had tucked inside his coat for safekeeping. "Let's go inside. If those creeps are coming after me, it'll be on my home turf."

"There's got to be some magic in that."

Diane blushed delightfully when he hurried to get out of the car and run around the front to open her door for her. Troy thought about all the places he wanted to share with her, all the things he
~~~~~

wanted to do for her, now that they were back in the real world. He didn't want to let her out of his sight. And not just because she had pulled some strings with her good relatives to put pressure on the bad relatives and clear up this problem with Allegiance.

His little sister was curled up on the couch in the living room, surrounded by textbooks and enough dirty dishes for half a dozen high school girls to have been snacking all night. It never failed to amuse and amaze Troy, how much Meggie could eat and still almost look like a famine victim. She had Turner Classic Movies on, with the volume turned down to whisper, and looked like she was half-asleep, bent over the book on her lap.

"You are in so much trouble," Meggie said, when Troy stepped into the living room. Then she looked up and her eyes widened as she saw Diane standing next to him.

"In trouble for what?" Troy asked.

"Well, if the call I got was legit, someone leaked our spy mission to the bad guys, so the Feds are gonna lock you away for about twenty years. Hi, I'm Meggie. Please tell me you're a date and not a social worker." She somehow managed to climb out from her tangle of dishes, books and blankets without disturbing anything.

"Ah, that would probably be Uncle Sydney or one of his lackeys, assuring you that Allegiance will not only be reforming, but helping you catch other violators," Diane said. "Hi, I'm Diane Rittenhouse, and yes... I think it's safe to say I'm Troy's date."

"Yes!" Meggie half-crouched, giving the downward-pumping arm motion that always seemed so incongruous with her delicate appearance. "Who's Uncle Sydney?"

"It's a long story," Troy said. "Your cousin works fast, doesn't she?"

"Mari is a total space-case and fashionista, but when she gets a bug in her ear, look out." Diane's smile froze and she glanced over her shoulder, toward the front door.

"Yeah, I sense them, too. Ah, Meggie, isn't it about time you get to bed?"

"It's not a school night." His sister looked back and forth between them a few times. "If you were just looking for a place to be alone so you can make out, you'd go to Diane's place, so what's up? What are you protecting me from now?"

"Told you so," Diane muttered.

The doorbell rang before Troy could respond. He made sure the disguised, substituted journal was secure inside his jacket and went to the door. Diane was on his heels, with Meggie right behind her. Troy was too tired and too keyed up from the events of the last few hours, or days, to argue with them.

The man who stood on his doorstep looked like someone's yes-man, conservatively dressed in a dark suit with a subdued, dark tie, white broadcloth shirt, and carrying a briefcase. Troy flinched at this proof he was indeed sensitive to magic. He sensed there was much more to the briefcase than just leather and lining and locks. He had a momentary image of a slit in the back of the case that opened into a deep, dark space.

"Mr. Richards." The man, who had only introduced himself as Carpelli the first time they met, managed a thin, flattened twitch of his lips in lieu of a smile. If it hadn't been past eleven at night, Troy suspected he would have been wearing dark glasses. "How nice to see you're...unharmed. We had a moment of worry earlier this evening."

"I'm sure I have no way of explaining whatever worried you," Troy said. A number of theories half-formed in the back of his mind. He was going to have to have a long talk with Angela, maybe even take lessons, before he could make any of those theories coherent. All that mattered was that these people blackmailing Meggie to make him their errand boy had no idea what had happened inside the shop. "You know more about what's involved with Divine's Emporium than I do."

"Hmm. Yes, that's certainly true." Carpelli glanced over his shoulder, at the dark, expensive-looking sedan sitting by the curb. Whoever was inside didn't give him any signals Troy could see. "Did you succeed this time?"

Troy chose not to speak, but first pulled out the coin they had given him, to help him find the book inside Divine's Emporium, then withdrew the journal with the switched-out cover as his answer. He gave both to Carpelli, then crossed his arms and waited as the man checked the cover with the designs they had drawn for him, so he could identify the book. Then Carpelli opened it and flipped through the pages. Troy looked away after a few moments, because he could have sworn some of those drawings moved.

"Thank you for your help." Carpelli opened up his briefcase.

Troy saw something moving and could have sworn there were stars swimming in the blackness that lined the case. "As we agreed." He handed a thick accordion file to Troy and slipped the journal into the pocket where the file had been. He snapped the case closed.

Troy clutched the accordion file to his chest, pressing it hard enough to feel the video tape, the thick packet of what had to be photos, and several CD and DVD cases, just as promised. He responded to Carpelli's nod with a silent nod of his own, and stayed where he was, watching, until the big, dark car drove away. It was interesting, and a little disturbing that no light came on inside the car when Carpelli opened the door and got in.

"Okay, it's big bad confession time," Meggie said, when the car had vanished down the street and the soft quiet and natural chill of the night had seeped back through the neighborhood.

They settled down at the kitchen table, and Meggie insisted on making more food. Troy still felt hungry, despite the snack at Divine's Emporium. He supposed that was from stress.

He was more pleased when Diane offered to help and Meggie accepted without hesitating. It had already become clear to him that Diane was going to be a big part of his life from now on. Meggie's acceptance of her, with so little explanation, seemed like a signal, a promise that this would work out.

He got as far as explaining what had been exchanged. Meggie snatched the accordion file and took it to her computer in the office they shared. The surveillance tapes, computer files and pictures were all very convincing. Troy felt a little better, knowing he had made a wise choice to cooperate. Until Diane spoke up.

"Look at this." She slipped the mouse from Meggie's fingers and manipulated the screen, enlarging the photo of Meggie pushing a girl who looked terrified. "You can see the seams. What kind of jerk put this crap together and expected it to get past real investigators?"

In half an hour, using software that wasn't made specifically for the task, she highlighted and teased apart the various layers of the photos and DVD images meant to blackmail Meggie. Troy was impressed with Diane's skills, and infuriated that he had fallen for such blackmail. The problem was that he wouldn't have known where to look, or even how to prove all the evidence against his sister was false, if Carpelli had let him look at the evidence first.

"How did they expect experts to buy all this junk?" he growled, after Meggie put the disks and photos back into the accordion file.

"Magic?" Diane offered. "Maybe our trip made us able to see through the illusion they have wrapped around this."

"Magic?" Meggie looked back and forth between them. "Okay, what have you two been up to? And why didn't you take me along?"

It was nearly 3 in the morning by the time they finished telling the tale of what had happened to them. Meggie was more upset that she had missed out on the adventure than that she had been used against Troy, to force him to take the risk.

"You gotta promise me, we're going to visit Divine's Emporium. I want to see what's going on there and especially meet Angela," Meggie said. "I wish we lived in Neighborlee. Darbyville is okay, but Neighborlee sounds like a lot more fun."

"Actually..." Diane nodded, seeming to come to a decision. "I think it would be a pretty smart move to do just that. Now that we've been touched by magic. There's a protection that surrounds Divine's, and another layer of protection that goes around the whole town. I've always felt that way, even though I could never put my finger on it. Now I know it's true." She offered Troy a hesitant smile. "Now that we've been touched by magic, I don't want to lose it. I can't imagine you do, either. Move to Neighborlee."

"We'd be a lot safer, once Carpelli and his friends realize I gave them the wrong book," Troy mused, thinking aloud.

"Who the heck cares about the goons?" Meggie said. "I want to meet Maurice and Angela."

Later, Troy finally slipped into his own bed for the first time in a week, from one viewpoint, but only twenty-one hours since he got out of it, from another. His body ached, not just from the bouncing and tumbling he had done, but from exhaustion and tension. He was tired enough his vision was fuzzy by the time he'd made sure Diane was comfortable in the guest room. Once he had showered and crawled between the sheets, he couldn't sleep. Maybe he found the bed too soft, after six nights of sleeping on the ground. Maybe it was too quiet in his room, without the sounds of nightlife, insects and night-hunting animals and the trickling of the stream that ran down the mountain.

No, he realized after nearly half an hour of trying to will

himself to sleep. It was Diane. Or rather, her absence. The last six nights, he had been able to look across the campfire and see her, sleeping peacefully, trusting him and the fire to keep her safe.

He couldn't sleep without her within arm's reach. The only way he was going to get any sleep from now on was to convince Diane to spend the rest of her life with him.

Troy knew he was rushing things, but peace settled in his chest and relaxed his limbs, once he made that decision. It might take a while to convince Diane they were meant to be together, but he thought he had a good chance. After all, she had been the one to recommend he and Meggie move to Neighborlee, and had even mentioned three houses for sale, all on her street. That had to mean something, didn't it?

That settled, Troy closed his eyes and went to sleep.

~~~~~

March turned into April and crept toward May. Maurice enjoyed the warmer weather and spent more time outdoors. He enjoyed story time on Saturday afternoons, when Holly took her groups of children for long walks, into the park or just to sit in the gazebo in the park. His favorite seat was on the shoulder of whichever lucky boy or girl got to sit right in front of Holly. For whole minutes at a time, Maurice could make himself believe she was looking at him when she told her stories.

Diane and Troy held onto their magic. They came into Divine's regularly and always made a point of talking to Maurice. He felt sorry for Troy's sister, Meggie, who wanted to meet him and see him, but couldn't. She seemed to think that moving to Neighborlee and spending several hours almost every day at Divine's would let her soak up just as much magic as her brother.

Once Lanie learned about Diane and Troy's adventure, she welcomed the Richards siblings to town. She put her brother, Pete in charge of helping Meggie settle in at Neighborlee High School, since they were in the same grade. The two of them became a team almost from day one. Still, that didn't totally cover Meggie's disappointment in not having her own healthy dose of magic.

Maurice talked over the problem of Meggie with Holly the next time he visited her dreams. She suggested that he do something for Meggie the next time she visited the shop, to prove he was there. Maurice kissed her, proclaiming her a genius. The next moment, he
~~~~~

staggered back from the Wishing Ball, feeling like he had been yanked halfway out of his skin by a hook caught in his wings. In the Wishing Ball, he saw Holly sitting up in her bed, eyes wide, panting, with the fingertips of one hand pressed to her lips.

"Yeah, sorry, kid," he whispered, pressing his hands on the Wishing Ball, as if he could cup her face between his hands and look into her eyes. "Stunner for me, too. But it was kind of nice, you think? I could go for it again."

Maurice dared to hope that underneath her fingertips, Holly smiled.

The next day, when Meggie came into the shop, he had a pen and a piece of paper waiting when she stepped up to the counter to buy some candy. There was no one else in the shop but Diane, and he waited until her back was turned before picking up the pen and bracing it against his shoulder.

Meggie stared, her eyes getting wider with every letter he scrawled on the paper, until he thought they would devour her face.

> *Hi, Meggie. I'm Maurice. I'm real. I can hear you -- you just can't see or hear me. But we can still be friends.*

Diane turned back to the counter with the bag of assorted candy. "Oh, Maurice, I'm glad you thought of that." She winked at Meggie. "I was really afraid you were going to start accusing us of playing a nasty trick on you."

"Wow!" Meggie sounded as if she had been holding her breath.

"Open the bag, Di," Maurice said. He waited until she complied, then leaped up, fluttering his wings, and swooped down to scoop a sour cherry chew from the top. Meggie took a step back, staring at the round red candy floating in mid-air. Giddy triumph swept over him when she held out her hand and let him put it down on her palm.

"Thanks, Maurice. It's nice to finally meet you," she said.

Angela was pleased, when he told her about it over dinner. That mattered more to Maurice than anything else, except maybe the pleased flush on Meggie's face and the shine in her eyes.

~~~~~

That night, Maurice caught up with Holly on a long, tree-lined field extending behind a cluster of old-fashioned buildings. It was
~~~~~

summertime, golden and green, the grass and trees lush with life. About two dozen assorted children played across the field, throwing balls and jumping rope and playing catch. At the far end was an old playground with weather-beaten swings, teeter-totter, jungle gym and slide.

Holly walked the perimeter of the field, pensively watching the children, dragging her fingers along the chain link fence.

Maurice tried to judge her mood. She didn't look happy or sad, just thoughtful. He wondered if she'd had a bad day at work. How could he cheer her up if he wasn't walking with her? He hurried to catch up with her.

"Wow, lots of kids. So, where are we tonight?" He clasped his hands behind himself as he fell in step with her.

"This is the Neighborlee Children's Home, where I grew up." Holly turned her head to watch the children as they gathered around two boys with a big, dusty red ball. Maurice guessed they were organizing to play kickball.

"Looks like a nice place. The kids seem happy enough."

"It was the greatest place in the world." Her smile widened, and some of that pensiveness faded from her eyes. "Mrs. Sylvestri made sure we all knew we were loved, no matter what."

"So, what are we doing here? What's on the agenda for tonight? What's wrong, sweetheart?"

Holly just shrugged and kept walking. Something knotted inside him at the thought that someone might have hurt her. He cursed his shrunken size and shrunken magical powers, because he couldn't do much of anything to protect or avenge her.

She stopped and turned to face him, so quickly it startled him.

"That's what's wrong."

"What'd I do? What'd I say?" He felt his wings fluttering in panic, but they didn't come with him into these dreams.

"How come I don't remember you, I don't remember any of this, when I wake up? I used to be able to remember all my dreams, but ever since you came into them, I don't remember anything during the day. Why?" Her voice wavered a little on the last word.

"Maybe..." He sighed. If she didn't remember anything, then it wouldn't hurt to be totally honest, would it? "I think it's to protect you. So you don't go crazy, maybe."

"I think I'm already going crazy. Remembering this, looking

forward to it, could get me through the really boring, dreary days." She managed a crooked smile.

That just twisted the knife in Maurice's gut a little deeper. "This? Dreaming about the orphanage where you grew up?"

"No! *This.* Even if it's just a dream, knowing that somewhere, someone handsome and good and clever calls me 'sweetheart.' That could get me through a lot of really low spots." She turned toward the fence, but not before Maurice saw the tears well up in the corners of her eyes.

"You don't need a fake like me to --"

"I know none of this is real." She shook her head, "But I wish it was. I wish you were real."

"What if I was?" The words caught in Maurice's throat. He caught her by her shoulders and turned her away from the fence. Holding her still, he gently brushed the tears off her cheeks.

"Wishes never come true for me," she whispered, visibly fighting to look into his eyes.

He wanted to pulverize whoever had made Holly believe that magic and happily ever after couldn't happen for her.

"What if I was real? Would you wish for me to be real?" He bent his head again and kissed the tears off her cheeks, slowly. When he raised his head, the blush had left Holly's cheeks and she stared at him, her eyes dazed.

"If I could have just one wish, I'd wish for you," she whispered.

"Take a chance, sweetheart."

When she opened her mouth to speak again, he pressed a fingertip to her lips. Slipping an arm around her shoulders, he nudged her to keep walking along the fence. He ached, and that pain was mixed with a shock that stole his breath and balance. Like he might step sideways and fall off the surface of the planet.

Chapter Twelve

What had happened to him? When had Holly changed from a playmate to someone whose pain could tear at his heart?

They walked in silence. The warm breeze and the sounds of birds and the wind in the leaves and the laughter of the children washed over them. Finally, when he felt the tension completely seep out of her body and saw the normal color had returned to her face, he said, "Tell me about growing up here."

Before the alarm clock yanked Holly out of her dreams, she had showed him around the orphanage and all her favorite places, and even some silly incidents in her childhood. She had laughed.

Maurice was relieved to know that when Holly woke up, she wouldn't be in pain. At least while she was awake. He seriously considered not going back to her dreams, to ensure she wouldn't think about him and wonder and hurt.

Two things stopped him. He knew he made Holly feel appreciated and wanted. And his insides clutched at the thought of never adventuring through her dreams again.

~~~~~

The morning of spring equinox, Maurice prepared, with full-size clothes and a blanket and pillow spread out on the couch in Angela's furniture room. He went to bed early and set the alarm to wake him up at midnight, so he could enjoy the whole twenty-four hours at full size. The alarm clock rang but he didn't hear it. He supposed changing his size was an exhausting process and he had slept through the ringing of the alarm clock. He woke to the sound of Diane coming into the shop around 7am. Maurice came into the main room with his shirt hanging open and fussing with his belt, and barefoot, as she emerged from behind the counter with the textbooks she had left there last night.

Diane screamed and flung a book at him.

Maurice shouted and ducked into the next room.

Angela's laughter stopped both of them in their tracks.

"Who is --" Diane's mouth dropped open and she shook her head twice. "Maurice? What happened?"
~~~~~

"Maurice gets to be full-size four times a year, and today is his day," Angela said. "I'm sorry. I didn't think to warn you."

"No, you didn't." She blushed when Maurice handed her the book she'd thrown at him. "Sorry. You scared me half to death."

"You're a good shot."

During breakfast alone with Angela, Maurice offered to run her errands in town.

"This is your day. It's lovely of you to offer, but don't waste it on chores."

"It won't be wasting. I want to see the town, all the places people have been talking about. Stop in and see how Eden feels while my magic is down. Lanie has a gig tonight, doesn't she? Maybe we can go see her perform."

"That sounds good." Angela nodded slowly, studying him.

"What? Did old Asmondius make my nose longer than normal? Is my skin turning purple?" he joked.

"Hmm? No. I'm just trying to reconcile this new, sedate you, to the person who first landed here."

"This is my home. I get to hear what everybody's doing all the time, but I don't get to see the town and be there with everybody, know what I mean?" Maurice shrugged.

Meggie was at Divine's when Maurice returned with Angela's groceries. The schools were off for spring break. She had been spending her afternoons in the shop, keeping company with Diane while Troy was tied up with business. Despite Diane's family's influence, there was still some fallout from the foiled blackmail plot and keeping Meggie safe was a priority.

Maurice heard the two girls giggling together when he came in the front door. He decided to go upstairs with his bags before dropping in on them, maybe joining their fun.

"Where's Angela?" he asked, when he came back downstairs. He hadn't seen her anywhere upstairs.

"Jane needed some advice, so she went over to the spa for a while," Diane said. "Do you need her for something?"

"Nope. Just wondering where she was." Maurice stepped up to the counter, where Meggie sat on a high stool, in front of a notebook computer. "What kind of trouble are you two getting into?"

Meggie gave Diane a questioning look. For a moment he wondered what was wrong with her. Then he realized he was the problem. He knew her, but she didn't know him. Not face-to-face, able to look at him and hear him speak.

He held out his hand. "Hi, Meggie. I'm Maurice."

Meggie said hi, shook, and let go of his hand.

Maurice's brain froze short of a smart remark. Diane snorted, muffling a giggle. She laughed aloud when Meggie frowned at her.

How to prove himself to her? He reached over to the cherry sours jar at the end of the counter, plucked one out, and tossed it to Meggie. She caught it.

"Maurice," he said again.

"No." Her expression of hope mixed with doubt brought more giggles from Diane.

"In the flesh, for today only. Kind of." He snagged another stool with his foot, dragged it over, and sat down.

"Yeah, I felt the same way when I saw him walk out," Diane said. "It's kind of like *Brigadoon*."

"Oh." Meggie's confused expression faded.

"Briga-what?" Maurice said.

They were still laughing and explaining the play about the village that appeared and disappeared when Angela came back.

She seemed pleased to see him entertaining Meggie. He suspected Angela was more worried about the girl than she had let on to anyone. When Meggie had to go to the library to do some research, Maurice offered to walk with her.

"I can check up on Holly while I'm there," he said. "And I'll bring Meggie right back and make sure no evil biker dudes sweep her off her feet, or some muscle-bound sports hero doesn't try to corrupt her on the way."

Angela's approving smile and Meggie's laughter were all the reward he needed.

Maurice was able to clown to cover up a sudden dropping sensation of pure guilt. How could he have forgotten about Holly? Why hadn't he run over to the library first thing, to see her?

Fear? What if he introduced himself to Holly, and she didn't remember him from Angela's Christmas party? What if she didn't care that he was supposedly back in town?

"So..." Once they were out of sight of the shop and heading toward the center of town, Meggie turned around and skipped backwards a few steps. "Nobody has ever really told me why you're here, and why you're not full size all the time."

"It's part of my punishment. Angela is my probation officer."

"For what?" The disbelief on her pretty face warmed him.

Maurice entertained her on their short walk with the basic details of what landed him in front of the Fae Disciplinary Council. He was amused to find how little time it took to give her enough details to understand his background.

He caught a glimpse of a dark car slowing as it passed them, just before they crossed the street to the library. Maurice instinctively reached inside himself to gather his magic, just in case. He stumbled when there was...nothing.

He needed magic. What good was he to Meggie if someone came after her? He thought he was used to the limits of his exile, until now.

"Watch yourself, kiddo." He hooked his arm through hers as they stepped into the street.

Meggie laughed and tugged her arm free. "I'm not going to fall on my face."

"It's not you I'm worried about." He yanked her close to his side. No way was he going to admit he felt less than useless.

Sure, he could do Tai Kwan Do and knew all the ins and outs of hand-to-hand combat and barehanded self-defense. That was in controlled circumstances. That was sparring with friends who wouldn't grind his face into the cement. And he'd always had magic, before, if some damage did get done to him.

"Do you see somebody?" She looked all around as they stepped into the deeply shaded porch of the big old house that held Neighborlee's library.

"Not yet. Sorry," he said, when his over-zealous assistance up the steps made her stumble.

"You're nervous. Why?"

"Honey, just how calm would you expect James Bond to be if you took away all of Q's gizmos and blindfolded him?"

Meggie giggled. She stopped with her hand on the doorknob. "Maurice, you're cute, but you're not James Bond. You don't even have the accent."

"I'm a Fae, right? But on the one day every three months when I get to go around without wings, full-size, I don't have any magic." He wiped sweat off his forehead. "I never should have volunteered to walk with you. I'm useless."

"Hey." She rested a hand on his shoulder. "I didn't think... Ouch. That's got to be pretty rough. But you don't have to worry about me. Really. We'll just stay inside the library until Diane can come pick me up, okay? I have lots of research to do. And didn't she say something about you being interested in Holly?"

"Not ... yeah, I want to check on her." Maurice caught the glint of mischief in her eyes. "And so help me, if you say anything to anyone..."

"What are you going to do?"

"Just you wait. I've learned a lot of patience." He gently grasped her shoulders, poised to bracket her neck. "I know a lot of ways to make you --"

Shadows swooped around them. He saw Meggie's eyes widen and her mouth open. He turned -- and saw stars.

He struggled up through darkness, swinging arms and legs, desperate to drive away the attackers. He had to get to Meggie. Was that a bag over his head?

"Maurice!"

Meggie's yelp set off a reverberation through his head like broken glass rattling around and piercing tender spots in his skull.

"Wha-- Who-- Are you okay?" Maurice managed to find his eyes and get one open. He groaned as light speared into his skull. "Did somebody get the license plate of that truck?"

"Uh ... sorry." That was a thick male voice.

"I'm okay." Meggie stepped into his field of vision and he managed to get his eyes to focus. Why was she hanging from the wall?

No, he was lying on his side. He managed to lever his arms under himself.

"Hold it," a girl said in a breathy voice. A long, bony hand entered his field of vision and reached over him. Maurice winced at new pressure, this time coming from the outside of his aching skull. She had adjusted a big, drippy icepack on the side of his head. When she leaned closer, he saw delicate features, pale skin and frizzy, white-blond hair, a tiny nose and sharp, elfin cheekbones.

"Florence Nightingale, I presume?" He reached up to hold the icepack in place as he sat up. "Hey, Doni, thanks."

"Do I know you?" Doni Longfellow settled back on a bench.

"Hey, it's me, Maurice. My one day out of four." He could almost laugh when her eyes went almost as wide as her mouth, in a perfect 'O' of amazement.

Then she glared at the people outside of his field of vision. "We're really sorry. The Keystone Kops here thought you were kidnapping Meggie, so they clobbered you. Or tried to. Godzilla Junior fell on you. Otherwise, you probably would have clobbered them instead."

"That ain't fair," the boy with the thick voice said.

Maurice turned around and looked up, and up. Godzilla Junior was a good name for the huge teenager who leaned against the wall, meaty fists jammed into the pockets of his jeans. Somehow, he managed a hangdog, ashamed expression.

"I swear, I'm a friend."

They were in the three-walled shelter in the park, across the street from the library. Meggie, Doni, Godzilla and four other teens, all boys, blocked his view. Knowing how guilty parties thought, he guessed Meggie's friends and rescuers were trying to keep any interfering adults who might be in the area from finding out what they had done, while they tended to his injuries.

"Yeah, Meggie just about tore shreds out of their hides," Doni said with a breathy giggle.

"I don't suppose you guys want to sign on as bodyguards, do you?" He took a couple deep breaths and braced himself to stand up. Fortunately, the world didn't fall out from underneath him. He had never quite appreciated his inborn magic until he didn't have it to heal himself.

"Maurice, these bozos couldn't fight their way out of a wet paper bag," Meggie said.

"They were more alert than I was, and more alert than I can be now, with the way my head is feeling. I figure, they'll at least scare away anybody who wants to come after you." A new thought penetrated the aching that kept trying to drop into his stomach and create a volcano. "Hey, how come these guys even know you've got the boogie man coming after you?"

"Athena," Doni said. "She was helping us in the computer lab and we kind of..."

"They were checking out the new girl in town and managed to get information that the police don't even know about." Meggie's grin proved she wasn't upset.

"So they decided to jump in and help look out for you?" He shook his head, and only slightly regretted it. Either his head was going numb, or he was feeling better. "You gotta love this town."

"We're really sorry," Godzilla Junior said.

"Hey, better you guys than the bad guys." He gestured at the library. "How about we move this herd across the street, and find a quiet place to sit and plan, work out a schedule for looking out for Meggie?" He sighed. "Especially since I'm only in town today."

Maurice thought better about his optimistic response when they got to the library. He found out that he had not only lost an hour of his afternoon, but Holly had left the library and no one was quite sure of her schedule. He considered calling her when he got back to Divine's, but he could imagine her reaction to someone she probably didn't remember from Christmas, calling her while he was visiting the town for a single day.

When he returned to Divine's Emporium, Angela commiserated and Diane made a fuss over him getting hurt defending Meggie, even if it was a big, stupid mistake. Angela made him a mug of tea with a tingle of something extra in the brew. Maurice retreated to her quarters and slept off the remainder of his headache, while Angela and Diane worked with the Keystone Kops to set up an escort schedule for Meggie.

He felt rather proud of himself that he had that idea, but it didn't soothe his disappointment at not being able to talk to Holly. He went with Angela to watch Lanie's comedy routine that night. He enjoyed sitting in the audience and being able to laugh with people who saw him and talked to him and even bumped into him and spilled a drink on his leg. Still, the evening felt flat when Maurice curled up on the couch in the furniture room and willed himself to fall asleep before midnight struck and he returned to his reduced, winged state.

~~~~~

Dressed like characters from *Heidi*, Maurice and Holly strolled through an Alpine meadow in her dream, carrying a huge picnic basket. They laughed together as he related how Reggie Grandstone had utterly humiliated himself in front of not just Doni Longfellow and her friends, but the Willis-Brooks athletic department and the blossoming young athletes in the elementary
~~~~~

and middle schools of the surrounding communities.

Reggie and his scheming aunt had let Doni's scheming Halliday relatives manipulate them yet again. They had learned Doni was helping with a sporting event at the college stadium to celebrate the approaching end of the school year. A mini-Olympics for grades four through eight. Reggie had showed up with roses and champagne and settled on the track where the 400-meter race quarter finals were taking place. He also brought reporters. None of them worked for the local newspapers and TV stations, which had learned to ignore the Grandstones.

"I didn't get to do a dang thing." Maurice pretended to be upset. "The guy set himself up good. He nearly went into hysterics when Doni didn't present herself, front and center, after screaming for London Halliday to come out of hiding. He insisted they were childhood sweethearts and she was being totally unfair, torturing him so long, making him wait for the -- get this -- consummation of their long-time, enduring, passionate, holy, pure love."

"Oh, gag me." Holly fought so hard not to laugh, tears squeezed from the corners of her eyes.

"The guy went on for maybe twenty minutes, with the reporters catching everything, and all these parents and teachers bringing out their smartphones to record it. Then he stomps over to the teachers and demands they stop hiding his true love from him. The guy still didn't get the message from last winter, that Doni is like half his age! Her own moron Hallidays relatives can't even keep straight how old she is. So Lanie wheels out, and the big goofus is all, 'Hey, what do you think you're doing, you're not my London,' like Lanie would ever *want* to get within a thousand yards of the guy? I swear, single-digit IQs are contagious, y'know?"

"Yeah, just look at Congress. Half the country's problems would be solved if they would put up quarantine barriers around Washington and block all communication."

"Oh, you are so bad." He grinned and then dove in for a quick, pecking kiss. "Anyway ... what was I saying? Oh, yeah, Lanie holds out her phone and asks Reggie, in front of witnesses, to identify 'his' London from all the pictures she was taking for the *Tattler*. The guy couldn't. He's having a meltdown, insisting his London isn't there. And Lanie says he's right, there is no one named London Halliday living in the town of Neighborlee.

"It should have ended right there. Reporters were leaving and putting the Grandstones on the 'never on pain of death' list at a dozen more newspapers and magazines. But his twitchy aunt starts shrieking victory. She was sneaking around behind the scenes while Reggie was melting down. She at least had the brains to get a picture of Doni. She grabs the poor kid by her wrist and drags her out, and suddenly Doni is in the national spotlight. Reggie is all, 'Hey, what are you dragging this scrawny kid here for?' and she's snarling, 'This is London Halliday, you big idiot, jam the ring on her finger and let's get going.'"

"She didn't!" Holly giggled.

"Pretty much. Not those words, but heck, enough people recorded the whole thing. Good old Gordon is working security, so he stomps forward and he gets them to answer enough questions to implicate themselves in a kidnapping and forced underage marriage plot. Then to put the cherry on the whole enormous, delicious ice cream extravaganza of humiliation, Doni pulls out her new driver's license. It states right there her name is Doni Longfellow, not London Halliday. Reggie and his auntie are shrieking about how the Hallidays set them up again, and they were going to sue the school district for humiliating them and ..." He tipped his head back and spread his arms. "It was glorious."

"Good for you."

"Huh?" He shook his head.

"You enjoyed the whole ridiculous situation and didn't care one bit that you didn't help engineer it. You're growing up."

"Daaang!" He managed to twist his face in a mask of dismay. It held for about three seconds. "Proud of me, babe?"

"Definitely yeah." Holly went up on her toes and kissed his cheek. Then she blushed and kissed him lightly on the lips.

Maurice understood why champagne bottles popped their corks. Laughing, they linked arms again and continued walking. Soon, though, her laughter and smile faded. She grew thoughtful. Maurice waited, and when she didn't speak for a few more minutes, he asked what she was thinking.

"Sometimes," Holly said slowly, "when I manage to fall into a really horrid, scary-ific dream, I wish I could bring the really nasty people from town in here, like the Grandstones, to pay them back for what they did to me and my friends in high school. You never met Sylvia. She got herself killed last New Year's Eve. But there were times I just wanted to tear her hair out by the roots and make Reggie sing soprano. And that's just for starters."

"Gee," he drawled, "somebody'd think you didn't like them."

"I hope when I wake up tomorrow, I find out everything you've been telling me was real. That would be great, even if I don't remember that you told me now."

"Miracles happen all the time," Maurice offered, wishing he could put the sparkles back into her eyes.

"True ..."

"So why the sad face, Holly Berry?"

"Miracles never happen for me, that's all," she said, and shrugged.

"What kind of miracle would you want?"

"Nothing big and impossible. Little things like this. The picnic and spending time together and just being happy."

"Ah ... correct me, but isn't that what we're doing?"

"It's not real." She shrugged and cast a brave little smile up at him. "I know it's not real. A guy like you would never give me a second look, in the real world."

"Who says?" Maurice hadn't felt hot, righteous indignation in a long time, but it rose up now on Holly's behalf. "If this could be real, if I was real--"

"I'd think you were a set-up. That you were playing a really nasty trick. That someone had asked you to help them trick the brainy girl."

"Somebody did that to you once, didn't they?"

"Just once. That's all it takes." She swung the picnic basket a little harder.

"Someday, Holly Berry, I promise, all of this will be real."

"I learned to stop wishing for anything to change in the real world. This is enough for me. Dreams are better. If you're careful, they last forever." She forced another smile and pointed at a pretty little level spot, sheltered by pines, with a glistening pool in one corner. "Look. Up there is the place I wanted to show you. When the sun sets, it's the most spectacular light show in the entire world." She ran to the spot.

Maurice kept up with her, his heart on the verge of shattering.

~~~~~
~~~~~

Two weeks later, Maurice hovered over Holly's shoulder in Angela's backyard garden. He watched her face, as Gina laughed and chattered with her and Angela and Diane, talking about the grand opening plans for the latest phase of the long-term renovation of the old factory that housed Eden. Part of the next phase to take place over the summer would include a branch of the Neighborlee Public Library, and Gina promised Holly she would lobby to have her the liaison between the library and the city.

"And I've got the firepower to back up my promises now," Gina added, with a happy chuckle for punctuation.

"You're speaking of that new partner at Carr, Cooper and Crenshaw?" Angela said.

"She better not be talking about anyone else," Diane said. "After the torture you put the guy through before you tossed him a bone?"

Maurice grinned, knowing it wasn't nearly as bad as she made it sound. An old school friend of Gina's, the proverbial boy from the wrong side of the tracks, had returned to Neighborlee just before Christmas. He had worked his way up the ranks in a prestigious Los Angeles law firm. Then he decided what he really wanted was to come home, work for the lawyers who had helped him straighten out his life, and find out if the girl who encouraged him to make something of himself was still as wonderful as he remembered. Gina had been burned too many times, and she had forced Calvin to prove he was for real.

"It's better than a dream," Holly said, when the four finished laughing together. She sighed and raised her glass of iced tea in a toast. "To having all your dreams come true, and snagging the cutest guy in town, on top of it."

"I hope you're talking about me," Diane said. She fluttered her hand, showing off the tasteful diamond and emerald engagement ring Troy had given her the week before.

"She's talking to both of you." Angela tipped her head to one side and met Maurice's gaze for a moment before nodding to Holly. "And she's talking about all of us."

A merry chuckle burst from her when all three women gave her astonished looks. "Why so shocked? I'm just as liable to find true love as you, and I know Holly has a real, live, enchanted prince waiting to sweep her off her feet."

"Only in books." Holly sighed. Her smile was genuine. Maurice looked deep into her eyes and didn't see the pain he dreaded.

"Can she wait that long?" He fluttered to a landing on Angela's shoulder. "Can I wait that long?"

Patience, Angela said, her mental touch soothing. *If I can wait for centuries for my true love to return to me, you can wait two years.*

"Your true love?" He tried to laugh. "I knew it. You're an enchanted princess under a curse."

Who knows? All I can be sure of is that magic is constantly moving, and I can feel someone longing for me, seeking for me, through time and distance. What else could keep him looking and working so long, except true love?

Chapter Thirteen

Jon-Tom Castle saw the cradle by accident, when he dropped off an order of wooden toys at Divine's Emporium that June day. Old pain shot through him, just as sharp as it had been two years ago when Caryn broke off their engagement and tried to clear out his bank account by misrepresenting herself as his wife.

He knew better, but he still crossed the furniture room and knelt to examine the cradle. He remembered all the dreams he had enjoyed while he made that cradle. Carved faeries danced along the golden oak sideboards and flowers twined down the spindles and across the rockers. He had dreamed of their children sleeping in it, and all the stories he would tell them as they grew up.

Caryn had loved the cradle when he gave it to her two weeks before their wedding. His joy had shattered when she exclaimed over the money he could get for it. She had laughed when he stammered that the cradle was for their children, not for sale.

During the next two hours, while her laughter turned to scorn and harsh words, he'd realized everything he thought he knew about her, everything she'd told him during their whirlwind romance, had been lies. She didn't want or even like children. She didn't want to live in Neighborlee. She wanted him to expand his woodworking business, make connections with high-priced interior designers and art galleries, and rake in the money.

Jon-Tom ran one stained fingertip over the faerie perched on a mushroom. He still marveled that Caryn hadn't shattered the cradle to matchsticks when he refused to let her sell it.

He hadn't wanted the cradle either at the family farm or in his little cottage in town. He had brought it to Divine's because he trusted the magic of the shop to match the cradle with someone who would love it. Caryn would never walk into Divine's in a million years, so she would never know he was selling it. She had never understood the difference between the treasures of the heart and soul, and material wealth.

"That cradle's just waiting for the right person," Angela called from the vintage clothing room, where she was conducting inventory. "Don't you worry. It'll sell when the time is right."

"I'm not worried." He jammed his hands into the pockets of his overalls and strode up to the counter. Angela had left the check for this newest order lying there. *I'm not worried. I don't need to sell that cradle any more than I need another lying, spoiled rich brat in my life.*

He heard Caryn's scornful laughter in his memory when he checked the dollar amount written on the check. The money wasn't for him, but for the fulfillment of his dream. That enormous, childhood-dream-come-true playground he was building would take more years and more money to be complete. He was happiest when his world was filled with children. What did it matter if they were other people's children? He didn't have to be related by blood to love children and want to make them happy.

The Wishing Ball sat on the counter, right under his nose. It had held down the check so it didn't fly away in the gentle breeze from the open windows, making the wind chimes shimmer.

He remembered coming to Divine's Emporium with the half-dozen foster-brothers and foster-sisters his parents had taken in. They bought penny candy and explored the treasures hidden in the shadows of the house-turned-store. There was always something new, every time they came.

He remembered when Angela told him how the Wishing Ball was strongest when it was used to help others. He had been upset over the bully who had just moved into their home. Jon-Tom hadn't really believed in the power of the Wishing Ball, but he had been desperate and made his wish. Not too much later, the bully had become his friend. He had made other wishes through the years, until he got too busy in high school and had spent his summers apprenticing with a master craftsman in Wisconsin.

Grinning at his own foolishness, Jon-Tom pressed his hand over the top of the ball. A chill flittered up his arm, pleasant on a humid June day.

"I wish," he whispered. And stopped. He certainly didn't believe in wishes at the ripe old age of thirty-one.

And yet, magic did happen at Divine's Emporium. Even if they had all been coincidences, his wishes *had* come true. What would it hurt, to make one more wish?

"I wish I could find the perfect woman. One who doesn't care about money. Who loves kids. Who doesn't care about fancy clothes and going to New York every week and..." He sighed. Making a list of Caryn's flaws wasn't going to help him. "I want a real girl, who cares about the important things. I want a girl who will love me for me, and not the guy she thinks she can make me into."

Just like the first time he'd wished, lights seemed to swirl around the Wishing Ball, inside the dark rainbow swirls, and the bronze dragon that formed the base winked one ruby eye at him.

Jon-Tom laughed softly at his over-active imagination and looked around. Sure enough, the lights had flickered because the front door had opened, letting in the blinding afternoon sunlight.

"Got it, Angela," he called, and stuffed the check into his overalls pocket. "See you next week."

"I'll be here," Angela called from the back room, and a whisper of musical laughter filtered out to him.

He remembered when he'd first heard that laughter. He'd thought fairies were hiding in the shadows of the shop, eager to come out and play. If only...

~~~~~

"Guy's got a world of hurt resting on him." Maurice glided down the hall on the freshened breeze. "What are we gonna do about him?"

"Maurice, I'm proud of you." Angela emerged from the clothing room, a pleased smile lighting her face.

"What? What'd I do?"

"Sympathy. Wanting to help. And thinking of it as teamwork from the start, instead of seeing yourself as a lone vigilante." Her smile faded a little. "Short of giving his ex-fiancé a heart transplant... I've felt some things shifting throughout Neighborlee. New people moving in. Let's see what the winds of change bring us, shall we?"

"So, tell me about this wicked witch he almost married. Any chance of her coming back to town and ruining his day?" He followed her back into the clothing room.

"Caryn hated Neighborlee. You could feel the strain of the town trying to push her out, from the moment she followed him from the East Coast and started setting up housekeeping in that lovely old farmhouse Jon-Tom's parents left him. She thought she could change him. But he was stubborn about the things that mattered. She gave him an ultimatum, and when he wouldn't bend,
~~~~~

she left, just before the wedding. Fortunately for Jon-Tom."

~~~~~

The morning dew was still sparkling on the grass when Jeri tripped over a basket on her porch and nearly nose-dived into the new mulch she'd spread last night before it got too dark to see. She slammed hands and knees into the sidewalk, inches from disaster. A cry split the air when she stood up and looked at her cement-burned palms.

She held her breath, but the cry continued, so it hadn't come from her. Closing her eyes, she turned, and counted to three.

When she opened her eyes, the basket was just where she had glimpsed it before she did a full-gainer down the three steps. Jeri wiped her blood-spotted hands on the thighs of her pajamas and forgot about retrieving the morning paper. She stared at the basket while the wail increased in volume. She couldn't be so lucky to have something disposable in there, like a puppy or a bunch of kittens she could take to the shelter, could she?

Absently, she noted the torn knees in her pajamas and the blood seeping across one skinned knee. She kicked some disturbed mulch back into the flowerbed and took two steps to the porch. Holding her breath again, she looked down.

Red face, curly black hair, a pale blue baby blanket pushed to one side, and a chubby little body dressed in nothing but a diaper. The baby kicked and writhed and wailed loud enough for an entire frat house during Rush Week.

The opening sequence of a spoof Western, *Evil Roy Slade,* popped into her mind. Roy had been abandoned as a baby, but he'd made so much noise the coyotes wouldn't adopt him. Jeri understood why. How could something so tiny be that loud?

"Hey, I'm the one who should be screaming here," she said. "You're not bleeding."

The kid jerked and went silent. He opened enormous gray-blue eyes and stared up at Jeri. Judging from the blue blanket and those long, killer eyelashes, she guessed the baby was a boy. Girls never got lashes like that without cosmetic help.

"How'd you get here?"

The last thing she wanted to do was touch the baby. Suppose he was kidnapped? Who would believe her when she said she had no idea how he landed on her porch? She was a newcomer in the
~~~~~

sleepy little college town of Neighborlee. Nobody for hundreds of miles could vouch for her.

Police investigations and accusations of kidnapping invariably led to newspaper stories and getting her picture posted on the Internet. She didn't want the people she left behind to know where she was, thanks very much. She refused to contact those soulless bloodsuckers, even to get a lawyer to keep her out of jail. Her former friends and unwanted relatives made vampires look downright cuddly.

The corner of a sheet of paper showed from under the blanket. With thumb and forefinger, she gingerly grasped the corner and yanked it free. The boy just lay there, blinking sleepily now, and watched her.

"'Jerry Hollis, you low-life,'" she read aloud. She glanced over at the baby. "Well, they got the name right even if it's spelled wrong, but I take exception to the rest of it."

The baby blew raspberries at her. Did he find her aggravated tone amusing? Well, that figured. Nobody else in her past life took her seriously, either.

"'Here's your son,'" she continued. "'It took me long enough to track you down, but you're not skipping out on me again. You have enough money for a whole houseful of kids, so pay up. Maggie.'"

Jeri glanced at her cottage, not one of the more upscale houses on the winding, tree-lined street. She had money, true. It had helped her escape her old life and set up here without worrying about little details like a job. But enough for a whole houseful of kids? Hardly.

"I hate to tell you, Junior, but you aren't mine. I mean, if I had a kid, I think I'd know it, and I certainly wouldn't have a kid with someone named Maggie." Jeri squatted, ignoring her aching knees. "So, what're we going to do, huh?"

In the movies and in books, the hapless fool stuck with a surprise baby tried to take it to the orphanage or some authority. She supposed that was the next step.

Just as soon as she had some breakfast, washed up and put Bactine on her hands and knees.

She supposed the baby would be happier with some food in his stomach. What did babies eat, anyway? She couldn't give him her breakfast of peanut-butter-and-honey on a bagel and iced coffee. Plain milk probably wasn't good for babies, either. Unless they were baby cows. Maybe juice? She remembered her nanny giving her apple juice when she was little.

"Juice it is, Junior. You don't happen to be packing a bottle in there, do you?"

The baby grinned at her, and something went all twisty and warm inside her in response.

Her hand shook a little as she grabbed the handle to take the basket inside. After all, she couldn't spend the day kneeling on her porch in her pajamas. Her neighbors hardly knew her after only a week of residence in Neighborlee, and Jeri wanted them to have a nicer image of her.

"There's probably some legal obligation that landed on me the minute I picked you up," she told him as she crossed the porch. "But I bet there are worse legal implications if I leave you outside all day." She sighed, reflecting that even here in quiet little Neighborlee, she couldn't avoid worrying about what people would demand of her.

Inside, with the door safely closed, she investigated the basket. The angry mommy had left ten diapers, a plastic box of damp wipes, three filled bottles, one which went immediately into Junior's mouth, a rattle, a pacifier, and one change of clothes. Memories intruded, of entire closets filled with just frilly dresses, not to mention drawers full of lacy socks, bonnets that dripped with ribbons and other baby paraphernalia. Even if other babies weren't forced to be fashion plates as she had been, Jeri felt sure Junior had been short-changed. Maybe that was why his mother dumped him at her house. Mommy expected the low-life Jerry to take care of his son because she didn't have the resources.

"Okay, how hard can it be to find a guy named Jerry Hollis in a town this size?" she muttered, thinking aloud as she unscrewed the top of the empty bottle. Junior just gurgled contentedly and drained his second bottle with lightning speed. "Hey, you want to slow it down? If you keep that up, you're going to be a chugging champ before you get into high school."

Her words earned another happy giggle from the baby. That melted, hollow feeling dropped to the region of her toes. All the books she had ever read had described that feeling as *love*.

No guy had ever made her feel hollow and dizzy unless he had spiked her drink at a party. Then she barfed all over him. For about two weeks she'd fooled herself into believing Foster made her feel that way, but she had awakened from that fool's dream before disaster struck. She hadn't really felt love before in her entire life. Why did the feeling have to come from a baby she couldn't keep?

"Oh, no," she whispered. "Get hold of yourself, girl. You are not equipped, mentally, emotionally or otherwise, to handle a baby. You can't keep him. He's not a puppy. You killed your goldfish. What makes you think you can take care of a baby?"

Still, childhood memories of playing quietly in her suite made Jeri smile. She had loved dressing up her two dozen baby dolls, feeding them, rocking them, singing to them. They didn't cry and wriggle and smell like baby powder and grin at her, though. There was a big difference between dolls and babies.

She knew better than to take the time to find out just how big that difference was. This kid needed to be dropped on the authorities, pronto. Before she starved him or dropped him or broke something.

With one thing and another going wrong, she didn't get the baby his refills on juice or get herself dressed until after 10. Jeri chalked another one up to sleeping late, after staying up until 1am to finish reading the last book in the stack she had taken from the library. The title of which, she couldn't remember now. Why had she gotten out of bed, anyway?

Oh, yeah. To get the paper.

With a sense of dread, she stepped outside with her purse over her shoulder and both arms looped through the handle of the baby basket. Just as she feared, her newspaper had blown into three other yards. With a groan, she put the basket down on the porch and went to chase down the scattered pages before they traveled any farther.

She couldn't even handle a daily newspaper delivery without making a mess. The garden she was putting in, aided by books from the library, would probably die by the end of next week. There was no way she could keep a baby. Even though he certainly was adorable. And warm. And grinned at her as if he actually liked her.

The lack of traffic at nearly 11 in the morning cheered Jeri as she strolled toward downtown Neighborlee. This was exactly why she had moved here. She had feared a town named Neighborlee would be anything but, yet the pictures the realtor had sent her and her Web searches revealed an idyllic town where Century houses and slate sidewalks met a nice chunk of the Metroparks, and the trees were tall and old and drooped over the streets.

Most of the commerce centered in downtown, with old-fashioned storefronts and apartments over stores, plenty of offices, and buildings with bay windows and recessed doorways. Jeri had fallen in love with the town even before she'd made her escape flight from the other side of the country. No one in her old life would ever expect her to come here. They always assumed that if they didn't like something, she wouldn't like it, either.

They were wrong, as usual. Maybe, in another six months, she would grow the backbone to actually tell them they were wrong. Of course, she would do it via a letter sent through an indirect route, so they couldn't trace it back to her.

No matter how long she had been established in her new home, with new friends and new identity, if anyone in her old life found out where she was, they would come drag her back to the Hell of high fashion and high society, where money and time were wasted at the speed of sound. It wasn't as if any of those people actually liked her. They liked her money and family connections.

If hiding here in Neighborlee, Ohio didn't work, she would run to the ends of the Earth. How about Australia? How about a convent? Not that she wanted to live by anyone else's rules but her own, ever again. That was something she intended to avoid with every speck of energy left in her.

She turned down the street that should have held the government complex, a low sprawl of sandstone buildings that included the fire and police stations. Instead, she saw a big olive and gold Victorian house, some empty lots, and a dead end. Yes, the dead end gave way to a gorgeous view of the slope down into the Metroparks, but it wasn't what she wanted. How could she turn Junior over to the proper authorities if she couldn't *find* them?

Sighing, she shifted the basket to her other hand. Her shoulder ached from the weight. At least Junior was asleep, lulled by the warm day and the swaying of the basket as she trudged down the slate sidewalk. Jeri turned around and tried to get her bearings.

Three turns later, she ended up at that same dead end street. That made no sense, because she'd turned left, then right, then left again. Not left, left, left. What was going on here?

"Hey, you okay?"

That voice was deep, rumbling and male, and didn't sound familiar. That made it a beautiful sound. Jeri didn't tense and clench her hands into claws, ready to dig her false nails into any male hand that tried to touch where he wasn't invited. Besides, she didn't have her false nails anymore.

"No, not really," she admitted, and forced a cheerful, false smile onto her sweaty face.

She looked up. And up. Into chocolate brown eyes not quite shadowed by oak brown hair streaked with gold by the sun. The owner of those eyes had a wide, cheerful face, fringed by maybe three days' growth of beard. He had a streak of blue paint across one cheekbone, smears of gold paint in his hair, and a fingerprint in white paint on the bridge of his nose. He wore overalls, sans shirt, and his bare arms were spattered with more paint.

The big crate resting against a truly buff, tanned chest, held a dozen old-fashioned toys, all made of wood. A tractor, a tiny rocking horse perfect for a Barbie doll, and a jointed clown on a stick. Junior would laugh at those toys, especially the clown.

"You like?" Mr. Chocolate Eyes grinned, revealing perfect teeth, except for a crooked right incisor that made him totally human and safe. Unlike some people who were so physically perfect their brains rotted in revolt.

"They're great -- Umm, could you tell me where I am?"

"About fifty feet away from Divine's Emporium. Lost?"

"Unfortunately. Could you tell me how to get to City Hall?"

"I can take you there. After I make my delivery." He hefted the crate of toys to demonstrate. "Why don't you come on inside, get something cold to drink, put down that baby basket for a little while? I'll show you the way after Angela and I get everything squared away."

Something cold to drink sounded wonderful. Both arms ached like they wanted to come off at the shoulders. The warmth in his eyes and the thought of getting out of the sun convinced her to do what she had sworn not to: talk to strangers and trust their advice.

"What does Divine's Emporium sell?" she said as she followed him through the wrought iron gate in front of the Victorian house.

"Anything and everything. Seems like, whatever you need, it's there. And even things you didn't realize you needed, they just show up." He laughed and paused to brace the crate between the wall and his hip as he reached to pull the door open. He gestured for Jeri to go ahead of him.

Her face warmed at the courtesy. She tiptoed through the doorway. Bells above the door chimed in whispers and were echoed by wind chimes hanging from the ceiling all through the store. A soft sigh escaped her as she walked across the wooden floor and stared in delight at the crowded, old-fashioned display shelves on either side. This was the kind of place she had always dreamed of visiting, of playing in, maybe even owning someday.

Old-fashioned apothecary jars full of a rainbow assortment of candy sat on shelves behind a marble counter. Rag dolls. Teacups. Kitschy knickknacks. Souvenirs and cold remedies. Junk and collectibles. Candles lined one wall and filled the store with fragrance. Signs hanging from the ceiling pointed to other rooms with vintage clothes, games, toys, books, and housewares.

"Jon-Tom." The words, spoken in a sweet, low voice came from seemingly out of nowhere. "You're right on time."

Jeri turned. She could have sworn the woman had materialized from the empty space and shadows behind the main counter. She had long, dark blonde hair, flame-blue eyes, and a smiling face.

"You must be the new girl in town." The woman turned her warm smile on Jeri next.

The habitual icy stiffness that came on encountering strangers defrosted and spilled down Jeri's spine. Or was that just the sweat she had generated, turning chill in the shade?

"I figured she needed to meet you," Jon-Tom said. "This is Angela." He sidestepped the basket still hanging from Jeri's hands, took his crate of toys to the counter, and put it down with a soft thud. "Whew! It's hot out there."

"I bet you both could use a cold drink." Angela beckoned.

Jeri looked where Angela gestured. She could have sworn the white wrought iron soda fountain tables and chairs hadn't been there two minutes ago. She mentally kicked herself. Maybe she had hit her head when she tripped over Junior's basket, or she was having heatstroke. It wasn't like her to miss things, or to thoughtlessly do what strangers told her. Somehow, she found herself setting the basket on the closest table and sitting next to it.

"He's adorable. Is he yours?" Angela bent over the basket. She didn't pick up the sleeping baby, which eased the jolt of possessiveness and concern that shot through Jeri.

"Temporarily." Jeri wiped her sweaty hand on her thigh and held it out. "Hi, I'm Jeri Hollis."

"You're kidding," Jon-Tom said, with a snort of laughter.

"Nope." The hairs on the back of her neck bristled. She had thought long and hard about the new name she wanted to wear for the rest of her life, and she liked the name enough to fight for it.

"My best buddy's name is Jerry Hollis."

"He is? Do you know where he is? Because this is his kid."

Jon-Tom gave her a look that clearly said he thought she was crazy. Jeri wished she could rewind the last few minutes and start over.

Angela just stepped back and looked her over. "How do you know this is his baby?"

Over iced coffee loaded with vanilla syrup and cream, Jeri spilled the whole story. She hadn't meant to tell anyone her business. Something about the understanding and humor in Angela's expression yanked out the plug she had mentally inserted in her vocal cords over the years. Once she got started, and that first taste of vanilla coffee and cream had slid down her throat, she couldn't stop until she reached the end of the story.

Jon-Tom had put the toys away in another room and done some paperwork at the counter while she talked. Now he came to take the other chair. He grinned and looked down into the basket. "Sure is a cute little guy. I can't imagine Jerry ever abandoning his kid, if he knew he even had a kid."

"Maybe that's the problem," Jeri conceded. "He didn't know, and the mother thinks he should know, and now she's mad." She stroked a finger down the baby's soft, plump leg. "She sure didn't leave much with him."

"Jon-Tom, does this baby look like Jerry?" Angela said.

"Give him a butch cut and put him in uniform... Well, he needs a constant five o'clock shadow, but yeah. I've known him since sand box days." He nodded once, decisively. "I think this is Jerry's kid."

"Where can I find him?" Jeri felt a little breathless at having her problem solved so quickly. She wouldn't have to go anywhere near the authorities.

"Got a plane ticket to Germany? Jerry's a Marine, on guard duty at the embassy. Won't get back for another year, I think. He left about ten months ago."

"Ouch," Jeri whispered. "So I guess the best thing to do is take Junior to the police and let the authorities take over."

"If you put that kid in the system, Jerry'll never be able to find him when he gets back," Jon-Tom snapped.

"What do you expect me to do? Take him home and babysit for a year?"

"Children." Angela flattened her lips, but a smile glinted in her eyes. She rested one hand on the shoulder of each. "Why don't we sit back and relax and take it slowly for a minute? All right? You know Jeri will be in a great deal of trouble with the authorities if she keeps that baby without the proper people knowing. What if it's some horrid trick somebody played on the mother, dumping that baby on her doorstep this morning? She could be frantic, tearing her hair out, trying to find her baby."

Jon-Tom glowered for a few moments, then nodded. The storm clouds left his eyes, and Jeri was strangely glad. She didn't like him being angry with her, even if it was for a good reason.

Wait a minute. Where had that thought come from? She didn't care what anybody thought of her. She just wanted to be left alone to live her own life and make her own decisions. To watch the movies she wanted to watch and wear the clothes she wanted to wear, without having to dodge paparazzi and dynastic marriage plans while relatives fought to control her mind and her money.

"Now," Angela said, when they'd managed half-hearted smiles for each other and had agreed to the truce. "The first thing we need to do is outfit this baby of ours."

Chapter Fourteen

"Ours?" Despite herself, Jeri smiled. The weight that had settled on her shoulders when she picked up that basket full of baby lightened considerably. *Ours* implied others would help her and share the responsibility. "What do you mean, outfit?"

"Clothes, diapers." Jon-Tom grinned, nearly flattening her with the full wattage of his smile. "Lots of diapers. And powder and ointment and wipes and--"

"Toys," Angela said. "Something to sleep in besides that basket. You're new in town. You took the Harris place, right?"

"Right." Jeri nodded, though she was only vaguely sure the previous owners had been named Harris. Her college roommate, one of the few people she trusted simply because Rita hated the "Establishment" so badly, had been her go-between to obtain the house, to keep her name out of official records as much as possible. The publisher of an underground newspaper was the best kind of friend to have, if someone could only have one trustworthy friend.

"So, I bet you haven't any place to put a baby, even if you only agreed to take him overnight." Angela stood up and looked around her shop. "You two stay right here while I go hunting." She strode out of the room. Jeri heard creaks that sounded like someone climbing old wooden stairs.

"Whatever you need, you can find at Divine's," Jon-Tom said. He rested his elbows on the table. "So, how new to town are you?"

"Week or so." Jeri glanced at the baby. "What makes you think your friend Jerry didn't abandon his girlfriend and kid?"

Somewhere during a recital of Jerry's heroism in middle school, pulling two children out of the river during a flood, the heat and long walk and stress of the morning finally got to her. Jeri felt like someone had attached weights to her eyelashes. She bowed her head, resting it on her palm. Vaguely, as the dimness took over, she heard Jon-Tom chuckle, felt his hand guiding her head down, crossing her arms to form a pillow on the table. He had nice hands, big and warm, calloused but not rough. Gentle.

She dreamed about the baby. He leaped out of his basket and

landed on her lap. He hugged her and giggled and called her Mommy. Something turned hot and fierce inside her, where Jeri had always imagined herself to be empty, cold and dusty. They ran through the shop, playing with toys. They found all sorts of treats she never had as a little girl because she was always on display, always expected to perform, or sit quietly in the corner.

Jeri dreamed the baby taught her to dance and sing silly songs. They had a tea party with Angela and a handsome little man with enormous, glittery wings. Every time the baby hugged her and called her Mommy, Jeri wanted to laugh and cry.

~~~~~

Jon-Tom trusted Angela to look after Jeri. With three orders to finish and four customers coming throughout the day to pick up orders, he had to get back to his shop. He had worked hard to build up a good reputation and couldn't let one black mark threaten it now. Not even for his best friend.

That didn't mean he couldn't pull every string, follow every lead to track down Jerry and let him know what had happened. By 4:30 that afternoon, frustration burned a hole in his stomach from hours of phone calls in the gaps between customers. He'd often tucked the phone between his ear and shoulder, waiting to talk to a human being, while he sanded or painted or worked on sketches for new designs. The comforting smells of sawdust and linseed oil didn't work their magic. All he got for his efforts was a gigantic phone bill and four messages left for Jerry at his quarters, two with his superiors, and one with the chaplain.

His heart was in his throat as he walked up the slate walk to Divine's door, because he feared Jeri wasn't there. His fear the baby would land in the hands of the authorities was a very close second to not seeing Jeri there. And that just didn't make sense.

There was nothing particularly unique or compelling about Jeri. Fashionably ragged-cut hair made her look like a lost kid on an adventure. She had big, muddy green eyes framed in lashes so pale they were almost invisible. Not skinny, not plump, she had a few extra curves in her bottom and hips, but he liked a girl who felt soft inside the curve of his arm. He didn't like girls who looked like a stick or a piece of dandelion fuzz that would blow away at the first stiff breeze.

Jon-Tom stopped short with that thought echoing in his head.
~~~~~

Since when did it matter how Jeri might fit into his arms? He was too busy for relationships. Especially with a girl who didn't know a thing about kids and obviously didn't want one.

With a growl rumbling silently in his chest, he shoved the front door open and strode into Divine's. He hurried down the aisles to the table where he had left Jeri and Jerry's baby.

The basket was gone. Jon-Tom's heart plummeted and his stomach tied into a knot.

Jeri was still there, however, in the same position where he had left her. He tripped over a non-existent seam in the wooden floor. She wasn't dead, was she? Angela hadn't drugged her to make her stay, had she?

No, Angela wouldn't do anything sneaky like that. Weird things happened in Divine's, but nothing illegal.

He knew he grinned like an idiot. Just standing and looking at Jeri was rude, but he didn't care. Seeing her still here sort of paid for the rotten day he had. But the baby was still missing. He reached out to shake Jeri. How could she just sit there and not know someone had taken the baby away?

"Don't panic," he muttered. "Nothing bad ever happens at Divine's."

"There you are." Angela came through the doorway from the back room, all smiles, the baby basket in one hand and a bulging shopping bag in the other. "Did you get everything done?"

"Yeah." He let out a long breath, and hoped his face wasn't as hot as it felt. "How's the kid?"

"Jerry Junior is just fine. We had a long talk, and then we had a long nap. He ate all his lunch and loved every bit of it. Didn't you, sweetheart?"

Angela had an admirable talent for being able to croon to a baby without sounding like her IQ had dropped by half. The baby gurgled at her, kicked his pudgy little legs, and waved a glistening, drooly fist.

"How's--" Jon-Tom jerked a thumb at Jeri, afraid to say her name, and ashamed of what he had been thinking.

"Jeri." Angela rested a hand on the sleeper's tousled head. No reaction. "Jeri Hollis, wake up." She shook her slightly, and still no response. "Natalie St. Germaine Hollister."

"Leave me--" Jeri sat bolt upright and raised her arms as if warding off a blow. For two heartbeats, her eyes were wide, her face alabaster pale, and she froze. Then her face went red and she subsided, drooping as if her fright had exhausted her. "Uh. Hi."

"Have a nice nap?" Jon-Tom dropped into the chair next to her, fighting the urge to wrap an arm around her and ask who had hurt her. It didn't take much imagination to guess, from the long name Angela had used, Jeri was trying to escape trouble of some kind.

Did he want a woman in hiding to take care of Jerry's baby until he got hold of his friend?

"What time is it?" Jeri blushed even darker when her stomach rumbled loudly.

"Time for something to eat." Angela sat down in the third chair, after depositing the basket on the fourth chair, and the enormous shopping bag under it. "You're just worn out, aren't you?"

"Not anymore," Jeri mumbled. She rubbed at her neck, then raked both hands through her hair. "I don't want to impose. And I'm really sorry about falling asleep in your store. Hope I didn't scare off any customers."

"Don't worry about it. People get exactly what they need and what they're looking for when they come here." Angela winked. "I guarantee, nobody was looking for you, so they didn't see you. Now, why don't we get this little guy settled for another nap, and we'll go get comfortable upstairs and have something to eat?"

Angela didn't lock the front door when she led them up to her living quarters, even though Diane wasn't in today. Jon-Tom had learned long ago that she always knew when someone came into her store, and nobody ever stole. They might temporarily borrow something, but they never stole.

He gladly followed Angela and Jeri up to the second floor. The table was already set for three. An open drawer in the bureau under the fantasy landscape painting made a temporary bed for the baby. His hands shook a little when Angela handed the basket to him, but he liked the warmth and softness that filled his arms when he picked up the baby, cuddled him a few seconds, and put him down in his makeshift bed. The little guy gave him a wet baby grin, blew a few bubbles, and closed his eyes.

"I just... Thanks but... Where I come from, people aren't this nice to total strangers." Jeri slid into the chair Angela pointed out to her. Discomfort was bright and clear in her eyes, so Jon-Tom felt sorry for her.

"Don't you worry about anything. Neighborlee doesn't do things quite the way the rest of the world does. People come here for quiet, for peace, for safety. It's a nice town even though it has its flaws. You couldn't find a nicer town to visit." Angela brought a platter of sandwiches from the refrigerator. She set it down and added a fruit gelatin, a bowl of potato salad and a pitcher of iced tea loaded with lemon slices.

"Oh, no, I'm not visiting. I'm here to stay," Jeri said quickly. She glanced at Jon-Tom, caught him grinning at her, and looked away.

"So, Jon-Tom," Angela said, "any progress?"

While they ate, he gave them a quick run-down of the people he had managed to talk to, and all the computers he had fought with while trying to track down Jerry. Every few bites, Jeri stopped eating and gave him a look that clearly said she couldn't believe he'd gone to all that trouble for someone, even a good friend.

Jon-Tom decided to pity her bad experiences rather than feel angry over her lack of faith in people.

When Angela asked him about his woodworking business, he got carried away, as usual, about the woods he was working with, his new designs, the fun he was having with the summer apprenticeship program for the kids in town. Before he knew it, Angela had refilled the iced tea twice and they'd started on their dessert of raspberry sherbet and lemon cookies.

The big grandfather clock downstairs chimed six.

"What?" Jeri leaped from her chair, but instead of running away she stood still, legs trembling. "I thought we were having lunch. I spent the whole day here? City Hall is closed," she wailed.

"I wouldn't worry about it," Angela said. "You have more than enough supplies to get you through the night."

"But I don't know anything about babies." She sank down into the chair. "I'd kill him without meaning to. I can't even keep a goldfish alive."

"I'm sure Jon-Tom will help you." Angela sent him a meaningful glance.

"Sure. Be glad to," he hurried to assure her. "We're neighbors, anyway. I'm in the house behind you, to the right."

"Your right or my right?" Jeri mumbled.

"Doesn't matter. Our fences touch. You call for help and I'll be over the fence and at your back door before you know it."

"You're just trusting me with your best friend's baby?" Her pale face flushed red, then paled again. She turned to Angela. "I mean, I'd love to take him, but there has to be some laws, right? I don't know the first thing about babies, but I know they can get sick and you have to feed them and keep them clean and warm. I don't want to hurt him."

"But you do want to keep him, don't you?" Angela asked. There was something in her tone that made Jon-Tom think she was making a statement rather than verifying something.

"It's crazy, but yes, I do." Jeri's voice cracked on the last word, and she took deep breaths, visibly fighting panic. She sat back in her chair and raked her fingers through her hair again. "I'm sorry. I'm not making a very good impression, am I? Considering that when I came in, the most important thing in the world was passing the little guy on to someone else."

The wobbly smile she gave them did something to Jon-Tom's insides. What kind of a deprived life had she led, that the thought of taking care of a baby terrified her? Didn't all girls fight to babysit? Didn't all girls love babies?

No. He knew that was a lie, didn't he?

"You're going to be all right." He reached over and squeezed her hand. "I don't know much, but I'll help you all I can. And I bet Angela can give you a few lessons."

"Whatever you need, you can get it here. Supplies, furniture, advice." Angela nodded for emphasis. "Especially friends."

~~~~~

"Thanks." Jeri almost added "want to come inside?" but she knew better. She stepped onto her porch and dug in her pocket for her keys.

Jon-Tom had walked her home after a long, bewildering crash course in baby care from Angela. Who would have thought when she got up that morning she would end up with a baby in her house, even if only for a few days? Who would have thought she would spend the evening with a shopkeeper and consider her the closest thing she had to a friend, outside of Rita the Rebel? Her aunt would die of embarrassment if she knew Jeri socialized with a "mercenary" shopkeeper. And took lessons from her, no less.

If Aunt Eleanora were here, she would have swept into the
~~~~~

nearest hiring agency-- No, strike that, she would have sent her secretary to the nearest hiring agency to get a nanny for the baby. She would have dragged Jeri out of her cozy little cottage, entirely out of the town of Neighborlee, taken her to the richest suburb of Cleveland and deposited her in a penthouse apartment. Then she would have dragged her to a spa to get her hair and nails done, along with a whirlwind shopping trip to replace all the fashionable outfits Jeri had dumped at the Salvation Army store on her way out of town two months ago.

Aunt Eleanora would never understand the warm feeling Jeri got every time the baby smiled at her. Nor the butterfly, giddy feeling when Jon-Tom laughed at her attempts at humor, or when he looked into her eyes. Definitely, Aunt Eleanora would have a stroke if she knew Jeri liked this woodworker who wanted her to watch the baby until his buddy came back to claim his son. It wasn't just that Jon-Tom wore paint-smeared denim, and sneakers without socks. He wasn't a blueblood who could trace his ancestors back to some medieval warlord.

Hadn't that been part of the biggest reason she changed her name and hair and her entire lifestyle? Aunt Eleanor was determined to marry her off to someone with the right bloodlines. Someone so inbred he couldn't do anything except wear fancy clothes, drive expensive cars, and escort models to movie premiers.

Not a man who would fight for a baby's right to be tended by someone who cared, instead of a cold, unfeeling System. Who would fight for his best friend's child. Who made furniture and toys for children, with his own hands, instead of telling someone else what to do. And walked her home instead of calling a taxi. And promised to jump over the fence separating their back yards the moment she called for him.

It didn't really matter, at this point, if Jon-Tom actually did it or not. The fact that he'd offered was enough for her.

Why couldn't she ask him inside and offer him some lemonade? It was hot out. It was only neighborly to offer him something to drink, right?

Jeri hardly recognized herself in those thoughts. She hadn't been raised to think about anyone, except when it would ultimately make her look good or benefit her in the long term.

"I don't know what I would have done without you today," she said, after gazing into his eyes a few seconds longer than was safe.

"Probably not got yourself saddled with a kid that isn't yours?" he offered with a grin.

"Junior's a sweetheart. And you did say Jerry would get back to you as soon as possible, and he'd take over."

"You believe me?"

"Yeah." She wanted to laugh when his face lit up. Why did her belief mean so much to him?

"Do you want me to carry all this gear inside? If you don't feel comfortable with me in the house, I understand. First date and all."

"No, that's okay." Jeri knew she was tired, but not too tired to know that denying they'd had a date at all would be the wrong thing to do. And honestly, she had more fun today than she had known on dates with ten socially acceptable men, combined. "Um, let me unlock and you can just...um, put it inside the door."

No way in the world was she going to admit she didn't have any place to put the baby except the basket where he was already asleep. She had a mattress on the floor, a folding table and two folding chairs, a makeshift sofa of cushions and throws, and milk crates for shelves and tables. Bad enough he had to step inside and see her bare living room.

"Need some help with the floors?" Jon-Tom laughed when she took two hasty steps backward and put the baby basket down behind her. "Refinishing the floors. They're gorgeous. Need about twenty coats of varnish and ten years of dirt stripped away, but you've got beautiful wood underneath all that. A few scatter rugs and you won't need much decorating."

"What are you? Carpenter or interior decorator?" She managed to laugh. The end of the effort was much more assured than the beginning.

"In the winter, when things slow down and people aren't coming from out of state to buy furniture, I do a lot of remodeling, renovations, things like that." He shrugged. "It's a good rainy day project. And I just thought, since you haven't put your furniture in here yet, you were waiting until you'd done the floors."

"I don't have much furniture to speak of," she admitted. Her heart skittered a few beats at that reckless disregard for her cherished privacy. What about Jon-Tom made her want to open up?

Maybe it was as simple as the warmth in his eyes and his

crooked smile when he looked at his friend's baby. What would it be like to have a friend so good, he'd step in and watch out for her interests even when she had done something stupid?

Jeri sighed, knowing better than to go in that direction.

"Starting over, huh?" Jon-Tom nodded and stepped back, over the threshold. "Takes a lot of guts to just drop everything and take a chance. Angela has a lot of great furniture in the back room. If you want anything brought over here, just give me a holler."

"You'll bring it over the fence?" It felt good to laugh with him, and then muffle the sound for the sake of the sleeping baby.

"I have a truck. G'night, Jeri. See you in the morning." He winked, turned the button on the lock, and pulled the door closed behind himself.

"'Night." She waited until she saw him pass the front window, then turned off the overhead light, picked up the basket, and stumbled by moonlight to the back of the house. Her bedroom had sheets over the windows and another sheet under the mattress, to protect it on the floor. She checked the baby to make sure he was sleeping straight and wouldn't strangle himself on his thin blanket, and then got ready for bed.

In Jeri's dreams, she wandered through Divine's Emporium, finding dishes and linens, vintage clothing, curtains, a dozen items that snatched at her imagination. Anything that would brighten her empty, echoing little cottage and make it hers. She had never been allowed to choose her own style before, or even decide what that style should be. Now she had a chance.

When she woke, she let out a cry of dismay that her house wasn't decorated in bright colors against white, pristine walls, furnished with mismatched dishes and retro furniture.

She thought about her dream. Angela couldn't possibly have all the things she wanted. Still, was there any harm in looking? For once, she would listen to her interests and whims instead of bowing to the dictates of those who claimed they knew better.

Who knew what she would find at Divine's Emporium?

She stumbled through changing Junior's diaper and felt some measure of triumph. Not bad after only one lesson. Jeri managed not to gag at the unusual smell when she mixed enough formula to fill all the bottles Angela had found and sterilized for her yesterday. She mixed enough juice and water to keep Junior hydrated for the entire day, and filled the three original bottles that had come with the basket and baby.

Jon-Tom arrived in time to help her figure out how to bathe Junior in her bathroom sink. Jeri had an unreasonable fear of the slippery, wriggling little boy sliding out of her hands and drowning, even though there was barely enough water to cover his chubby little toes.

"Not so bad, was it?" He laughed at her when they were finished, both of them spattered with water and suds.

"Not at all. Were you serious about helping me furnish this place?"

"Absolutely. Where do you need to go?"

"Just check in with me at Divine's this afternoon." Jeri sighed, mostly to fight the self-deprecating laughter trying to bubble up. "I'm going to need a lot of baby advice from Angela, and you have a business to run."

"That's the nice part about being self-employed. The boss likes me and he's flexible."

Her heart gave that funny little skip again, directly connected to the warmth of his smile.

~~~~~

Jon-Tom thought about Jeri's smile all morning. He considered offering her the set of chairs and table Mr. Albersythe had ordered for his fiftieth anniversary next month. That startled him. But not enough to stop him from looking through the odds and ends sitting around his workshop, things that hadn't turned out as he originally planned, or experimental items he had worked on when business was slow.

He had kicked himself on the walk home last night, for not realizing her living room and dining room weren't empty by choice. Those shadows in her eyes were from fear. She had come to Neighborlee with very little, to start a new life.

Jon-Tom admired Jeri for having the guts to strike out on her own and escape whatever or whoever had hurt her. But was it just admiration that made him want to throw out today's work schedule in favor of helping her?

The phone rang, clashing with the fading scream of his table saw. Jon-Tom jumped, nearly dropping the length of cherry wood right on top of the slowing blade. Muffling a curse, he scrambled
~~~~~

across his shop and snatched up the phone.

"Hey, what's this about a baby with my name on him?" Jerry Hollis roared.

Jon-Tom told his best friend all about his meeting with Jeri and the note and how much the baby looked like him. Jerry interrupted with curses and questions, and forced him to repeat portions of the story several times.

"This reeks of Maggie's stepbrother. I tell you, the guy wants her for himself. I don't know how many times I left messages on her answering machine or sent her cards and presents she never got. Her slime bag stepbrother gets into her apartment and opens her mailbox, takes everything I send, and erases my messages. Then he keeps pounding her with how I never take care of her and leave her alone all the time. The guy's sick, that's all I can say," Jerry snarled.

"You didn't know she was pregnant, did you?" That was the most important part of the conversation, to Jon-Tom.

"You think I'd be here if I did? We had a big fight just before I shipped out. She was supposed to come with me. I was planning on marrying her over here. I figured I'd take her on a trip on my first leave, propose in a castle, do the whole romantic deal, but all of a sudden she changed her mind. Or got it changed for her. I gotta find her. You'll watch out for my kid, won't you?"

"What do you think I've been doing? You are such a screw-up, it's a miracle the Marines let you hang around."

They laughed together, like they used to when they were just boys, getting in trouble over stupid pranks and adventures.

His laughter died the minute Jon-Tom hung up the phone. What was he going to do with Junior until Jerry found Maggie and straightened things out? Jeri had been willing to help out when it seemed like only a day or two of tending him. What if it took a week, or weeks? What about months?

Whatever happened, Jon-Tom had to get to Divine's and see how Jeri felt about the baby. Remembering what she'd said about furnishing the house, he drove his truck there, instead of walking the few blocks over.

John Stanzer, the town's one private investigator, was just coming out of the front door of Divine's when Jon-Tom arrived. They nodded to each other, but didn't speak. He had made the mistake of asking Stanzer to investigate Caryn when his ex-fiancé tried to clean out his bank account. Stanzer made it a policy to avoid investigations into any kind of domestic trouble. Jon-Tom respected him for that, but at the time, he had been furious. The two were friendly now, but he suspected it would be a long time before they were friends again.

Inside Divine's, he found the baby lying on a blanket on the counter, and Angela leaning over him, making him giggle. A moment of pure panic knotted his throat. That counter couldn't be a safe place for a baby. But Angela was watching him, and nothing bad ever happened at Divine's Emporium. Jon-Tom suspected if the baby were totally alone and rolled off the counter, he would slowly float down to the floor like a puff of dandelion fuzz.

"Well, you're just in time for the fashion show," Angela said, before she turned around. "What do you think, Uncle Jon?" She scooped up the baby and settled him on her hip.

Jon-Tom laughed, which made the baby laugh. The little boy wore a white sailor suit, complete with a little flat cap.

"Hey, buddy, your daddy will just love that outfit on you." He tweaked the baby's nose, prompting giggles.

"So you got hold of Jerry?" Angela said.

"Yeah. He believes the kid is his, but he hasn't heard from Maggie since before he went overseas. It turns out her weird stepbrother has been running interference. Jerry's going to get some leave time and go find Maggie, see what's up."

"Maybe she's in the area."

"I suggested that. Jerry said he'd email me some photos, so I could start looking around. He's terrified she dumped the kid and ran home." Jon-Tom sighed, trying not to hate the poor, mixed-up girl. Jerry didn't blame her at all, and was certain her psycho stepbrother left the baby on Jeri's front step.

Chapter Fifteen

"I should know by now not to doubt you," Jeri called, as she came down the stairs. "I love it. I'd never think to get it for myself."

Laughing, she twirled down the aisle, holding out her arms. She looked like a butterfly, in a gauzy, multi-colored, kerchief-sleeved top and pristine white shorts. Her sandals glittered with gold, blue and green beads. She stopped short when she saw him, blushing a shade that made Jon-Tom think of pink lemonade. And kissing her to see if she tasted like sweet lemons and strawberries.

"I couldn't resist trying on all the great clothes Angela has."

"Sounds like a good idea to me." He cleared his throat, mostly to fight words he hadn't let fall from his lips since Caryn. He wanted to give those compliments to Jeri, but they felt used. Such words should be fresh for her. "Umm, did you find any dishes or furniture or anything? I brought my truck."

"Our resident knight in shining armor," Angela said with a rich chuckle. "I hope you have a big truck. Jeri found everything she needs for her house."

"It's a small house, and I don't need that much," Jeri hurried to say. Her eyes sparkled.

He was glad to see she was comfortable again.

"It's amazing. I dreamed about how I wanted to do the house, and practically everything I wanted was here." She offered a little laugh. "Who would have thought Divine's would have so much?"

"It's bigger inside than outside," he said, echoing an observation he had heard others make.

Caryn had hated Divine's. She'd turned up her nose at the eclectic mix and called all the treasures junk. Something that had felt cracked and dried inside him warmed and softened now, like soil in the springtime rains. He grinned at Jeri and she grinned back. Would she laugh or be pleased if he said she looked like a butterfly?

"Why don't we finish up the fashion show and have lunch?" Angela said.

"No, really, you've done too much already. I mean, you have a business to run," Jeri began.

"Sweetheart, it runs itself. Diane always gets here just about the time the afternoon rush starts. And with Divine's, that means more than two people in the store at one time." Angela handed Junior to Jon-Tom. "Why don't you take a seat and tell this little guy about his daddy, while we pack up everything Jeri picked out?"

That sounded more than good to Jon-Tom. The warm, soft weight of the baby boy felt exactly right in his arms. Not too delicate, not damp or limp or too soft. He liked the smell of the baby, sweet with powder and clean skin, and the faint cedar scent from the little sailor suit he wore.

He went upstairs to Angela's living quarters without having to be told and settled in the front room. Something about having those big, blue-gray eyes focused on his face made everything else vanish. He couldn't remember back to the time he and Jerry had been this little. He couldn't honestly imagine Jerry looking this sweet, innocent and trusting.

"Okay, buddy, what do you want to know about your old man?"

Jon-Tom lost all track of time as he rambled through memories. The boy grinned wetly at him, and when he got restless, all it took was shifting him from one arm to the other, or bouncing him a little on his knees to make him happy. Jon-Tom didn't realize Angela and Jeri had arrived and got to work on lunch in the next room, until he related the time he and Jerry got caught skinny-dipping by the high school girls' varsity swim team, when they were twelve. Laughter rang out from Angela's kitchen.

"Oh, very funny, just shred my fragile ego," he snarled in mock anger. His face burned. "Traitor," he added, when the baby giggled and tried to snatch at his nose. "You were supposed to warn me when the ladies showed up, remember?"

"I hope you aren't giving him any bad ideas," Jeri said. She deposited a bowl of fruit salad on the table.

Angela brought in a platter of sandwiches and turned the conversation to Neighborlee. All the things Jeri needed to see, the summer fun to be had in town. The lake in the park. The deer that came up the hill to graze in Angela's backyard. Hundreds of simple, small details. The joys of quiet, small town life and neighbors looking out for each other.

She embarrassed Jon-Tom, telling about the toys he made for

the children's home. The children he gave part-time jobs to, to teach them a trade and a hobby to train their creativity. The woodworking classes he taught at the high school.

He liked Jeri's admiring looks. He thought he had trained himself not to need a woman's approval, ever again.

When lunch was over, he began loading pieces of furniture into his truck.

"You weren't kidding," he said, laughing, as Jeri helped him heave a drop-leaf table with beveled edges into the truck, followed by six matching chairs with butterflies carved across the backs.

"Do you think I can get away with stripping off the old finish and just rubbing in tung oil? I mean, under all that glop, there's a beautiful wood grain." She paused a moment to run her fingers lovingly over the tabletop before wrapping old blankets around it for padding.

"Sounds like a plan." Jon-Tom liked the warmth of satisfaction that came from her words. She was a woman who appreciated natural beauty, so different from Caryn.

No, he refused to even think her name. She was out of his life.

Next came several apple crates of dishes. Muted colors and slightly varying styles, slate blue and burnt orange, pale yellow, avocado green, cinnamon. They were all the heavy, sturdy kind that reminded him of the dishes at summer camp, and standing in line outside the dining hall in the dew and chill, smelling oatmeal and sausage cooking.

Jon-Tom froze when Jeri moved a paper grocery bag of gauzy, brightly colored clothes and he saw the cradle she had bought. He stared too long. He almost turned away.

"It's gorgeous, isn't it?" Jeri said quietly. She came back from checking on Junior, asleep in a third-hand car seat in the truck, and bent to gently brush her fingertips along the fanciful flowers carved on the spindles. "Angela offered to just let me borrow it, until your friend takes care of things with Junior, but..." She shrugged and couldn't meet his gaze. "Something like this doesn't deserve to be just borrowed. It shouldn't sit in a store, even one as great as Divine's. It should be used."

"So..." He turned to heave a bag of linens into the back of the truck. "Are you going to give it to Jerry when he finds Maggie and settles down to play house?"

"No." She laughed and bent to pick up the cradle. It was light, easy to lift, because he had built it that way. Somehow, it hurt to see her pick it up, because she was so careful. Caryn had refused to touch it when he refused to sell it. "Kind of silly, huh?"

"Not much need for a cradle where you are." The words clogged in his throat.

"Right now. Who knows? Maybe I'll have kids someday. And when I rock them to sleep every night, I'll tell them all the faerie tales I never got when I was a baby." Jeri wrapped a sheet around the cradle slowly, as if reluctant to hide it from sight.

"I thought you didn't like kids."

"I don't know much about kids. Especially babies. I know they can't all be as great as Junior, but ... well, if I don't have kids of my own, maybe I'll be a foster mother. Just for babies. After I've had lots of lessons from Angela and lots of practice with Junior." She shrugged and bent to pick up a box of all sorts of baking and cooking pans and pots and bowls and utensils.

"That sounds like a great job. Considering how much Junior likes you."

"How could anyone not be a great mother, with a cradle like that? They just don't make them like that anymore."

"Actually --" He stopped short, his face suddenly hot, when she stopped and looked him in the eyes.

"You made it, didn't you?" Her smile, her admiration soothed away the rest of his pain. "Jon-Tom, it's the most beautiful thing I've seen in years. You should be proud."

"We're all proud of him," Angela said, appearing in the doorway. "He's had offers to go to lots of places and make four, five times as much money."

"Living in a big, smelly city and working for someone else," Jon-Tom said, with a grin. "No, thanks. I'm happy just like I am."

"Really?" Angela's smile turned sly. She slowly shook her head, as if she knew all the wistful thoughts and feelings that had been plaguing him. "Nothing you want in the whole world?"

"Well..." He glanced at Jeri.

She caught her breath, as if she knew the image that flashed into his mind. Jon-Tom saw himself holding Jeri on his lap, kissing her. They were sitting in front of a fireplace in the family farmhouse. A handful of children played around them, along with a couple dogs, on a snowy winter night.

That was Jon-Tom's idea of paradise.

~~~~~

Jeri let out a cry of dismay when they pulled into her driveway. The screen door hung crooked, like someone had tried to yank it off the hinges. She leaped from the cab almost before Jon-Tom put the truck into park, and flew up onto the porch. When she shoved at the front door, it banged open without needing to be unlocked.

Someone had broken in. Why? A glance through the front window would show there was nothing to steal.

She looked around once she was inside. The intruder hadn't been a thief, but a vandal. Food, plastic plates, the folding table and chairs had been flung out of the kitchen and across the empty living room. Her few groceries had been opened, emptied, scattered and spilled. The refrigerator door hung open. Orange juice and milk cartons were ripped open and their contents spilled across the floor to mix with macaroni and dry cereal. Her bananas were smashed on the floor, smeared, brown globs in big, heavy boot prints. A rotten smell hung, fermented, heavy and sick in the air.

Jeri looked at the window over the sink, sure she had left it open at the top for ventilation. It was closed. She shivered despite the humidity. Someone had deliberately closed the windows to make it hot inside the house. Who could be so nasty? Who could be so thorough in destroying everything?

Actually, she knew quite a few people who would enjoy planning the destruction of her shabby little house, just for the fun of seeing her distress. The problem was, they were all hundreds of miles away. No one knew where she was, and they would never risk getting their hands dirty, literally and figuratively.

"Jeri?" Jon-Tom tapped on the screen door's frame. "You okay?"

"I'm ... fine. Furious, but fine," she added, choking on the mix of laughter and stomach-burning fury rising from deep inside.

Jon-Tom whistled when he came in with the car seat cradled in his arms. He set Junior down on one of the few clear spots on the floor and set about righting her table and one of the chairs. The other one was mangled and bent, totally unusable.

Jeri couldn't take the mess or the smell in the kitchen any longer. She went down the short hall to her bedroom. The door was closed. Another shiver went up her back.
~~~~~

"Jon-Tom, could you --" How could she ask him to take the risk, if the person who broke in was still there, hiding in her bedroom? Shaking her head at herself, vowing once again to live her own life, take her own chances, she grasped the knob and turned.

The stench that rolled out of her hot, humid bedroom was unlike anything she had ever smelled before.

"That smells like you left something sitting in the diaper pail too long," Jon-Tom choked out, coming up behind her. He swore a few times, tripped over something, and finally got to the window to open the drapes and push up on the old-fashioned sash.

Her few Salvation Army clothes lay in heaps on the floor. The plastic milk crates she used as shelves were shattered into hundreds of pieces. Bedding had been torn off the bed, her sheets ripped. A yellow stain and a brown pile lay in the center of the mattress.

"Is that --" She gagged and took a step backwards. It didn't help against the stench.

"Yep. Looks like your burglar doesn't know what a bathroom is. What kind of a loony is this guy?" Jon-Tom muttered.

"How do you know a guy did this?" Jeri could name at least six relatives, all female, who would point out that if she chose to live in a shack that was only fit for a cat's litterbox, it would be used as a litterbox.

"Name one woman who would take the time to squat on a mattress? Hate to tell you, but some guys never grow up, and they love to show off their aim, if you know what I mean."

She took another step backwards, fanning herself to try to dissipate the stench. "Why would anybody do this to me? I don't know anybody in town yet, besides you and Angela. Did anybody hate the old owners of this house, and they don't know someone new moved in?"

"This place has sat vacant for the last five years. The folks on this street are the kind to bake you cakes to thank you for moving in, not try to drive you out."

"Oh. So that's why." Jeri felt her face heating. She had wondered why her new neighbors on each side had brought over cakes and cookies and homemade preserves the first two days after she moved in. So, that destroyed her only explanation.

"Well, let's get to work. You got a bucket in all that gear you bought today?" Jon-Tom grasped her shoulders and turned her to face the front door.

"No." Her face heated. Well, honestly, why would she think of a cleaning bucket? She was barely used to doing her own laundry and washing her own dishes.

"You sure?" He reached over the side of the truck and lifted out a bucket.

Jeri could have sworn the bucket, scrubbing brushes and mop hadn't been there when she loaded the truck at Divine's. When she told Jon-Tom so, he just shook his head.

"Let me clue you in. When it comes to Divine's, you always find what you need, even if you weren't thinking about it at the time. Angela probably figured you'd need it, and threw it in when your back was turned." His grin got wider. "I don't suppose she threw some disinfectant and soap in there, too?"

It comforted Jeri a little when she checked the crates of supplies and discovered Angela hadn't thought of everything. While she got to work with the broom she couldn't remember buying, Jon-Tom ran up to the closest grocery to get soap and disinfectant and anything else he thought of along the way, to clean up the mess.

"I guess it's true, huh, Junior?" She paused after sweeping out the kitchen. "Whatever you need, you can find at Divine's. I certainly found my knight in shining armor there."

Junior blew bubbles at her. She laughed and wondered at the person she had been just a few days ago. How could she have ever wanted to get rid of the little boy? How did people without babies in their lives survive?

She tiptoed into the bedroom to avoid the wet smears all across the floor, and glimpsed the message written on the bathroom mirror in her lipstick. Her laughter died, caught in her throat.

Great place to raise a kid. Get rid of the slut before the cops come.

Her mind stuck on the second sentence. What slut? What cops?

Fury took over. Her house might not feature in *House Beautiful,* but she kept it clean and she checked for bugs and she was getting all sorts of furniture and things to make it much nicer. She even had a cradle for the baby now. Jon-Tom was going to help her refinish the floors. She hoped to paint the walls and maybe learn to stencil.

Her house *could* be a great place to raise a kid. But someone had come in and trashed it. He had peed and dumped on her mattress and then criticized her house. Who was he to talk?

Then something struck her and she staggered out of the bathroom without watching where she put her feet.

The vandal thought *she* was a slut.

The message had been left for Jerry, just like the baby was left for Jerry, but both had landed with the wrong Jeri.

Her hands and legs still trembled, but she went to the kitchen and got to work wiping out the denuded cupboards so she could put away her new dishes.

The creep wouldn't come back and destroy all her lovely new second-hand things, would he?

Jon-Tom answered that question an hour later, when he finally returned with plenty of soap and disinfectant, sponges, rags, window cleaner and groceries. He also brought new locks to put on the front and back doors, and a battery-operated alarm system to put on any windows accessible from the ground.

"It won't go to the cops," he explained, "but it'll make a whole heck of a lot of noise, and the neighbors are great on this street. They'll come running and somebody'll call the cops. Nobody will get very far into your house, no matter what."

She tried to smile, but her teeth started chattering. She couldn't even get out a "Thanks."

"Hey, what's wrong?"

He slipped his arms around her and guided her head to rest on his shoulder. Jeri shivered, but not from fear. She had been here, in Jon-Tom's arms, in her dreams last night. Reality was much better.

"It's okay. That jerk won't be back. While I was out, I stopped to ask Stanzer if he'd help out. He's our local PI, and he's pretty ticked that someone would pick on you."

"Not me," she finally managed to say. "I think it's the same person who dropped Junior on me. He thinks Jerry is living here. I don't think Maggie left her baby here at all."

Jon-Tom's confused look was almost amusing. She reluctantly slipped out of his arms, caught his hand and led him to the bathroom. He swore, immediately muffling his voice, as if the sleeping baby could hear him. He pulled out his cell phone.

John Stanzer showed up in ten minutes, making Jeri reflect on the benefits of living in a very small town.

Stanzer walked around, studying everything, taking pictures of the bathroom and bedroom and what remained of the mess in the rest of the house. He asked questions. Lots of questions. When he had everything he needed, he called the police on his cell phone. Jeri groaned, thinking she would have to wait until tomorrow to start cleaning up her house.

To her surprise, Stanzer rolled up his sleeves after he put his phone away. "What should I do first?"

~~~~~

The sun was setting when Stanzer and Jon-Tom finished installing the last lock and alarm on Jeri's windows and doors. The smells of tomato soup, toasted cheese sandwiches and something chocolaty drifted on the cooling breeze. Jon-Tom's stomach rumbled, making both of them laugh.

"Never seen you so angry before," Stanzer commented, as he stepped back and gave the window alarm an approving nod. "Not even when I refused to do that job for you."

"This is different. Jeri didn't do anything to deserve this." Jon-Tom took a deep breath, reassuring himself that Jeri's little cottage smelled of pine and lemon cleaner, not some immature slime bag's idea of fun.

"You scared her a little, with how mad you got a few times."

Jon-Tom didn't like that idea. He'd scared Jeri? He was here to protect her, to take care of her.

Jeri stepped out of the kitchen. "Are you almost done?" She had a towel tucked into her waistband in lieu of an apron, and a smear of what Jon-Tom hoped was chocolate frosting across her left cheekbone. Her feet were bare, and her hair was damp from the humidity. He remembered how she felt in his arms a few hours ago. What would she taste like when they kissed?

He knew they were going to kiss, and soon. He had to get rid of Stanzer, though.

"Done," Stanzer said. He tipped his head back and sniffed loudly. "Sure hope I'm invited to dinner."

"I insist." Then she grinned. "Of course, I'm not too steady on my cooking yet, so you might want to take the easy out, if you have one."

Tomato soup with rice and oregano, toasted cheese sandwiches with thin slices of ham and tomato, and brownies. Jon-Tom knew he was hungry, but that couldn't explain how good everything tasted. Stanzer agreed with him, repeatedly. Until Jeri
~~~~~

laughed.

"You two are going to drive me crazy." She opened up the door under the sink, pulled out the garbage bag, and took a cake mix box from it. "This is what you're supposed to be eating, not brownies. I can't even get a stupid cake mix right."

"Poor little rich girl," Stanzer muttered. "Never learned how to cook."

Jon-Tom expected Jeri to laugh more, but instead she went white and dropped the garbage bag all over the floor. He leaped out of his chair to help her.

"He was just teasing," he said, and nearly pulled her into his arms right there in front of Stanzer, to comfort her.

"You two have no idea how close to the truth..." Jeri forced a smile and shook her head. "Doesn't matter. I'm going to learn how to cook. I just hope it doesn't take until Junior needs lunches for school."

The mental image of Jeri, Junior and him, together as a family, stayed with Jon-Tom all through the evening. He had a hard time shaking it because Stanzer went home soon after that revelation, leaving them alone.

Jon-Tom helped Jeri put together the frame for her bed and carted her ruined mattress to the street. Fortunately, trash day was the next day. He could only be grateful Angela had insisted they take the mattress and box spring that fit the frame. Otherwise, Jeri would have nothing but the couch to sleep on tonight.

Jon-Tom had other plans for it.

~~~~~

Jeri finished putting sheets on her new bed and came out into the living room. She muffled a gasp when she found Jon-Tom making up a bed on the floor. She had fashioned a couch with cushions on a narrow bed frame and covered it with multicolored throws. Now everything was haphazard.

"Um, Jon-Tom, what are you doing?"

He paused, looked at her, and then at the floor. A crooked grin lit his face.

"Sorry. We've been working so smoothly together, I just figured ..." He shrugged. "I'm planning on spending the night, to make sure the creep doesn't come back."

"You think he will?"
~~~~~

"Somebody is out to get you, because they think you're with Jerry."

"Yeah, I'm a slut, keeping Junior in a dump." Amazingly, she managed a dry wisp of laughter.

"So, maybe he'll decide to break in and take the kid. Then he can call the police, tell them you didn't report the kid being dropped on the porch, and now you've lost him, and really get you and Jerry in trouble."

"Except Jerry isn't here."

"If he was, I wouldn't worry."

"I'm glad -- I mean, I'm glad you're worried -- I mean --" She took a deep breath and wished she could cool her face off. By about fifty degrees. "I'm glad you're here."

"Yeah. Me too. And not because you're such a great cook."

"I'm not a great cook."

"Didn't hear us complaining, did you? By the way, no more brownies left. Me and Stanzer finished them off while you were giving Junior his bath." He winked and turned back to finish making his bed.

Jeri wished she had some place better to offer him to sleep. The couch was too short for him to stretch out, but with the cushions lined up on the floor, he had enough length. He would be relatively comfortable, as long as he didn't roll over.

"By the way, Stanzer thought about the creep taking the kid and reporting you to the police. He's stopping at the station on the way home, to let them know what's up."

"Won't I get in trouble, anyway?"

"Jerry asked us to take care of his son. According to that note, that's his son until someone tells us otherwise. Legal enough for me." He paused in tucking one of her multicolored throws into place over the cushions. "It's going to be okay. I promise."

Funny, how that stern look in his eyes, the solid weight of his voice, helped her sleep better than she had since she decided to get out of Dodge and start a new life.

~~~~~

Jon-Tom woke before the sun, with dreams lingering in his mind, of Jeri smiling and cuddled in his arms, and children playing around their feet. He lay there on his narrow bed, imagining a life with her, until he realized he had built three rooms and a dormer
~~~~~

onto the cottage in his daydreams. Time to get moving and give himself something else to think about.

Jeri had liked his ideas about refinishing and sealing the floors, so he went out to his truck and pulled out the equipment he had picked up last night. He laid out the first coat of stripper, leaving her a wide swath of dry floor to walk on. That could sit and work all day while he finished two furniture orders.

Jon-Tom grinned, thinking how nice it would be to work in here and hear the baby laughing and Jeri working in the kitchen, making dinner. Maybe it was ridiculous, making plans like this, but something told him she would like the idea. At the very least, if she made dinner, she wouldn't feel so obligated to repay him for all his work. That had almost caused trouble last night, when she started talking about paying him back for the cleaning supplies.

Now, how to make sure Jeri and Junior were out of the house all day, so the stripper fumes wouldn't make them sick?

That was easy enough. Divine's Emporium, Angela, and baby lessons. He wondered if Angela guessed what had happened and what would happen, when she made the offer to Jeri. For just a moment, it occurred to him how odd the everyday coincidences at Divine's Emporium might look to outsiders. But that was the thing: outsiders never noticed. The wonders and coincidences and little miracles never happened for them.

Some of that magic must have been at work, because Jeri just laughed when she came out of her bedroom and saw what he was doing. She suggested getting Junior out of the house during the day by taking a tour of Neighborlee and visiting Angela before Jon-Tom could tell her his idea.

Yes, things were working out better than he could have hoped. If he didn't live in Neighborlee and didn't believe in miracles, he would have been frightened by how everything fit together.

What was he going to do when Jerry came for his son and he didn't have an excuse for spending time with Jeri?

Chapter Sixteen

Three days later, Jeri realized she had fallen into a pattern. Waking to Junior's laughter, bathing and feeding him. She ate breakfast with Jon-Tom before helping him with the next step in refinishing a section of floor. It was an unspoken agreement that he worked on her floors to thank her for watching Junior. Maybe, she hoped, also because he wanted to spend time with her. Once the floor was drying or the stripper was working, Jon-Tom headed for his shop and she took Junior to spend the day at Divine's and get baby lessons.

Half the women in Neighborlee found an excuse to come to the shop and cuddle Junior. They brought baby food and baby dishes, toys and clothes their own children had outgrown, and offered advice. No one thought it strange she was taking care of a baby belonging to someone she had never met.

Everyone had stories about Jerry and Jon-Tom growing up. Jeri liked the absent Marine, the more she heard about him. She couldn't imagine him as someone who would abandon his pregnant girlfriend. That, combined with what Jon-Tom claimed about his friend, convinced her that Jerry hadn't known his Maggie was pregnant.

She loved coming to Divine's Emporium, even if she didn't need baby lessons or something absolutely essential for the cottage. There was magic in the very air of the big old house. It was a safe, cozy feeling. She felt as if she belonged.

When several women blessed her for taking responsibility for Junior, hugged her and told her she was never allowed to leave Neighborlee, Jeri choked on tears. When had anyone ever praised her for doing something just because it was right and good and helped someone?

She laughed when her new friends told her how the Hollis family and the Harris family kept getting each other's mail for over twenty years. Jerry Hollis' old house was at 1751 Baker, and the old Harris house was at 1751 Bader, and the two streets backed up to each other. What made it truly silly was that Grandma Harris had been the Neighborlee Postmistress for nearly eighty years and often delivered her own mail wrong.

That was Neighborlee, Jeri decided. And she decided she would listen to and learn from these women, who treated her like someone they had known all their lives. She would never leave. She had finally found her home.

The women who came to give her baby lessons all agreed Jon-Tom was completely in character to watch out for his best friend's interests. When the conversation drifted into Jon-Tom's personal life, Jeri didn't know whether to stop them or beg for more details.

Jon-Tom loved kids. That much was obvious. His parents had fostered several dozen children at the big family farm on the edge of town, until he graduated from college and they moved to Arizona. He'd earned a degree in early childhood education and occasionally helped out some friends who ran a daycare in Medina.

His first love was woodworking, though, and it showed in the beautiful pieces he made. Jeri thought of the cradle and wondered why something made with so much love and creativity had been sitting in the shadows at Divine's.

When a few women mentioned Jon-Tom's ex-fiancé, Jeri definitely didn't want to hear more. She tried to say so, and most of the women listened. A few insisted, however, on talking about the generally disliked Caryn. Jeri got the impression Jon-Tom's ex had only cared about life in the big city with its fast pace and everything she desired at her fingertips.

"She was an idiot, wasn't she?" she whispered as she put Junior down for his nap that afternoon. "And you know what's really sad?" She made her voice a sing-song. He smiled and cooed. "I was just as big an idiot, once upon a time. I thought I was in love. I thought he was different, that he cared about real things. But when I asked Foster to help me break free..."

She sighed and brushed curls off Junior's forehead. "I thought he loved me, but he wanted to be reasonable instead of running away. Sometimes you gotta run away instead of wasting your whole life negotiating and being civilized. What's so reasonable about letting people turn you into a brainless doll without a heart?"

"Who's Foster?" Angela said. Jeri had thought she was downstairs, ringing up a customer. After several days at Divine's Emporium, she'd have been more surprised if Angela didn't respond to her unspoken thoughts and didn't appear at the oddest, most unexpected moments.

"Foster Alsworth is the biggest phony in the whole world. What's really ironic is that he showed me how fake I was, and I didn't like it. So I ran away."

"I hear a broken heart in there."

"Wounded pride and a lot of self-loathing. The girl I used to be wouldn't have cared one little bit what you thought of me. She would have asked for hand sanitizer if you ever asked me to touch someone else's baby, let alone feed him or change a diaper." Jeri exchanged a soft smile with Junior, just before he closed his eyes, sighed, and relaxed into sleep. She turned to face Angela. "Foster wanted the girl I was supposed to be. She doesn't exist anymore."

"I'm sure Junior and Jon-Tom will be very glad to hear that."

"Oh, don't ever tell them. Please?" Jeri tried to smile through the panic that shot a bolt of ice through her chest. "I don't like her. I'm sure Jon-Tom would loathe her."

"All right. I won't tell him. But you need to."

Jeri nodded, immediately pushing aside the entire idea of confessing her deep, dark, self-centered past to Jon-Tom.

Maurice fluttered into the room to check on Junior. The two of them had worked out a truce. The baby wouldn't try to grab him, and he wouldn't put the boy to sleep every time he flew by. He settled down on the baby's slowly rising and falling chest and watched Angela and Jeri leave the room.

"Foster Alsworth, huh? How many bozos can there be in the world with a handle like that?" He patted the sleeping baby. "Feel the need for a showdown, to move things along? The sooner we get you a real mom and dad, the happier you'll be, you think?"

~~~~~

Four days later.

Jon-Tom's phone rang while he helped Jeri load Junior into the truck. He had been talking about renting a movie to watch, after they put another coat of stain on the floors. He grimaced and looked at the display. His grimace turned stern as he answered the call.

Jeri rested a hand on the baby, half-afraid the caller was Jerry, saying he was in town and coming for his son.

Jon-Tom said little during the conversation, mostly grunts of agreement, ending with, "We'll be right there." Then he closed the
~~~~~

phone, put it in his pocket and climbed in the truck.

They were halfway home before Jeri spoke. "Bad news?"

"Stanzer's at your place. Got a call from Mrs. Dunsmoore. Some shady character skulking around outside. He's got the guy cornered." Jon-Tom sighed, his shoulders slumped, and he finally turned to look at her. "The guy claims he knows you."

"Knows me?" Jeri looked down at Junior, lying in his car seat wedged securely between them. The baby blew bubbles and giggled at her.

"Claims he's your fiancé."

"I am not engaged. See?" She spread her hand, wiggling her fingers to show there was no ring on them.

Her heart sank. Aunt Eleanora had been pressuring her to choose among five eligible young men when Jeri had flung her old life to the winds and bolted. It would be just like her aunt to promise that whichever of those well-dressed, manicured, perfumed, in-bred idiots found her could marry her. That didn't mean the winner actually had the intelligence to track her down, or knew her well enough to guess where she would go. It just meant whoever hired the best investigator.

It wouldn't matter if Jeri said no a thousand times. The inbred twit and Aunt Eleanora would consider it a done deal. The winner of the treasure hunt would get the prize, no matter how unwilling the bride turned out to be.

If they had to forge her name on the marriage license, they would. They had the money and lawyers to get away with it, too.

"Something you want to tell me?" Jon-Tom pulled the truck to a stop at the end of the street. Stanzer's car and a low-slung red sports car were parked in front of the cottage. "Like maybe how long you were planning on playing house before you got bored and dumped Junior?"

"Dump?" Jeri couldn't breathe for a moment.

"Must be a lot of fun for you rich girls to slum it for a while. Cooking for yourself and buying second-hand clothes must be a real adventure, huh?" Jon-Tom didn't look at her, just gripped the steering wheel hard enough to turn his knuckles white.

He thought she was slumming? Fury cleared Jeri's head and let her breathe again. For half a second, she was tempted to take his dare, to jump out of the truck, just hit the road and leave

Neighborlee behind. But that would mean leaving her house and Angela and the friends she had made, and Junior.

And Jon-Tom.

I don't want to leave. I like it here. I even like Jon-Tom, even though he's being a total moron. What is wrong with him? What makes him think I'm playing games? I'm not his ex.

That thought stopped her cold. Jeri took another look at Jon-Tom, who still wouldn't look at her. Was he afraid she had been lying, just like Caryn? Was he afraid of her leaving? Did it make him angry? Did he care that much?

"I am not engaged." Somehow, she managed to say it in a calm tone of voice. She remembered times she would had been unable to speak, choked by imminent tears. Aunt Eleanora had trained her to fear scenes of any kind, so she gave in rather than argue or cry or scream in public. "I ran away from home to avoid whichever creep Stanzer has cornered. I'm not the girl I was three months ago. Can we leave it at that?"

"Sure." He shrugged and still didn't look at her as he took his foot off the brake and gunned the engine.

Jeri felt sure Jon-Tom would have swung into the driveway, spitting gravel, except for two things. First, there was a baby in the truck. And second, that ugly sports car and Stanzer's car blocked her driveway. He probably wouldn't have hesitated to ram the sports car, but Stanzer was a friend. Besides, Jeri felt sure Jon-Tom loved his truck more than the creep who had been spying on her house ever truly cared about her. Whoever he was.

The creep loved her trust fund, her family's money, and the social standing that would come from combining two old and prominent families. Loved her, Natalie St. Germaine Hollister? Hardly.

Jon-Tom pulled the truck up so the passenger door was lined up with the slate path to the curb. He was always thoughtful like that, even when he was angry. She knew he had to be angry, because he'd never been this silent and tense with her.

A figure dressed in white slithered around the roadblock of Stanzer, and darted toward the truck. "Natalia, darling!"

"Foster," Jeri groaned. She didn't need to see him in his summer "ice cream suit" to recognize him. He insisted on using his fake French accent and changing her name, as if that gave him a special claim on her. For a short time, he had convinced her he cared about things that mattered, and helping her escape the cage her aunt and high society had built around her. Slowly, she came to realize all Foster's encouragement was just to coax her into slipping from one cage into another. She hated being Natalia because Foster loved Natalia. Pretty much along the same lines that a sexual predator loved the children he abused.

"So you know him." Jon-Tom stared straight ahead, still gripping the steering wheel.

"Nope. I'm not Natalie or Natalia. I'm Jeri." She took a deep breath, grasped the door handle, and swung it open into Foster's fashionably rippled chest. He had gained his muscles by way of a gym and personal trainer, whereas Jon-Tom had his through honest hard work. Jeri preferred nature, whenever possible.

She didn't hit Foster on purpose, but Jon-Tom snorted and his eyes lit up. If he thought she had meant to do it, well, then she meant to do it.

"Darling." Foster didn't have the sense to realize what had happened. He flashed her a twenty-thousand-dollar smile. She knew it cost that much because he had told her. Did he think that would impress her? "What are you doing here?"

"I have no idea who you are." She unhooked the seat belt holding Junior's car seat and shoved harder on the door.

This time Foster stepped out of the way, nearly losing his balance on the curb. He staggered backwards when she emerged backwards from the cab, dragging Junior's car seat with her.

Usually, Jon-Tom carried the car seat for her. Right now, Jeri wanted to hold it, and she hoped he understood why.

"What is that?" Foster choked.

"It's a baby. Please go away. He doesn't like strangers."

"Is this why you disappeared before our engagement could be announced?"

"Since I don't know who you are, how could we be engaged?"

"The lady says she doesn't know you," Stanzer said, coming to her rescue. He reached for Foster's arm, to get him out of the way.

"Natalia, darling --"

"Jeri." Jon-Tom held out his hand. "Want me to take care of Junior?"

"No, I want you to take out the trash." She headed toward the house.

"Sweetheart." Foster twisted free of Stanzer and darted around in front of her. She could either detour around him and walk through the flowerbeds, or let him say his piece. "I've come to take you home."

"I am home."

"This?" He curled his upper lip, glancing at the cottage. "Your servants wouldn't condescend to live in this hovel."

"Then it's a good thing I don't have any servants."

"No, you have an instant family. This ..." He gave up searching for a word, and pointed at Junior, who was waking up cranky, judging by his reddening, wrinkled little face. "This can't possibly be yours. Did this cretin talk you into something you and I will both regret?" He glared disdainfully at Jon-Tom.

Who just stood there, thumbs looped over his belt, rocking a little on his heels, waiting.

Jeri didn't know who made her angrier. Even Stanzer didn't look like he would help now. Well, just as she had three months ago, with a choice between slitting her wrists or ditching the life she had never wanted, she would just have to rescue herself.

"Look at you." Foster's lip curled even more. She rather hoped it would stay that way. It was an improvement over his bland prettiness. "You're dressed like a peasant."

Jeri liked the Bohemian look she had chosen today, with rainbow patches all over her faded, worn jeans, a rainbow print tube top, thong sandals with lots of beads decorating them, and a dozen glittery, chiming bracelets on each arm. It was a look and a feeling of freedom she had dreamed of since she was a little girl and had to endure hours every few months with the dressmaker.

"Next thing you know, you'll think you're actually happy, spending your time cooking and cleaning and changing diapers. No time for yourself. Nothing worthwhile accomplished."

Jeri's mouth dropped open. Nothing worthwhile? Every time Junior smiled at her, she felt like she had just been crowned queen. If Junior grew up to be a worthwhile person, like Jon-Tom, even if he did just stand there instead of throwing Foster into his car, her life would be more than well-spent.

Just who did this arrogant, rich, overdressed booby think he was, to pass judgment on a simple, fulfilled life?

"Need some help, Jeri?"

Jon-Tom put his hand on her shoulder, and suddenly everything was right with the world. She smiled at him, throwing in all the wattage she could summon. It must have done the job because Jon-Tom's lips curved up in a goofy-looking grin.

"Hold Junior for me?" She batted her eyelashes at him and that goofy look turned downright nasty and gleeful. That meant he understood her message, if not her intention.

Right that moment, she loved Jon-Tom.

She handed the car seat to him, took two steps closer to Foster, and metaphorically rolled up her sleeves.

Foster's smile turned smugly triumphant.

Did that arrogant booby actually think she was giving up and throwing herself into his arms? The only thing she planned to throw his way was a right hook.

Which she did.

Foster slid through the mulch of her flowerbed and out the other side into the grass, juicy and green in the shade. Only when he stopped moving did he lift both hands to his nose, as if he couldn't believe it spurted blood until that moment.

"I'll sue your family for everything they've got!" Foster shrieked, sounding like he had been gelded. "Thousands of dollars of plastic surgery, and you ruined it! Not to mention my suit will have to be dry-cleaned and even then I doubt --"

"I'll testify to the cops that this bozo threatened you," Stanzer said, sounding downright bored.

Junior whimpered for punctuation, that little hiccupping sound that meant he was winding up for a full-blown wail.

"And disturbing the baby, on top of it," Stanzer added.

"You're going to lie to the police?" Foster yelped.

Jeri didn't know much about bloody noses or broken ones, but from the small amount of blood she had raised from Foster's nose, she seriously doubted anything was broken. She made a mental note to work on her right hook, so it did more damage next time.

"Next time," she said, "I'll do more than try to break your nose. For the hundredth time, Foster, we are not engaged. I am not going back with you, I am not going back, period, and the sooner you get out of my town, the happier everybody in the county will be. And you can tell all your creepy friends, and especially Aunt Eleanora, the next one who comes here will get even worse."

"What makes you think I'd tell anyone where you are?" Foster snarled. He would have sounded more threatening if whimpers didn't leak through his pique.

That was the problem with Foster and his gang, and everyone her aunt approved of. They didn't get angry. At the most, they had snits and tiny temper tantrums, and then went out to soothe their nerves with manicures, massages, and herbal tea. Until it was time to go to the clubs or gentlemen's bars, where they did ungentlemanly things to girls who got paid to be stupid, and everyone got filthy, stinking drunk.

They were the product of good breeding, according to Aunt Eleanora. Every time Jeri had tried to break free, even if just for an afternoon, her aunt had lectured her again on her mother's three years of insanity: when she fell in love with a man of "common stock" and had his child.

Aunt Eleanora had seen the death of Jeri's parents as righting a cosmic social imbalance. She had often mocked Jeri as a child when she cried for her parents.

Would bloodying Foster's nose finally convince Aunt Eleanora she was a lost cause, and her "accident of breeding" was impossible to correct? Would Aunt Eleanora write her off once and for all?

Maybe she should have punched someone years ago?

"You can stay here in the boondocks and rot, for all I care. I hope everyone you ever cared about forgets you even exist. I know I will, as soon as I get on the highway." Foster hauled himself to his feet, ignoring the hand Stanzer held out to him. He stomped down the slate sidewalk to his sports car.

The smears of mulch and grass stains on his white suit gave it some character. Jeri doubted any of it would rub off on Foster.

"From now on, Natalie St. Germaine Hollister, you are dead. Socially, and every other way that matters." He emphasized his words by slamming his door. The expensive hinge didn't allow for more than a muffled thud.

Jeri held her breath, waiting, refusing to even blink, until the engine turned over and the brake lights flashed, and Foster headed down the street.

Stanzer broke the silence first. "You going to be okay?"

"She's going to be ... just great." Jon-Tom held out the car seat.

Just taking the handle wouldn't be enough. Jeri scooped up Junior and cuddled him close. He let out a little giggle and dug his tiny fists into her tube top. So what if he decided to gum her shoulder to death? She was washable.

Jon-Tom slid his arm around Jeri's shoulders. They walked up the sidewalk to the house. She heard Stanzer's car start up, and realized she had forgotten all about him. She looked over her shoulder in time to see him grin and give her a thumbs-up sign.

For some reason, when she got into the house, her legs started shaking. The last thing she wanted was to drop Junior. She shoved the baby into Jon-Tom's arms and ran across the bare wooden floor of the living room and into her bedroom. She hit the bed and buried her face in the pillows half a second before the tears came.

At least she didn't wail or sob. She just lay there, shivering, while tears soaked her pillow. She gasped for breath and felt like her heart wanted to pound out through her ribs.

Somewhere in all the dizzy spinning, the nauseating mix of relief and glee and outright terror, Jon-Tom's arms wrapped around her and pulled her upright. She wrapped herself around him and let her tears soak his shirt.

Too soon, the tears slowed and the world stopped spinning. Jeri clung to Jon-Tom, eyes closed. She wished she could just sit in his arms, forever.

"Hey, it's okay," he whispered.

"I know," she whispered back.

He didn't ask about Foster while they made dinner and hung the curtains she had learned to hem at the shop that afternoon. She hoped it was because he'd caught enough of the story through her exchange with Foster, and not because he didn't care. She wanted him to care. A lot.

Chapter Seventeen

The next morning, Jeri left Junior snoozing in her bedroom in his cradle. Breakfast and the kitchen table and chairs sat in the living room. She stepped into the kitchen, where Jon-Tom was sanding the kitchen floor.

"Is my cooking that bad?" She laughed and stepped backward. She wriggled her bare toes, feeling the fine dust from the sanding clinging to her feet.

"I happen to like your cooking, but you can consider the kitchen off-limits for the next day or two."

"Continental breakfasts and picnics, then." She wiped her feet on the rug Jon-Tom had thoughtfully put in the doorway between the kitchen and living room, and went in search of her shoes.

"Where are you going?" he asked, when she came back to the kitchen, shod, with her purse over her shoulder.

"Since I'm banished from the kitchen, I'm going shopping for provisions. Junior should stay asleep for another hour. Try not to get into any trouble while I'm gone?"

"You're in deep trouble, woman. Just you wait."

"Promises, promises."

Jon-Tom let out that hearty, rumbling laugh that made her feel like flying. Jeri grinned as she stepped outside.

Stanzer was waiting on the curb, just getting out of his car. Her stomach dropped, followed by her purse hitting the porch step.

"Foster's suing?" Jeri guessed. Somehow, she made it down the sidewalk to his car without stumbling.

"Him?" He wrinkled his nose. "I figured you didn't need two doses of bad news yesterday, so I waited until now. That wimp wasn't what brought me over yesterday. Mrs. Dunsmoore's been calling in prowler reports the last few days, so I set up a couple cameras to try to catch whoever it was."

"Not Foster." Jeri's spirits did an upswing. Foster wouldn't be caught dead sneaking through this neighborhood. Cat-burglar wasn't a fashionable Halloween costume. He'd never try out the role for real.

"Nope. Caught some creep sneaking around, trying to get pictures of the inside of your house. Thought it might be the same guy who broke in before. Called out like I was the police." Stanzer grimaced. "He ran for it, and he dropped his camera."

"And?"

"Prints?" Jon-Tom said, startling them both. He pushed the screen door open.

"They're still being researched," Stanzer said. "I got permission from the police to upload the photo files. This guy's been following you two around for a couple days, judging by the different clothes Jeri's wearing in the pictures. He stayed in the shadows when I saw him, so I'm having a hard time matching his face to any records. The fingerprints ought to be good evidence, along with the photos."

"You think it could be Caryn, trying to blackmail some money out of me?" Jon-Tom said.

Jeri's heart did a few skips when he spoke his ex's name so calmly, without any anger or hurt.

"Blackmail you with what?" Stanzer just grinned. "She doesn't have any claim on you. She can't charge you with infidelity. Besides, she lied to bank officers, and tried to take a truck of your custom furniture when she left town."

"She sounds pretty vicious to me," Jeri muttered. "Some people will kill their own mothers, for enough money."

"Don't worry. Miss Fashion Plate doesn't have a slimy leg to stand on."

"Then who does the Peeping Tom with the camera work for?"

~~~~~

Maurice knew he was in trouble when Angela crooked her finger at him, beckoning for him to follow her into the kitchen. Diane, Holly, Jeri and the baby were having lunch in her apartment. Jeri had just shared the exciting events of the day before.

"Want me to set up some booby-traps for the guy stalking Jeri?" Maurice said, when Angela crossed her arms and looked at him, rather than refilling the lemonade pitcher, which had been her excuse for leaving her guests in the other room.

"Why do I have the feeling we'll find your fingerprints on this?"

"Me? Why would I waste magic on illusions of guys spying on them? Jon-Tom doesn't need any help being a white knight, if you ask me. He's hooked solid on Jeri, and I say good for them."
~~~~~

"Not the spy. The former suitor who showed up on Jeri's front step without any explanation."

Maurice considered playing innocent for about two heartbeats, then common sense won. Besides, he didn't like lying to Angela. There were times when the ends still justified the means, but how could he convince her of that before he got in trouble?

"Had to test her, for Jon-Tom's peace of mind. I've heard what people have said about the skinny witch he almost married, and I've eavesdropped on Jeri when she gets in a blue funk and thinks about the creepazoids she left behind. Until she made the big choice and kicked the wimp out of her life, Jon-Tom was going to always wonder, y'know?"

"So you contacted Foster and let him know she was here." Angela nodded. The very calmness of her expression frightened Maurice just enough to make his wings twitchy. "How?"

"Diane's computer. I borrowed it while she was busy last week and she left the Internet open." Maurice snorted. "You know how long it takes to type out an email, hopping from one key to another?"

A tiny bubble of laughter escaped Angela. One corner of her mouth twitched. Then she closed her eyes and shook her head.

"Your technique... Well, it's improving. And your reasoning is somewhat logical." She opened the refrigerator to get the lemonade. "You're learning. Just don't help matters along and call Caryn to come test Jon-Tom for Jeri, all right?"

"Hey, the last thing we need is her trying to sweet-talk him to get her claws into his money again. Even though all that woodworking of his could make big bucks with interior decorators."

Maurice caught his breath when her gaze bored into him. "Not my idea. Jeri's. She was saying it just the other day, gushing to Holly about all the detail he puts into things, and how much her buddy loved the little table she sent her as a thank-you for helping her find Neighborlee and putting together her new identity and... I wouldn't invite that witch to invade our town. Cross my heart and hope to die." Maurice drew the X over his chest and pressed both hands over his heart.

"I believe you, but if Caryn walks through my door one of these days, I'm going to wonder. You do realize that?"

"How about if I promise to never, ever again manipulate the creeps without clearing it with you first?"

Angela tipped her head to one side and studied him for several long moments. Maurice felt pressure building up around his wings like invisible fingers ready to pull them off. Or maybe pull him away by his wings and lock him up somewhere much worse than the holding room when he faced the Fae Disciplinary Council.

"You have a deal," she said, and picked up the pitcher to take out to her guests.

Maurice slumped down on top of the refrigerator and let out a sigh. Then he sneezed from the dust.

~~~~~

Two days later, Jeri, Diane and Megan, a high school girl who worked part-time, took over the counter with their jewelry project. Jeri was picking through the glass beads Angela had suggested she use to make a bracelet. When the wind chimes gave off a sour note, she turned to see a sleek, black-haired woman in a wine-colored silk suit saunter through the door. She recognized the designer, mentally shrugged, and went back to her project.

Diane inhaled sharply, making Jeri turn to look again.

"Caryn. It's been a long time." Angela appeared around the corner from the back room. "Jon-Tom's not here." Her voice lacked its usual warmth.

"I know." Caryn continued her runway stroll to the counter, flexing her mile-long legs. "I saw him go into the hardware store. I just thought I'd check and see what he's been selling here before I go to our house to wait for him." She turned to survey the store. "I can't believe you're still making a go of this place. How can anyone find anything in this disaster zone?"

"People who know what they need always find it at Divine's," Jeri said. "Maybe you just don't know how to look."

"You're new around here." Caryn pursed her collagen-enhanced lips and looked her over from head to toe.

"You've been gone a long time." Diane placed herself on Jeri's right hand, like a guard.

"Not long enough," Megan said.

The door slammed open, making the chimes jangle and the bells clatter. The floorboards shook. A subliminal chord in the air, a scent of freshly cut wood, told Jeri who had arrived just seconds
~~~~~

before Jon-Tom came into view. His face had settled into deep, dark scowl lines.

"What are you doing back in town?" he growled.

"Oh, honey, can't we let bygones be bygones?" Caryn's syrupy chirp made Jeri's stomach twist. Her petulant look turned warm and seductive. Her hips swayed in a definite come-on as she walked toward Jon-Tom and held out her arms.

"No. I just want be-gones. As in, you will be gone." He took a step backward. "What do you want, Caryn?"

"Well ... I was hoping to make up with you." She fluttered her eyelashes. On anyone else, Jeri might have believed the sorrowful look. "I guess I can't really expect you to welcome me with open arms when it's been just silence between us for so long, huh?"

Jeri flexed her fingers, wanting to claw Caryn when the supermodel wannabe ran a long fingernail tip down the middle of Jon-Tom's chest.

She caught her breath when he grabbed Caryn's wrist and shoved her hand away. Jeri grinned, delighted far more than she thought she had any right to feel.

"You said you wanted nothing to do with me, remember?" Jon-Tom said quietly.

"Well, yeah, but... Well, you scared me."

"The only thing you've ever been afraid of," Angela said, "is not getting your way and all the attention."

Caryn turned to glare at Angela, but caught herself. She resumed her sorrowful mask and turned back to Jon-Tom. "Please, sweetie, can't we be friends? I realize what a mistake I made --"

"Your mistake was thinking I'd believe your repeat performance." He glanced around the shop, seeming to see Angela, Diane, Megan and Jeri for the first time. "You always preferred being as public as possible, to try to get people on your side."

"Oh, now that's not fair!" Caryn stomped her high-heeled feet.

Jeri gave her points for poise. She would have fallen over and broken at least one ankle, if she had tried that move.

"I want you back. And you're being so mean. I thought you loved me."

"Past tense." Jon-Tom moved past her to the basket on the floor, where Junior still slept, amazingly undisturbed. "You throw something out, it's kind of hard to get it back in the same condition."

"But we can fix things." Her tone turned wheedling again. "You were always so good at fixing things. Let's see if you can fix us. In spite of all our arguments, I really do want to be married to you."

"There is no 'us'." He glared at her and stopped short, as if her presence kept him from getting any closer to the baby.

"Oh, why are you so mean to me?" She stomped her foot again, wobbling a little this time. "I want you back. I want it all back. Our house and all the gorgeous furniture you made for me. Especially the cradle. You'll let me have the cradle, won't you? Please? Pretty please?" She wriggled a little and took mincing steps closer to Jon-Tom, reaching as if she would put her hand on his chest again.

"Jon-Tom, you know what I think?" Jeri said. "Your reputation is growing, and she wants to cash in on it."

"Oh, what do you know?" Caryn snapped.

Jeri knew right then, under her sleek sophistication, Caryn was nothing but heavily lacquered and polished trash.

"Everything Jon-Tom makes is a work of art," she said. "I got four phone calls last week from a designer who wants everything Jon-Tom can give him. I gave his sister a table Jon-Tom made, and she showed it to him. This guy sells to the rich and famous and his interior design work gets into all the magazines. He wants an exclusive contract for Jon-Tom's work. And I'll just bet you heard, and you're here to get your claws into all that money."

"I don't care about that." Caryn fluttered her eyelashes. "Please, Jon-Tom? Honey? Let me have my cradle? You made it just for me. It's special to me."

"Can't have it." Jon-Tom flicked a glance at Jeri, then down at the baby. "It's being used."

Caryn followed his look. Her expression hardened into something sharp and glacial. Her lip curled up when she saw the baby. She took two steps backwards.

"Well, it didn't take you long to find some sap to start shooting out babies, did it?"

Diane and Megan gasped, sharp little sounds of exasperation and fury. Angela smiled serenely and leaned forward to rest her elbows on the counter.

"Of all the nerve," Caryn continued, and pointed at Jeri. "I'll bet you had her waiting in the wings. You couldn't wait to get rid of me, could you?"

"That's not the story I've heard," Jeri said.

"You were just waiting to snatch up what belonged to me."

"You didn't know what you had! Jon-Tom is mine and I'm not giving him back. So just climb onto your broomstick and get out of town." Jeri managed to keep a pleasant expression on her face as she spoke, though it took all her self-control not to spit.

"I want --"

"That's always been your problem." Jon-Tom sounded tired more than angry. "You couldn't get what you wanted, so you dumped me and ran. You have no claim on me."

Caryn's mouth opened and closed a few times, but no sound came out. Under her expertly applied makeup, she had gone sickly white. Then red fury flooded her face.

"Fine! I don't know why I cared so much to try to drag you out of the sticks so you could make something of yourself. You had a great chance, but you're blowing it. You'll never get anywhere." She stomped toward the door, wobbling now on her high heels. "Just waste your life taking care of other people's snot-nose brats and making toys for kids who'll only break them over and over and --" She let out a scream when the door refused to open, no matter how much she pushed on it.

"Pull," Jeri called sweetly.

The look Caryn shot her was nearly potent enough to kill. Then she yanked the door open. The chimes sounded like birds singing as the door thudded closed faster than usual.

"And stay out!" Maurice roared, brushing his hands against each other, as if he had physically pushed the door closed.

Diane saluted him. Angela let out a long, gusting sigh that turned into soft laughter. She slid down into the nearest chair and turned a beaming face to Jon-Tom.

"I've been waiting years for you to rip strips out of her hide."

"He didn't yet," Megan muttered sourly. "Not as much as she deserved."

"What did she mean?" Jeri said. "The stuff about taking care of other people's kids?"

"That's Jon-Tom's dream," Angela said. "He's got this huge house on the edge of town, lots of land, and a playground he's built over the years. He's going to have a daycare someday, and a nursery school. He's already making quite a living as a toymaker.

And someday when he's old and white-haired and fat, he can grow a beard and convince everyone he really is Santa Claus."

"A daycare, huh?" Jeri smiled even wider. Her heart skipped a few beats when Jon-Tom finally smiled and visibly relaxed. She noticed he hadn't looked toward the door once his ex had slammed her way outside. That made her more glad than she liked to admit. "What's the big hold-up right now?"

"Funding, mostly. And getting my staff." Jon-Tom stepped over to the basket and knelt to scoop up Junior. "Hey, buddy, did that old witch scare you?"

Junior belched loudly and slapped Jon-Tom's nose. The laughter from everyone in the room broke the last bands of tension.

Then Jon-Tom's grin froze. He turned and frowned at Jeri. "What interior designer?"

"Oh... Ah... Well, I have this friend and I told her about your furniture and she didn't believe me, so I sent her that little plant table you made. To thank her for helping me find this town."

"And?" His face seemed to close up, all the warmth and laughter not so much fleeing as hiding behind heavy doors.

"Well, her brother went absolutely crazy about it, and she gave him my new phone number and, well, I'm sorry. I meant to tell you, but you've been so busy and I didn't want to bother you and I wasn't sure how you'd react to finding out someone wanted to put you under a contract..." Jeri wished she had picked up Junior first, because she really needed a hug and she doubted she was going to get it from Jon-Tom any time soon.

"She's heard enough of what Caryn did to you," Angela said, "so she has a good idea how you feel about wealth and fame."

Jeri nodded, praying Jon-Tom wouldn't throw her out of his life as quickly and easily as he had his ex-fiancé.

"See? It wasn't me this time." Maurice landed on the top of the cash register. "Other people like to interfere, too. Not just me."

Angela turned her head just enough to silence him with a look.

Jeri swallowed hard and tried to smile when an embarrassing need for tears burned her eyes. "I just thought Rita would love that table and she's about the only friend I have outside Neighborlee. Honestly, Jon-Tom, if I had thought she would bother you--"

"Jon-Tom, if you don't get down off your high horse and tell Jeri you're not angry with her, I don't know what I'll do," Angela said. "Both of you, just think for a minute. Your problems are solved. Be glad about it, will you?"

"Solved?" Jon-Tom's voice cracked.

Jeri dared to hope when one corner of his mouth started to curve up.

"You've been living in dread of Caryn coming back and trying to wheedle her way back into your life. Well, she came back and she tried, and she failed. And Jeri, now you know you're free of all those people in your past. Don't you feel better knowing you can stand up to them?"

"Yeah," Jeri admitted, letting out a long, gusting sigh. "I do. I'm sorry, Jon-Tom. Honestly, I am. I wasn't thinking about money when I sent Rita your table."

"Yeah, I know." He shook his head, then shifted Junior over to one arm and wrapped the other one around her.

Something cold and hard and afraid, deep inside, melted at his touch. She wanted to stay safe, wrapped up in his warmth, held close to his side, for the rest of her life.

Jeri didn't really believe the stories Angela had told her about the Wishing Ball sitting on her counter, but she knew better than to dismiss anything that might help. That evening, just before she left the shop, she rested both hands on the rainbow-streaked globe and thought about all the things that would make her life perfect. Jon-Tom was at the top of the list.

~~~~~

"So, how come you've never asked me to see your place?" Half-asleep, Jeri spoke slowly, as Jon-Tom started his truck down the few short streets between Divine's Emporium and her cottage.

He understood exactly how she felt. It had been a rough day. He still felt the aftershocks of the encounter with Caryn. Mostly because he hadn't *felt* anything. Not the hurt and anger she'd left behind, or the disgusted shame he'd felt for admiring anything about his ex.

He liked the way Jeri had flayed Caryn with only a few words and that amused little smile. He had asked Stanzer to do a little investigating, based on Jeri's encounter with her pseudo-fiancé, and had learned a few things about the woman riding in his old truck.

Natalie St. Germaine Hollister had vanished three months ago, leaving all ties clearly severed, with no trail for her alleged friends
~~~~~

and family to follow and force her back into high society. She was rich and cultured and had a reputation as a quiet little mouse who let others do her thinking. Her aunt, who had raised her, was a mover and shaker in the art world, sponsoring concerts and charity events.

Stanzer openly admired her for the brains and guts it took to cut free like that.

Jon-Tom remembered the glimpses of fear she had showed before she pulled herself together and slapped Foster back on his expensive heels. He preferred the woman slouched on the seat next to him, spotted with baby formula, dusty from digging through the treasures at Divine's, her hands rough from helping him re-finish the floors of her house, who changed diapers now without gagging.

"Nothing special about my place," he finally said. But he turned left when he should have turned right, and drove his truck past the cluster of school buildings, toward the edge of town where all the greenhouses and farms stood.

"It's your place. I thought pals share everything." Her lips curved up just enough to notice as she spoke.

"Pals, huh?" Jon-Tom liked the sound of that. He even more liked the sound of *share everything.*

When they reached his family homestead, he slowed enough for her to get a good look at the big old farmhouse with its wrap-around porch, twice the size of Divine's Emporium. Her smile got bigger. He remembered that Caryn had blinked once when she first saw the house and never smiled. That was a good sign.

Slowly he drove down the long gravel driveway and out into the big turnaround behind the house. He stopped the truck so Jeri's window faced his fantasy playground.

As she slowly climbed out, Jeri acted like someone in a dream, her mouth opening wider with every heartbeat. Her eyes got big enough to fall into. As if he hadn't fallen into and drowned in her eyes a dozen times since she walked into his life. Finally, he saw the sparkle fill her eyes and a grin of pure, child's delight.

The playground had forts. Two looked like Old West forts, two resembled castles and one mimicked a space station. Each had poles to slide down and rope ladders to climb.

There were five slides. Three were enclosed, curving, painted like snakes on the outside. A crow's nest had a ladder inside the column that supported it, and two rope ladders like rigging on either side. He had built swaying bridges and drawbridges and a miniature Golden Gate, climbing towers with pivoting arms to swing on, a pirate ship with three cannons that shot water, and ropes for swinging across shallow water-filled trenches. There was a maze made from four-foot-wide plastic tubing, like a hamster run. An enclosed pit was full of rubber balls and another pit was filled with sand and enough plastic buckets, shovels, sieves and other toys to furnish two beaches.

The playground spread out over an acre, and Jon-Tom had plans on his drawing board to expand it. Someday.

"Can grown-ups play there, too?" Jeri half-whispered. She flinched when Junior let out a questioning little coo, and grinning, reached back into the truck to scoop the baby out of his car seat.

"Grown-ups?"

"I never got to go to the playground when I was a kid. You go to amusement parks and you see the kids playing on things that are only a shadow of this, and you get so jealous. You realize, I never set foot inside a McDonalds until a few months ago. They had stuff like this, but all plastic and only a fraction of the size, and I was still jealous. Can I?"

"Go ahead." He gestured at the playground that had given him many happy hours of planning, designing and building. It had been a labor of love, taking the last four years. He had started it for his own children, and expanded it when friends shared their dream of opening a daycare. He was happier than he could fully understand that Jeri wanted to play on it.

Caryn had told him to sell it to an amusement park or go into business designing playgrounds. She had never wanted to touch it or even acknowledge its presence otherwise. Just before she left him, he realized the only reason she didn't demand that he haul it away as an eyesore was because she intended to get him to sell it, just like everything else that fed his soul.

No, he wasn't going to think about Caryn anymore.

To his surprise, Jeri didn't move. She still stood there, cuddling Junior, looking at everything and grinning. Jon-Tom had the frightening suspicion some of that sparkle in her eyes was tears.

"Does anybody play on this?"

"I let folks around here use it for parties. There are a couple companies that come out and rent the grounds for their company picnics. Things like that."

"Why aren't you running that daycare, when you have this for the kids?"

"Well, my friends are still getting their training and licenses, and you have to get approval from the state. And other considerations." He shrugged. Why, even when he was doing what he wanted, did everything always come down to money?

"Could you use a partner?"

"For what?" He could hardly speak for the huge lump in his throat and the thundering of his heart.

"Well, funding, for starters."

"Jeri--"

"I have a huge wad that's just sitting there, useless. You must have guessed that by now. I know you well enough to know you won't just accept it as a gift or even a loan. So I want to buy into this." She gestured with one hand, taking in the playground and the framework of the building that would be the main facility of the daycare in another year.

Jon-Tom hoped that gesture took in the farmhouse and all the dreams sleeping inside.

"Partner, huh?" He liked the images that sprang to life in his head. Not all of them having to do with hordes of children playing here every day.

"Of course, you're going to have to teach me an awful lot. And maybe I'll get my teaching certificate and work here." She shrugged and met his eyes, trembling a little, but smiling.

He rather hoped she saw in his eyes some of the ideas that were coming to him.

"I'm just a spoiled rich girl who didn't learn anything useful while I was growing up. Just like Angela and the folks in this town have had to teach me about taking care of Junior, well...you have an awful lot to teach me."

Jon-Tom nodded. There were quite a few things he wanted to teach her. And things he wanted to learn from her. Starting with the taste of her lips, how it would feel to kiss her while she laughed. He dared to hope that blush meant she had similar thoughts.

Chapter Eighteen

"Jon?" A familiar male voice rang out over the crunch of tires coming up the gravel drive to the barn.

He swallowed a groan and turned around in time to see an SUV jerk into park and the driver's door swing open. A tall, buzz-cut man in military blues hopped out.

"Jerry," he muttered.

"What?" Jeri looked from the stranger to him.

"He's Jerry." Jon-Tom sighed as his childhood friend ran around the SUV and helped a small, white-blonde woman get out. "I'm guessing that's Maggie."

"Timmy!" the woman shrieked, and flew across the yard to them. At the last minute, she stopped herself, just when Jon-Tom thought she'd yank Junior from Jeri's arms.

For five long heartbeats, the two women looked at each other. The atmosphere crackled as they sized each other up, questioning and judging and even a little begging for answers.

Tears sparkled in Jeri's eyes and her lips trembled, but she smiled and held out the baby. Maggie sobbed and clutched her little boy close. Junior cooed, and he held out his little hands to Jeri.

"Thanks, pal," Jerry said, coming up behind Jon-Tom.

"What's the story?" He watched Jeri, who helped Maggie sit down on the bench painted to look like a candy cane.

"Her slime bag stepbrother took the kid and thought he was dumping him on me, and then he hung around to take pictures and prove I was a bad father. So what's the story with the girl?"

"She's mine." Jon-Tom didn't flinch at the growl in his voice. Best friend or not, if Jerry criticized Jeri even by hinting, he was dead meat.

"Thought so. The creep sent Maggie dozens of photos, trying to prove I had kidnapped Timmy and taken up with some bimbo and she was hurting the baby and two-timing on me. Glad you have somebody, finally."

"Do you have somebody?"

"Oh, yeah. Maggie and me, we're fixing things and we're

talking about her coming overseas with me. Funny, but her brother actually helped us by taking the kid. Made us talk and get over a lot of problems. Most of them were his doing, anyway."

"Good." Jon-Tom watched Jeri, who watched Maggie cuddle and kiss her son. He remembered the day he met her, how reluctant she had been to even touch the baby. Now, the pain at losing the boy visibly radiated off her.

He hadn't counted on Jeri falling in love with Junior, and how hurt she would be when everything was settled.

She didn't cry until Jerry and Maggie drove away to their hotel. Jon-Tom didn't think the prospect of the newly reunited family coming back tomorrow for dinner and to talk was much comfort to her. He kept his arm around her as they watched Jerry's SUV go down the long drive.

She shivered a little, but didn't make a sound until it vanished beyond the trees lining the road. Then her knees buckled. Jon-Tom caught her and held her, letting her soak his shirt again.

"This is so stupid," she groaned when the tears slowed. "I knew Jerry was coming to take Junior away, but for some reason --" She hiccupped and tried to step back as she rubbed her face dry.

Jon-Tom refused to let go of her. To his delight, she didn't insist. He even imagined she relaxed a little against his chest.

"You'll see him again," he offered.

"Once a year?" She sniffled. "I want him all the time. I want to be surrounded by kids."

"You will be, once our daycare gets running. Or are you going to take back that offer?" He grinned, glad he had thought of something to catch her attention. She stiffened and tried to step out of his arms. He just held on tighter.

"Never," she finally said, after meeting his gaze for a few seconds. "I want to be your partner and learn everything about kids there is to know. Everything you can teach me."

"That ain't much." He relaxed a little when one corner of her mouth curved up in a trembling smile.

"You know the important things. I want to be a mommy someday. I want to go barefoot all the time and learn how to cook, really cook, and have a vegetable garden and --"

"And grow old with me?" he said, before he lost his nerve.

"Grow old with you?" She swallowed hard. "As in?"

"Everything. The ring and the license and having kids. You did say you wanted to be a mommy, didn't you?"

"Yeah." She blushed just enough to be noticeable.

"Here's something I want to teach you right away." He cupped her cheek in one hand and leaned down slowly, so he wouldn't frighten her.

Jeri's smile grew brighter. She closed her eyes, tipped her head back and curled her little hand around the back of his neck the moment their lips touched.

~~~~~

Somehow, Jeri wasn't surprised that Angela waited for them on the front step of Divine's Emporium the next morning. She beamed as if she had watched and listened last night as they made plans and kissed, cooked together and kissed, laughed and kissed.

"What brings you two here so early on this fine, bright summer morning?" She didn't wait for their response, but opened the door and led the way inside.

"We need a ring," Jon-Tom said. "The most beautiful ring in the entire world."

"But sturdy," Jeri hurried to add. "Something I can wear when I cook and clean and take care of babies." She sighed and leaned a closer to Jon-Tom, and his arm wrapped a little tighter around her waist. She hoped she never got used to the delicious thrill that shot through her every time he touched her.

"And what makes you two think I'd have something like that here?" Angela said with a chiming laugh.

"Everything anybody needs is here at Divine's." She looked up at Jon-Tom. "After all, we found each other here."

~~~~~

Holly and Maurice waltzed around a grand ballroom, straight out of Versailles. They were dressed in 18th century court costumes, glittering with jewels. Totally alone in the ostentatious room, they were surrounded by starlight and sparkles of magic.

Maurice thought they were having a wonderful time until the music coming from the invisible musicians ended.

"Oh, come on," he said, looking around, as if maybe this time some other inhabitants of the dream would become visible. "That's only our eighth dance. I can go all night, can't you?" By his reckoning, it was nearly 5 in the morning. He could cram days of fun and dancing into the next half hour, if he tried hard enough.

"It'll start in a minute." Holly seemed slightly distracted.

He scrambled for something to say to bring that smile back to her lips. "So, Holly Berry, what do you want for your birthday?" he said when the music resumed and they stepped out again.

"I don't need anything." She smiled, but that happy glow didn't quite fill her eyes like it had only a few minutes ago.

"Yeah, well, what's wrong with having something you want for a change, instead of just something you need?"

"I don't want anything ... except this. Every night. I can even put up with not remembering during the day." Her voice wavered a little. "I think."

"Dancing every night, huh?" He swallowed hard, fighting the thick sensation in his throat that tried to choke him. "You deserve a lot more, to my way of thinking."

"And you," she said, tipping her head back and giving it a defiant little shake.

"Me, huh? Flatterer. But I said you deserved more. As in better, not worse."

Holly giggled as she pulled a hand free and slapped his arm. "You!" She laughed more when he partially crumpled to the floor, pretending to be mortally injured. "Clown."

"Yes, my lady. Gladly, my lady." Maurice swept an extravagant bow, touching the floor with his fingertips. He stepped back up to her and held out his arms. In moments, the music resumed and they were dancing again, floating across the floor.

"So," she said after a few moments, "when is your birthday, and what do you want?"

"To be real for you, for just an hour," he said, feeling as if the words had been pulled out of him.

Holly stopped. He stopped. The music faded, and the grand ballroom darkened around the edges, as if the nighttime would swallow it up at any moment.

"Maurice, you're all the real I need," Holly whispered. She smiled with not a hint of that misery that sometimes darkened her eyes.

He bent to kiss her cheek. The grand clock in the tower high over their head ... clattered like Holly's alarm clock.

She froze, starlight in her eyes. And then slowly faded into mist.

"No!" Maurice howled, as the ballroom turned dark around him and he fell backward, out of the Wishing Ball and back to his seated body.

"Come on, give a guy a break," he groaned. With a surge of anger, he called up all his magic and vanished in a shower of sparks, to erupt into the air over Holly's bed.

Eyes closed, she turned off the alarm clock and curled back into sleep. She was smiling and her cheeks were flushed.

Maurice hovered over her for a few moments, watching her, breathless with an aching he had never known before.

He knew her habits, after watching her so many mornings. He didn't have much time. When he landed on her pillow, he leaned in to kiss her cheek.

"I promise you, Holly Berry, we'll see each other at solstice, and we'll have a great time, just you and me. Promise."

In Divine's Emporium, Angela rested her hand on the Wishing Ball and sighed, as she watched Maurice flutter away from Holly's bed and just hover there, watching her as she slowly woke. With her free hand, Angela wiped a few tears from her cheeks.

"Oh, Maurice, that's not what I wanted for either of you. Not yet, anyway. Now what are we going to do?"

Lips pursed in determination, Angela stroked the Wishing Ball until the image cleared, to be replaced by a soft lavender shimmer. She waited, but the face she wanted to see didn't appear.

"You can't avoid me, Asmondius," she muttered, and tapped at the Wishing Ball with the tips of her nails until it chimed. "I may not be Fae, but I've seen enough to know my way around Fae magic. At least, enough to modify Maurice's punishment. You and I are going to give him a very merry Christmas, whether you cooperate with me, or not."

END

Neighborlee, Ohio

(Title, Original Title, Release Date)

Confessions of a Lost Kid (Growing Up Neighborlee) 05/20
Semi-Pseudo-Superheroes (Dorm Rats) 07/20
Virtually London (London Holiday) 09/20
Living Proof (that no good deed goes unpunished) (Living Proof) 11/20
Night of the Living Proof, 01/21
Quitting the Hero Biz (Hero Blues) 03/21
Bride of the Living Proof, 05/21
Shrunk: The Exile of Maurice (Divine's Emporium) 07/21
Return of the Living Proof, 09/21
Allergic to Mistletoe (Have Yourself a Faerie Little Christmas) 11/21
Dawn of the Living Proof, 01/22
Angela's Knight (Divine Knight) 03/22
The Living Proof Gets the Blues, 05/22

About the Author

On the road to publication, Michelle fell into fandom in college and has 40+ stories in various SF and fantasy universes. She has a bunch of useless degrees in theater, English, film/communication, and writing. Even worse, she has over 100 books and novellas with multiple small presses, in science fiction and fantasy, YA, suspense, women's fiction, and sub-genres of romance.

Her official launch into publishing came with winning first place in the Writers of the Future contest in 1990. She was a finalist in the EPIC Awards competition multiple times, winning with ***Lorien*** in 2006 and ***The Meruk Episodes, I-V,*** in 2010, and was a finalist in the Realm Award competition, in conjunction with the Realm Makers convention.

Her training includes the Institute for Children's Literature; proofreading at an advertising agency; and working at a community newspaper. She is a tea snob and freelance edits for a living (MichelleLevigne@gmail.com for info/rates), but only enough to give her time to write. Her newest crime against the literary world is to be co-managing editor at Mt. Zion Ridge Press and launching the publishing co-op, Ye Olde Dragon Books. Be afraid … be very afraid.

www.Mlevigne.com
www.MichelleLevigne.blogspot.com
www.YeOldeDragonBooks.com
www.MtZionRidgePress.com
@MichelleLevigne

Look for Michelle's Goodreads groups:
Guardians of Neighborlee
Voyages of the AFV Defender

NEWSLETTER:
Want to learn about upcoming books, book launch parties, inside information, and cover reveals?
Go to Michelle's website or blog to sign up.

Also by Michelle L. Levigne

Guardians of the Time Stream: 4-book Steampunk series
The Match Girls: Humorous inspirational romance series starting with **A Match (Not) Made in Heaven**
Sarai's Journey: A 2-book biblical fiction series
Tabor Heights: 20-book inspirational small town romance series.
Quarry Hall: 11-book women's fiction/suspense series
For Sale: Wedding Dress. Never Used: inspirational romance
Crooked Creek: Fun Fables About Critters and Kids: Children's short stories.
Do Yourself a Favor: Tips and Quips on the Writing Life. A book of writing advice.
Killing His Alter-Ego: contemporary romance/suspense, taking place in fandom.
The Commonwealth Universe: SF series, 25 books and growing
The Hunt: 5-book YA fantasy series
Faxinor: Fantasy series, 4 books and growing
Wildvine: Fantasy series, 14 books when all released
Neighborlee: Humorous fantasy series
Zygradon: 5-book Arthurian fantasy series
AFV Defender: SF adventure series
Young Defenders: Middle Grade SF series, spin-off of *AFV Defender*

CPSIA information can be obtained
at www.ICGtesting.com
Printed in the USA
LVHW031642240621
691050LV00007B/492